The Extraordinary Powers of the Tarot

"Anyone who has examined a Tarot deck for the first time feels an indescribable attraction to the card images, the symbols and allegories which seem at once both foreign and arcane and also strangely familiar. The cards seem to speak directly to the soul, awakening a timeless wisdom once known and now forgotten, hidden somewhere within the deep recesses of consciousness, perhaps even deeper still within the collective unconscious of all humanity . . ."

This authoritative work initiates you into the secret world of the Tarot—one of the most ancient forms of divining the future and discovering meaning in our lives . . .

THE MYSTICAL TAROT

The
Mystical Tarot

Rosemary Ellen Guiley

A SIGNET BOOK

SIGNET
Published by the Penguin Group
Penguin Books USA Inc., 375 Hudson Street,
New York, New York 10014, U.S.A.
Penguin Books Ltd, 27 Wrights Lane,
London W8 5TZ, England
Penguin Books Australia Ltd, Ringwood,
Victoria, Australia
Penguin Books Canada Ltd, 10 Alcorn Avenue,
Toronto, Ontario, Canada M4V 3B2
Penguin Books (N.Z.) Ltd, 182–190 Wairau Road,
Auckland 10, New Zealand

Penguin Books Ltd, Registered Offices:
Harmondsworth, Middlesex, England

First published by Signet, an imprint of Dutton Signet,
a division of Penguin Books USA Inc.

First Printing, August, 1991
10 9 8 7 6 5 4 3

 REGISTERED TRADEMARK—MARCA REGISTRADA

Printed in the United States of America

For Bruce

Contents

Acknowledgments

I would like to express my heartfelt gratitude to my husband, Bruce, whose insights into the Tarot, both from individual study and from our work together, helped to shape this book. I would also like to thank Carol Tonsing, who played an instrumental role in bringing this book into being, and Bob Place for sharing his work in progress on the Alchemical Tarot.

Introduction

To work with the Tarot is to undertake a magnificent spiritual journey. The cards continually reveal new information, insights, and discoveries. My own involvement with the Tarot began in a typical way, with my first exposure occurring many years ago in a reading with a psychic. The deck used was the Rider-Waite version. I was immediately entranced by the images, which conveyed much more than was apparent on the surface. Intrigued, I wanted to learn the language of the symbols so that I, too, could read the cards. My work with the Tarot expanded over time to include other decks and other ways to use the cards. Using the Tarot is a rich and rewarding experience, constantly unfolding, never ending.

We can approach the Tarot in two fundamental ways: to glimpse the future, and to discover meaning behind the events and forces in our lives. The first approach, to divine the future, can be fruitful, but is only one dimension of the Tarot. The Tarot is much better suited to discovery, and through it we can gain knowledge of the Self, which helps us realize our fullest potential.

Mysticism is the belief in, or pursuit of, unification with the One or some other principle. It is also the immediate consciousness of the Divine. And, it is the direct experience of spiritual truth. Through the Tarot, we can experience, on some level, all of those things, or at least begin to contemplate them.

As profound, mystical, and mysterious as the Tarot

is, however, there is no reason why a guide to its mysteries, such as this book, cannot be simple and straightforward. Many of the books written on the Tarot seem to equate complexity and obscurity with profundity. They attempt to dazzle the reader with pseudo-esoteric prose that clouds rather than elucidates, or with a confusing assortment of keys attached to each card, or with card layouts that are so complex they virtually defy anyone to use them. For me, many of these approaches simply don't work. They are more dissuasive than conducive to using and learning the Tarot. In the search for knowledge, the straight and clear path is preferable to one that winds and curves and is cluttered with obstacles. That is the reason for writing this book: to provide a clear and uncluttered path of study for the Tarot. My intent is to help the beginner get a solid grasp of the cards and make rapid progress in using them, and to help the experienced student advance to new and higher levels.

Both beginner and experienced Tarot student can use this book. It will teach you how to maximize your work with the cards, regardless of which deck you use. The means for this are universal techniques for developing intuitive and meditative skills, understanding symbols, and making use of the psychology of ritual and patterns. The book also features clear, easy-to-understand interpretations of the individual cards; a guide for meditating with the Tarot; card spreads; and information on how to design your own spreads.

You'll get your ideas as you go along. Feel free to expand or modify the guide presented here, or create something entirely new. May your journey be one of wonder.

ONE

Mysterious Origins

Anyone who has examined a Tarot deck for the first time feels an indescribable attraction to the card images, the symbols and allegories which seem at once foreign and arcane and also strangely familiar. The cards seem to speak directly to the soul, awakening a timeless wisdom hidden somewhere within the deep recesses of consciousness, perhaps even deeper still within the collective unconscious of all humanity. No matter what the interpretation of the deck—and there are literally hundreds, each based on a particular theme or motif—the Tarot evokes a sense of awe.

Who created these cards, and for what original purpose? No one knows the answer. Today's Tarot, in all its incarnations, comes handed down to us through a mysterious history. The true origin and purpose are obscure and will remain so, perhaps forever. Numerous theories have been put forth since the eighteenth century, some of them plausible and some highly speculative. As the late occultist and Tarot authority Arthur Edward Waite once observed, much of the Tarot's alleged history is negative and clouded by "reveries and gratuitous speculations." In all likelihood, we will never know the truth about the origins of the cards, and will be left with only our most educated guesses. It is difficult not to imagine the cards were given some deliberate, occult significance, for whatever their origin, the Tarot cards contain ageless, esoteric truths couched in symbols. A great deal of fanciful information has been written about the Tarot's origin and purpose during the last two hundred or so years, and much of it survives today. Before one can grasp the true essence of the cards and put them to meaningful use, it is important to understand an outline of the Tarot's history, what is known about it and what has been theorized about it.

Tarot and Its Relationship to Playing Cards

Today's Tarot deck consists of seventy-eight cards divided into two parts. The Major Arcana, or trumps, includes twenty-two cards with mysterious, allegorical images. They have come handed down to us numbered save for one card, The Fool, whose later enumeration of zero and placement in the sequence of cards has been an ongoing debate for centuries. (More about that later.) The classic names of the Major Arcana are:

0	The Fool
I	The Magician
II	The High Priestess
III	The Empress
IV	The Emperor
V	The Chariot
VI	The Lovers
VII	The Hierophant
VIII	Strength
IX	The Hermit
X	The Wheel of Fortune
XI	Justice
XII	The Hanged Man
XIII	Death
XIV	Temperance
XV	The Devil
XVI	The Tower
XVII	The Star
XVIII	The Moon

XIX	The Sun
XX	Judgement
XXI	The World

The Minor Arcana includes fifty-six cards in four suits—traditionally wands, cups, pentacles, and swords—each with ten cards numbered one through ten (called the pips) and four court cards, traditionally the page, knight, queen, and king.

Some theorize that the Tarot is the ancestor of the modern deck of fifty-two playing cards, but it is likely that the Tarot and playing cards evolved independently of one another and converged. The Tarot probably originated as the twenty-two trumps now called the Major Arcana portion of the deck. At some point, the Tarot absorbed fifty-six playing cards to become a larger, two-in-one deck of seventy-eight cards. Judging from the few cards that have survived from medieval times, both playing cards and Tarot have gone through numerous incarnations.

The earliest surviving record in the West of any kind of cards dates to 1332, when Alfonse XI, the king of Leon and Castile, placed a ban on them. At that time, cards were making their appearance throughout Europe as gambling devices and were gaining great popularity. Since gambling was considered immoral, cards were banned by various rulers and condemned by the Church as instruments of the Devil. Playing cards were called—and still are by some—the Devil's Bible and the Devil's Picture Book.

There was no standard for the composition of these early decks of cards, and a great variety of designs and suits were employed. Even the number of cards differed greatly from one deck to another. In 1377, a German monk identified only as "Johannes," a resident of a monastery in Breveld, Switzerland, left behind a Latin manuscript describing the arrival of a card game used at the monastery. He said he did not know who invented the game, or where it came from, and he compared it to chess, "since in both there are kings, queens and chief nobles and common people." There were, however, more court cards than in the present playing card deck: six kings, four queens, and eight marschalli (knaves, which are now jacks). Johannes also speculated on the potential of the cards as a means of instruction in morality.

The appearance of other playing cards was recorded at about the same time elsewhere in Europe. Another early suited deck, the so-called Hunting pack of Stuttgart, Germany, which dates to around 1420, has for suit signs the hunting symbols of dogs, falcons, stags, and ducks.

Despite the opposition of the Church and the official bans on playing cards, Europe's royalty commissioned decks to be created for them, most likely for entertainment and amusement. Most of the surviving early cards come from such specially commissioned, hand-painted decks.

Early Tarot cards appear to have been used primarily in games of chance and fortune-telling. The earliest cards that may have been Tarot cards, and that still exist, may have been created and hand painted by Jacquemin Gringonneur in 1392 for the entertainment of King Charles VI of France. The Bibliothèque Nationale in Paris has on display seventeen cards said to be from the three decks created by Gringonneur, an allegation that has been disputed since 1848. Stuart R. Kaplan, a leading contemporary Tarot authority and collector, hypothesizes that the cards actually date from fifteenth-century Venice. The cards resemble the later Marseilles deck, which became the model for subsequent Tarot decks, but have no inscriptions or numbers to indicate their order. Whether they are true Tarot cards remains a matter of disagreement. Waite believed them to be Tarot, and linked them to some of the Major Arcana, including The Fool, Emperor, Pope, Lovers, Wheel of Fortune, Temperance, Strength, Justice, Moon, Sun, Chariot, Hermit, Hanged Man, Death, Tower, and Last Judgement.

The oldest known Tarot decks still in existence are the Visconti-Sforza cards from early fifteenth-century Milan, designed for the Visconti and Visconti-Sforza families. Eleven versions are in existence, none complete. One version, called the Pierpont Morgan-Bergamo deck, has seventy-four cards. The trumps bear no titles or numbers, and the Minor Arcana are divided into four suits of *spade* (swords), *bastoni* (wands), *coppe* (cups), and *denari* (coins or pentacles). One Visconti-Sforza deck, called the Cary-Yale deck, has sixty-seven cards, but in its entirety probably had eighty-six cards. Different artists created the various decks. The Pierpont Morgan-Bergamo pack, which is on display at the J. Pierpont Morgan Library in New York City, is believed to have been created by a Cremonese painter named Bonfacio Bembo. This deck has inspired some modern Tarot artists.

The name *Tarot* may have originated from fifteenth-century Italian decks. At that time, the trump cards were called *trionfi*, and by the early sixteenth century became known as *tarocchi* ("triumphs" or "trumps"), a name that eventually was extended to the entire deck of seventy-eight cards. *Tarot* is the French derivative of *tarocchi*. The *cartiers*, the guild of card makers in sixteenth-century Paris, referred to themselves as *tarotiers*. According to another theory, *Tarot* may have been derived from *tarock*, a German game with cards. Still another theory holds that the name derived from the term *tares*, small dots or points that bordered early playing cards, which were called *tarots*.

It is possible that Tarot cards, with their allegorical symbols of virtues, once may have been used as mnemonic devices for the instruction of children. This purpose is suggested by the Tarocchi of Mantegna, fifty Italian cards that are believed to date to the late fifteenth century. The Tarocchi of Mantegna are divided into five series of ten cards each, designated E (or S), D, C, B, and A, and which are oriented to a theme:

E (or S)—Conditions of Man

Beggar	Servant
Artisan	Merchant
Gentleman	Knight
Doge	King
Emperor	Pope

D—Apollo and the Muses

Calliope	Urania
Terpsichore	Erato
Polyhymnia	Thalia
Melpomene	Euterpe
Clio	Apollo

C—Liberal Arts

Grammar	Logic
Rhetoric	Geometry
Arithmetic	Music
Poetry	Philosophy
Astrology	Theology

B—Cosmic Principles

Genius of the Sun	Genius of Time
Genius of the World	Temperance
Prudence	Fortitude
Justice	Charity
Hope	Faith

A—Systems of the Heavens

Moon	Mercury
Venus	Sun
Mars	Jupiter
Saturn	Eighth Sphere
Prime Mover	First Cause

Twenty-two of the Mantegna cards bear a resemblance to sixteen Tarot cards, including thirteen of the Major Arcana and three court cards in the suits of swords, wands, and cups. Waite, however, found Tarot symbolism wanting in them. It is not known what the series letters designate.

By the end of the fifteenth century, Tarot decks in Italy and France (the "Marseilles" deck) and elsewhere in Europe had evolved with different designs. From the fifteenth through the mid-eighteenth centuries, both Tarot and playing cards underwent additional metamorphoses in content, style, design, and size. The invention of the printing press in the mid-fifteenth century helped the proliferation of cards, which now could be printed from wooden blocks rather than painted individually by hand. Playing cards continued to evolve on their own to the present-day deck of fifty-two cards (the Page was dropped as a court card), and the Tarot incorporated playing cards.

By 1748, the French Marseilles deck had become somewhat standardized; it is now considered to be the grandfather of all modern Tarot decks and is still in use today. The Major Arcana were titled and numbered, with the exception of The Fool. A game of Tarot was played in southern France, Spain, Italy, and Germany, but at that time had not reached Paris.

By the end of the eighteenth century, Tarot cards were used almost exclusively for fortune-telling. The Gypsies were instrumental in this development, for in their nomadic wanderings throughout Europe and England they used cards as one method of fortune-telling. In fact, a theory arose crediting Gypsies with either originating the cards or introducing them to Europe. The earliest extant record of the Gypsies in Europe dates to 1417, although it is likely that they arrived much earlier, perhaps as early as the tenth or eleventh centuries, probably emigrating out of northern India. They claimed to be Christian penitents who came from a land called Little Egypt. The Europeans dubbed them "Gypsies," a corruption of "Egyptians."

Occultists theorized that the Gypsies had come from Egypt, bringing the cards with them; the cards were said to be the remnants of the secret, esoteric wisdom of ancient Egyptian adepts.

That theory proved to be far-fetched, especially in light of more recent evidence of the Gypsies' Indian roots. When the Gypsies arrived in Europe, they merely made shrewd use of the cards they found there as a means to make a living. There is no evidence that they were concerned with deep, esoteric meanings in the cards.

The idea that the Tarot emerged out of Egypt was mysterious and appealing, however, and in the late eighteenth century it became one of the most widely promulgated theories speculating on the true origin and purpose of the cards.

The Egyptian Connection

The chief promoter of the Egyptian connection was Antoine Court de Gébelin (1725–1784), a French archaeologist and Egyptologist, who claimed the Tarot symbols were fragments of an ancient Egyptian book, the *Book of Thoth*. As a high-grade Mason, Court de Gébelin was well-versed in occultism, and was knowledgeable about ancient Egypt as well. But his theory was baseless because the Rosetta stone, which provided the key to deciphering the first Egyptian hieroglyphics, had yet to be discovered.

Court de Gébelin said he stumbled upon the Tarot and uncovered its Egyptian origins by accident while calling upon "Madame the Countess of H . . . ," who was from Germany or Switzerland and was visiting in Paris. Upon the arrival of Court de Gébelin and his friends at the home where the Madame was staying, they found the countess playing a card game with several others. She informed her visitors that it was the game of Tarot. The countess pulled out a card that she said was "the world," though Court de Gébelin could not see any resemblance of the card's image to the name. He wrote later, however, that he immediately recognized the allegory:

> Everyone put down his hand and came to look at this marvelous card [the world] in which I saw what they had never before seen. Each person showed me another card, and in a quarter of an hour the deck had been gone through, explained and proclaimed Egyptian. And since this was not a figment of our imagination, but rather the result of selected and sensible knowledge of this game in connection with everything that was known about Egyptian ideas, we promised ourselves to surely make it known to the public one day; we were convinced that it would be pleased to have a discovery and a gift of this kind—an Egyptian book which escaped barbarism, the ravages of time, accidental and spontaneous fires and ignorance which is still more disastrous.
>
> —from *Tarot Classic* (1972), by Stuart R. Kaplan

Court de Gébelin said that the word *tarot* was derived from two Egyptian words, *tar*, meaning "road," and *ro*, meaning "royal." (Don't forget that this "translation" of two alleged Egyptian words preceded the Rosetta stone.) The Tarot, he said, represented the "royal road" to wisdom. Furthermore, the twenty-two trumps were representations of twenty-two stone tablets hidden in a temple that at one time had sat between the paws of the Great Sphinx, but had long ago disappeared into the sands. The cards were either allegories of Egyptian philosophy and religion expressed in hieroglyphics or told the history of the world, beginning with Mercury (Hermes). The four suits of the Minor Arcana represented four classes of Egyptian society. Swords were rulers and military nobility; wands were agriculture; cups were clergy and priests; and coins were commerce.

Court de Gébelin found additional Egyptian connections with the number seven, which was sacred to

Egyptians: each suit of the Minor Arcana contained fourteen cards, or two times seven; the Major Arcana consisted of twenty-one numbered cards, or three times seven, plus the unnumbered Fool. He said the presence of The High Priestess confirmed their antiquity, as no modern deck would have such a pagan figure, and furthermore, she appeared with the horns of Isis. (It should be noted that horns are a virtually universal religious or esoteric symbol.)

According to Court de Gébelin, the Egyptians devised a card game with the Tarot, which they passed on to the Romans during the early Christian centuries. The game remained within Italy until the time of the Holy Roman Empire. The cards were dispersed throughout Europe by the Gypsies, who had saved all that was left of the ancient Egyptian writings.

If Tarot cards had existed in ancient Egypt, they would have been associated with Thoth, the god of magic, wisdom, learning, writing, healing, arithmetic, and astrology, who created the universe and transmitted his wisdom to mankind. An ibis-headed or baboon-headed deity shown in art with a pen-and-ink holder, Thoth was called the "Lord of the Divine Books" and "Scribe of the Company of Gods." According to myth, he restored the eye of Horus after it was torn to pieces by the evil Seth. Egyptian priests directed spells for the dead to him, because he recorded the weighing of the hearts of the souls in the underworld Judgment Hall of Osiris, and had the power to reanimate corpses.

The Greeks identified Thoth with his Greek counterpart, Hermes, the patron god of magic, the messenger to other gods and the courier of souls of the dead to the underworld. Thoth-Hermes in turn became identified with Hermes Trismegistus, the "Thrice-Greatest Hermes," a mythical figure credited with the authorship of from 20,000 to more than 36,000 sacred books of wisdom housed in the royal library of Alexandria. All but forty-two of the books supposedly were lost in fires when the city was sacked in the fourth century, and they survived through the ages as the Hermetica, the foundation of Western occultism, the secrets of which for centuries were said to be passed down orally from master to student. It is said that Thoth presented the *Book of Thoth*, or the "Key to Immortality," to his successors. It is said to contain the secrets for immortality—the quest of alchemy—and the means by which mankind can come into the presence of the gods. The book supposedly served as a text to the ancient mystery cults that flourished during the Hellenistic era, and after the demise of the mysteries was removed to some unknown and distant land, where it is still held in safekeeping by certain adepts.

Such beliefs were held among many occultists of Court de Gébelin's day, but in fact, the Hermetica was not of ancient Egyptian origin, but a much later Christian forgery. This had been demonstrated at least a century earlier than the time of Court de Gébelin, but the ancient Egyptian theories continued to have adherents, who preferred mystery to fact.

Court de Gébelin's Tarot theory, published as part of his nine-volume book, *Le Monde Primitif* (1773–1784), had an enormous romantic appeal and became quite popular. But the "Egyptian Connection" was never substantiated. Court de Gébelin's twenty-two stone tablets and secret temple between the paws of the Sphinx have never been found.

The lack of Egyptian evidence did not prevent *Le Monde Primitif* from becoming a definitive source on the Tarot for the better part of a century, although the images Court de Gébelin reproduced were primitive and differed somewhat from the Marseilles deck. As for the Major Arcana, Court de Gébelin placed the unnumbered Fool card at the beginning and gave it a Zero. He by no means had the last word on this.

The Egyptian theory was heavily promoted by an opportunistic follower of Court de Gébelin, a Parisian wigmaker named Alliette, who began spelling his name backwards—Etteilla—and rose to great fame telling fortunes as *Le Celebre Etteilla*. Waite labeled him an "illiterate and zealous adventurer." Never one to let facts and history stand in the way of a good story, Etteilla caught the public's fancy with his story of how the *Book of Thoth* was produced in the 1828th year of Creation by seventeen Magi, one of whom was Tri-Mercury, a descendant of Mercury and a great-grandson of Noah. Beginning in 1783, Etteilla inundated the public with his writings, claiming to have devoted some forty years to the study of Egyptian magic, the key of which had been discovered in the Tarot. Etteilla enthusiastically applied the Tarot to astrology, alchemy, and fortune-telling, and was a major influence in the raising of cartomancy to an exalted art.

Etteilla devised his own Tarot deck, distinct from other Tarot cards and apparently with little regard for any particular symbolism, and used them in his fortune-telling. He was later accused by the influential occultist, Eliphas Lévi, of using his cards to hypnotize his clients.

Many occultists who followed Court de Gébelin and Etteilla blindly accepted and reiterated the alleged Egyptian origin of the Tarot. Finally, in 1910, Waite—an illustrious member of the Hermetic Order of the Golden Dawn in London—attempted to put it to rest once and for all. Writing in his own commentary, *The Pictorial Key to the Tarot* (1910), Waite stated flatly that:

> . . . there is in fact no history [of the Tarot] prior to the fourteenth century. The deception and self-deception regarding their origin in Egypt, India or China put a lying spirit into the mouths of the first expositors, and the later occult writers have done little more than reproduce the first false testimony in the good faith of an intelligence unawakened to the issues of research.

14

As for Court de Gébelin, Waite said in another text:

> I respect M. de Gébelin for having conceived Egyptology by an act of the mind so long before it could have been conceived in any body of research; I respect him for having had, out of previous expectation, a vision concerning the Tarot, but as he did not marry his vision to any facts on this earth, I think he has only begotten a phantom son of the fancy.

The outlandish pronouncements of Court de Gébelin and Etteilla marked the beginning of a new stage in the evolution of the Tarot: the search for the truth about the purpose of the cards and their hidden meanings. The most creative theories were yet to come.

TWO

The Kabbalah Connection

In 1799, the Rosetta stone was discovered by troops of
Napoleon Bonaparte, and was so-named for Rosetta,
Egypt, near where the slab was found. Its hieroglyphics were deciphered by Jean Francois Champollion in
1821 and were found to have nothing to say about
anything remotely connected to Tarot cards. That
should have dashed Court de Gébelin's exotic theory
to pieces, but romantic ideas die hard, and the
Egyptian origin hypothesis resolutely survived.
Some occultists, however, did begin to look elsewhere
for explanations of the Tarot—and found them in the
Kabbalah of the Renaissance.

One of these individuals was Eliphas Lévi (1810–
1875), the pseudonym of Alphonse Louis Constant, a
French philosopher, occultist, and an Abbe of the
Roman Catholic Church, who helped revive interest
in ritual magic. Eliphas Lévi is a shortened version of
Eliphas Levi Zahed, Constant's name in Hebrew,
which he adopted for occult purposes. Arthur Edward
Waite dismissed him as an intellectual lightweight—
"only Etteilla a second time around in the flesh"—but
Lévi's peers regarded him as a man of great learning,
and his theories were given much credence.

Lévi's study of occultism naturally included the
Kabbalah and the so-called doctrine of universal correspondences. An important distinction must be made
here between the true, Jewish Kabbalah and other
Kabbalahs, which are amalgams. The true Kabbalah
is the mysticism of classical Judaism and is founded
on the Torah. It has absolutely nothing to do with

the Tarot. The term *Kabbalah* means "that which is received," and refers to a secret oral tradition which, according to legend, was passed from God to angels, and from angels to Adam in order to provide mankind with a way back to God after the Fall. Adam in turn passed the Kabbalah to Noah, who initiated seventy Elders, and so on.

The Kabbalah appears to have been influenced by Gnosticism and Neoplatonism, which also were influences upon the Hermetica. Although early Hebrew mystical practices date to at least 100 B.C., the historical origin and central structure of the classical Kabbalah come from a short book, *Sefer Yezirah* (*"Book of Creation"* or *"Book of Formation"*), which was in circulation in the tenth century, but may be much older, perhaps as early as the third century. *Sefer Yezirah* states that God created the world by means of thirty-two secret paths of wisdom, the ten *sephirot* and the twenty-two letters of the Hebrew alphabet. Originally the *sephirot* apparently referred to numbers, but later became the emanations by which all reality is structured, as symbolized in the Tree of Life. The twenty-two letters of the alphabet and their sounds form the foundation of all things. Thus, letters possess an enormous power to unleash formidable creative energies.

By the tenth century, practical Kabbalism, as it was called, employed magical ritual, prayer, meditation, and contemplation, and placed great importance upon the power of words. Various techniques were used—most notably gematria—to discover the truths and hidden meanings behind words. In gematria, numerical values are assigned to letters. The numbers in words are added up and are related to other words with the same numerical values. Gematria was used as early as the eighth century B.C. by the Babylonians, and also by the Greeks and early Christians. The Kabbalists used gematria to interpret the Old Testament, which they believed was written in code. For example, the passage from Jeremiah 9:9 says in part, "from the fowl of the heavens until the beasts are fled and gone . . ."

17

According to gematria, that really meant that no travelers had passed through Judea for fifty-two years, the Hebrew word for "beast," *behemah,* having a numerical value of fifty-two. Gematria commentaries on the Old Testament were quite complex.

In the late thirteenth century, another major Kabbalistic work, *Sefer ha-Zohar ("Book of Splendor")* elaborated on the *sephirot* as the language of God (this book was passed off as the work of a first-century rabbi). As the Tree of Life, the *sephirot* form the central image of Kabbalistic meditation, and depict the descent of the Divine into material form and the way by which man can ascend to union with God. Each *sephirah* is a level of attainment in knowledge: the seven lower are Sovereignty, Foundation, Endurance, Majesty, Beauty, Loving-kindness, and Judgment, and the top three are Understanding, Wisdom, and Crown (Humility).

The *sephirot* also are divided among the Four Worlds that constitute the cosmos: Atziluth, the world of archetypes, from which are derived all forms of manifestation; Briah, the world of creation, in which archetypal ideas become patterns; Yetzirah, the world of formation, in which the patterns are expressed; and Assiah, the world of the material.

Finally, the *sephirot* comprise the sacred and unspeakable personal name of God: YHVH (Yahweh), the Tetragrammaton, comprised of the letters Yod, Heh, Vau, and Heh. The Tetragrammaton translates to "That which was, That which is, That which shall be." The four letters correspond to the Four Worlds, as shown in Figure 1.

During the Renaissance, a Hermetic Kabbalah was formed as an amalgam of the Jewish Kabbalah and the Hermetica. A Christian Kabbalah also was created and purported to prove the divinity of Christ. The Christian Kabbalah mingled with the Hermetic Kabbalah, and eventually most of the Christian elements were dropped out. The Hermetic Kabbalah became

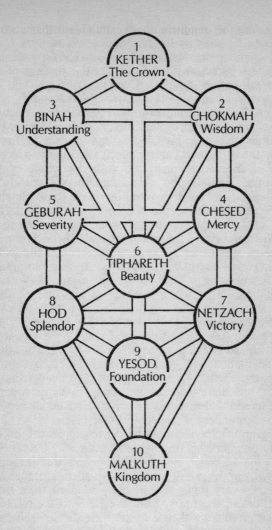

Figure 1   TREE OF LIFE
The ten *sephirot* and the paths connecting them

19

the basis of mainstream Western occultism, as it reached its peak by the late nineteenth century.

Concerning the doctrine of universal correspondences, Lévi was particularly influenced by the writings of the sixteenth-century occultist, Cornelius Agrippa, and the eighteenth-century mystic, Emanuel Swedenborg.

The doctrine of universal correspondences exists in some form in most esoteric texts and teachings. Most significantly, it is included in the central Hermetic text, the Emerald Tablet, which according to occult lore is an emerald inscribed with the whole of the Egyptians' philosophy. According to one version of the legend, it was discovered in a cave tomb clutched in the hand of the corpse of Hermes Trismegistus. The text of the alleged tablet has never been proved to be of ancient origin, but, like the rest of the Hermetic writings, was of later, Christian authorship. The text is by and large inscrutable (and no two translations agree), but its opening is held to be the axiom of Western occultism: "That which is above is like that which is below and that which is below is like that which is above, to achieve the wonders of the one thing." It also states that "all things were produced by the one word of being, so all things were produced from this one thing by adaptation. . . . Ascend with the greatest sagacity from the earth to heaven, and then again descend to earth, and unite together the powers of things superior and inferior." From this axiom evolved occult systems of correspondences and sympathetic magic.

Agrippa expounded upon correspondences in the first volume of his three-volume opus, *On Occult Philosophy*, in which he said that "every inferior thing should, in its kind, answer its superior thing . . . Hence, every thing may be aptly reduced from these Inferiors to the Stars, from the Stars to their Intelligences, and from thence to the First Cause itself from the series and order whereof all Magic and all Occult Philosophy flows . . ."

Writing some two centuries later, Swedenborg placed great emphasis upon the importance of correspondences. In *Heaven and Hell*, he stated that to the ancients, "knowledge of correspondences was the chief of knowledges":

> By means of it they acquired intelligence and wisdom; and by means of it those who were of the church had communication with heaven; for the knowledge of correspondences is angelic knowledge. The most ancient people, who were celestial men, thought from correspondence itself, as the angels do. And therefore they talked with angels, and the Lord frequently appeared to them, and they were taught by Him. But at this day that knowledge has been so completely lost that no one knows what correspondence is.
>
> Since, then, without a perception of what correspondence is there can be no clear knowledge of the spiritual world or of its inflow into the natural world, nor any clear knowledge of the spirit of man, which is called the soul, and its operation into the body, neither of man's state after death, it is necessary to explain what correspondence is and the nature of it. . . .
> . . . The whole natural world corresponds to the spiritual world and not merely the natural world in general, but also every particular of it; and as a consequence everything in the natural world that springs from the spiritual world is called a correspondent. . . .

Thus correspondences were seen as the way back to the Source, the means by which all great religions and esoteric systems could be unified. For Lévi, the origin of all esoteric teachings could be found in the Tarot and the correspondences between it and the letters of the Hebrew alphabet, the sacred name of God and numbers.

Lévi accepted Court de Gébelin's Egyptian origin theory, and considered the Tarot as a collection of symbolic "hieroglyphs" masking the inner truths of occultism. He was intrigued with the fact that there are twenty-two trumps in the Major Arcana and twenty-two letters in the Hebrew alphabet, which in turn has a numerical value and corresponds to the twenty-two paths in the Kabbalistic Tree of Life. He corresponded each Tarot trump to a Hebrew letter and devoted twenty-two chapters to these correspondences in his first and most important occult book, *The Dogma and Ritual of High Magic* (1861). Lévi described the Tarot as a miraculous book, the source of inspiration of all the sacred ancient books, and a perfect tool for divination "on account of the analogical precision of its figures and its numbers. In fact, the oracles of this book are always rigorously true, and even when it does not predict anything, it always reveals something that was hidden, and gives the wisest counsel to those who consult it."

Lévi opined that the Tarot was handed down by "certain wise kabbalists" who preserved their sacred knowledge "first on ivory, parchment, on gilt and silvered leather, and afterwards on simple cards, which were always the objects of suspicion to the Official Church as containing a dangerous key to its mysteries." He heaped praise upon Court de Gébelin for ferreting out the "truth" and criticized Etteilla.

Before he could draw his correspondences between trumps and letters, Lévi had to decide where to place the unnumbered Fool card in the sequence of trumps. In order to get the synchronization he desired, he moved The Fool from the beginning to between the last two cards, XX, Judgement, and XXI, The Universe or World. This enabled him to correspond The Fool with the letter Shin, the symbol of Life-Breath of the Holy Ones, or the Holy Spirit. The insertion did not change the number of the final card, which remained XXI. The sequence of the cards went from one to twenty to zero to twenty-one. In *Ritual*, Lévi provided his keys to the Major Arcana and their corresponding Hebrew letters as follows:

I The Magician. Aleph.
Being, mind, man or God; the incomprehensible object; unity mother of numbers, the first matter.

II The Female Pope. Beth.
The house of God and man, the sanctuary, the law, gnosis, Cabala, the hidden church, the binary, woman, mother.

III The Empress. Gimel.
The Word, the ternary, plenitude, fruitfulness, nature, generation of the three worlds.

IV The Emperor. Daleth.
The door of government among the Orientals, initiation, power, the tetragram, the quaternary, the cubic stone or its base [a symbol of the manifested universe; also, an alchemical symbol for salt, itself a symbol of the earth; also, a symbol of the fraternal Lodge].

V The Pope. Heh.
Indication, demonstration, teaching, law, symbolism, philosophy, religion.

VI Vice and Virtue or The Lovers. Vau.
Linking together, hooking, lingam, intermingling, union, embrace, struggle, antagonism, combination, equilibrium.

VII The Chariot. Zain.
Weapon, swords, flaming sword of the church, holy septenary, triumph, royalty, priesthood.

VIII Justice. Heth.
Balance, attraction and repulsion, life, fear, promise and menace.

IX The Hermit. Teth.
Good, fear of evil, morality, wisdom.

X The Wheel of Fortune. Yod.
Principle, manifestation, praise, manly honor, phallus, virile fecundity, the scepter of the father.

XI Strength. Kaph.
A hand in the act of taking and holding.

XII The Hanged Man. Lamed.
Example, teaching, public instruction.

XIII Death. Mem.
The heaven of Jupiter and Mars, domination and force, rebirth, creation and destruction.

XIV Temperance. Nun.
The heaven of the Sun, temperatures, seasons, movement, changes of life, always new and yet always the same.

XV The Devil. Samech.
The heaven of Mercury, occult science, magic, commerce, eloquence, mystery, moral strength.

XVI The Tower. Ayin.
The heaven of the moon, alterations, subversions, changes, weakness.

XVII The Star. Phe.
The heaven of the soul, thought emissions, moral influence of the idea on forms, immortality.

XVIII The Moon. Tzaddi.
The elements, the visible world, reflected light, material forms, symbolism.

XIX The Sun. Quoph.
Mixtures, the head, the summit, the prince of heaven.

XX Judgment. Resh.
The vegetative, earth's generative power, eternal life.

0 The Fool. Shin.
Sensibility, flesh, eternal life.

XXI The Universe or World. Tau.
The microcosm, the résumé of all in all.

Lévi found Kabbalistic associations for the Minor Arcana by corresponding the four suits and the four court cards in each suit to the four letters of the Tetragrammaton:

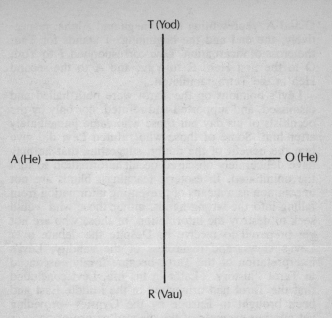

T (Yod)

A (He) ———————————————————— O (He)

R (Vau)

Figure 2   LEVI'S WHEEL OF LIFE TAROT

Yod—Sceptres (enterprise and glory); King
Heh—Cups (love and happiness); Queen
Vau—Swords (hatred and misfortune); Knight
Heh—Pentacles (money and interest); Page

Lévi also used another Kabbalistic letter-manipulation technique, temurah, to find meaning in the word *Tarot*. Temurah is the transposition of letters in a word to create new words. Thus, Lévi found that "Tarot" could be transposed to *rota*, the Latin term for "wheel," and "Tora," an incomplete spelling of "Torah," the holy scriptures and law of Judaism. The temurah was corroborating evidence to him that the Tarot was indeed a wheel of life or spiritual evolution, and was founded on Kabbalistic wisdom. Lévi represented this graphically as shown in Figure 2.

R stands for the Christ symbol, which lies between

O and A, representing the Omega and Alpha, respectively, the end and the beginning. T stands for Tau, the cross of incarnation. Lévi corresponded T to Yod; O to the first Heh; R to Vau; and A to the second Heh in the Tetragrammaton.

Lévi's opinions on the Tarot were both hailed and dismissed, and supported and refuted, not only by the occultists of his day but those who came immediately after him. Some of those who refuted Lévi did give him the benefit of the doubt, suggesting that he may have deliberately obscured occult information to fool the uninitiated. In esoteric teachings, blinds are not uncommon as a means of preventing information from falling into the wrong hands, either those who would seek to destroy the information, or those who are not yet prepared to receive it. Despite the debate over Lévi's views, and regardless of the validity, Lévi's interpretation of the Tarot became firmly ensconced in Tarot "history." Later in his life, Lévi concluded that the Tarot had originated in the Middle East and been brought to Europe by the Gypsies—providing yet another example of the diehard nature of popular fancies.

Lévi's work with the Kabbalah was expanded even further by another Frenchman, Gerard Encausse (1868–1916), a physician who went by the occult pseudonym, Papus. As a leading Martinist and member of the Kabbalistic Order of the Rose-Cross, Papus, too, was steeped in occultism. He saw the Tarot as presenting the spiritual history of man: the emergence of the soul from the Source, descending to the material, then returning to the Source. In his most important work on the Tarot, *The Tarot of the Bohemians: The Absolute Key to Occult Science* (1889), he optimistically predicted that society was on the verge of incredible transformation, and that materialism was on the way out. What was needed was synthesis, in the fashion of the wisdom taught by the ancients.

In ancient times, Papus said, knowledge was transmitted only to those who had proved themselves worthy by passing tests of initiation. The knowledge was transmitted in the secret rites of the Mysteries, upon which the adept became known as a Priest or Initiate. There came a time when the Initiates realized that their knowledge might be lost forever, and they established three ways for preserving it: through secret societies, the "cultus," and the people. The secret societies originated primarily from Alexandria, the great ancient seat of learning, and included such groups as the Gnostics, alchemists, Knights Templar, Rosicrucians, and Freemasons. The cultus was the means by which the one true religion was translated to religions that would suit the temperaments of all peoples, each with its own tradition and holy scriptures. The people were those entrusted with preserving and transmitting occult doctrines—specifically, the Bohemians, or Gypsies, whose card game of Tarot was the "Bible of Bibles . . . the book of Thoth Hermes Trismegistus, the book of Adam, the book of the primitive Revelation of ancient civilization," said Papus.

The key to the Tarot, he said, was the Tetragrammaton, YHVH, each letter of which not only had Tarot correspondences, but also correspondences with Christian symbols: Yod = the episcopal crosier; Heh = the chalice; Vau = the Cross; and Heh = the Host. The Tarot itself was based on the word ROTA, arranged as a wheel, each letter corresponding to a letter in the Tetragrammaton: R = Vau; O = Heh; T = Yod; and A = Heh.

Papus adopted Lévi's ridiculous placement of The Fool between XX and XXI of the Major Arcana, but he did have the sense to recognize that Etteilla's deck was "of no symbolic value" and "a bad mutilation of the real Tarot."

Papus also laid great stress upon the Pythagorean system of numbers in deciphering the meaning of the cards.

Papus soberly proclaimed that his Kabbalistic explanation of the Tarot was "for the exclusive use of Initiates." Undoubtedly, anyone who was not an Initiate would recognize this shortcoming immediately and, out of humility and respect, would not dare to open the cover of his book.

Thus, Lévi, Papus, and a few others, including the occultist, Oswald Wirth, laid the foundation for a Kabbalistic Tarot, which then was brought up to the state of high art by the Hermetic Order of the Golden Dawn.

The short-lived Golden Dawn, established in 1888 in London, placed the Hermetic Kabbalah and the Tarot at the center of its teachings. In its brief life span—by 1896 it was in eclipse—the Order possessed the greatest store of Western occult and magical teachings, and attracted the crème de la crème of occultists, including Waite, Samuel Liddell MacGregor Mathers, W. B. Yeats, and Aleister Crowley.

At that time, antiquity was still prized above all, and so to claim ancient roots, the Order was founded upon an "ancient manuscript" written in cipher that supposedly was discovered in 1884 in a London bookstall by Rev. A.F.A. Woodford, a Mason and member of an occult study group called The Hermetic Society. In 1887, Woodford sent parts of the manuscript to Dr. William Wynn Westcott and Dr. William Robert Woodman, officers in the Rosicrucian Society of England. Westcott contacted Mathers, an occultist, who, with the help of his clairvoyant wife, determined that the manuscript concerned the Kabbalah and the Tarot.

Westcott then followed instructions in a mysterious letter attached to the manuscript to contact "Sapiens Dominabitur Astris," in care of a Fraulein Ann Sprengel in Hanover, Germany. Sprengel advised Westcott that he and his associates could establish "an elementary Branch of the Rosicrucian Order in England." In so doing, the Golden Dawn claimed to be directly descended from Christian Rosencreutz, the fictitious founder of Rosicrucianism.

The purpose of the Golden Dawn was "to prosecute the Great Work: which is to obtain control of the nature and power of my own being." Teachings were given on ritual magic, the Kabbalah, the Tarot, astral travel, scrying, alchemy, geomancy, and astrology. Mathers adopted "Qabalah" as the spelling for Kabbalah, stating that it was closer to the original Hebrew term.

Of great importance was a set of Tarot papers called *Book T*, which was given to initiates. *Book T* set forth the Tarot as the key to the Hermetic Kabbalah and all Western esotericism, and corresponded the Major Arcana to the Hebrew alphabet. According to Rosicrucian legend, *Book T* was found clutched in the hand of the perfectly preserved corpse of Christian Rosencreutz when his secret burial vault was discovered in 1604. He supposedly had died in 1484 at 106 years of age.

Golden Dawn Tarot teachings also corresponded the Major Arcana to the paths connecting the *sephirot* of the Tree of Life. Mathers, who claimed prodigious feats with the help of occult powers, designed a Tarot deck for the Golden Dawn, and his wife painted the finished product. Members copied the original. Decades later, the deck was reconstructed by artist Robert Wang, working under the direction of Israel Regardie, onetime secretary to Crowley and a member of one of the Golden Dawn's offshoot lodges, *Stella Matutina*. It was published in 1978, marking the first time the deck was made public.

The link between Tarot and Kabbalah also was put forth by another influential occultist, Paul Foster Case (1884–1954), a onetime member of the Golden Dawn and the founder of the Builders of the Adytum. Case composed a thoughtful and detailed analysis of the Tarot-Hebrew alphabet correspondences in his work, *The Tarot: A Key to the Wisdom of the Ages* (1947). His correspondences included not only the letters but the accompanying colors and musical tones associated with each letter, and the astrological signs that fit each Arcanum. With the letter correspondences, Case probed the hidden, occult meanings of Hebrew words by spelling them out with the Tarot, with the greatest yield coming from many words in the Old

Testament, divine and angelic names, and the names of the twelve tribes of Israel.

Although Case appreciated Lévi's efforts to associate The Fool with the Holy Spirit, he found Lévi's overall approach ridiculous. "The attribution of the major trumps to the Hebrew alphabet is the crux in Tarot study," Case stated. "Eliphas Lévi knew it but could not give it, because he received it from a secret order. He did, however, announce the fact that the major trumps correspond to the Hebrew letters, and then proceeded to give an attribution so patently absurd that one wonders how it ever gained credence." Case placed The Fool at the beginning of the Major Arcana, assigning it to the letter Aleph, which has the numerical value of one and represents Breath, the Life-Breath or Spirit. This is substantially different than Shin, the Life-Breath of the Holy Ones or Holy Spirit, but does give The Fool, as Zero, the symbolism of formless spirit, or that which precedes creative activities. Case observed that all the other trumps then logically fell into place.

Other Tarot scholars have been less enthusiastic about the associations with the Hebrew alphabet. Manly P. Hall termed such associations "far from convincing," and Waite stated, "I am not to be included among those who are satisified that there is a valid correspondence between Hebrew letters and Tarot Trump symbols." Case countered that Waite's own interpretation of the Tarot, published in 1910, showed that he agreed with the correspondence. "In his [Waite's] later writings he endeavored to throw dust in the eyes of the uninitiated by pretending to believe that the attribution of the cards to the letters . . . was not the true arrangement," Case stated. "Yet his own rectifications of the symbolism and numbering of earlier exoteric versions of this picture-book of Ageless Wisdom are sufficient evidence that he understood and accepted the validity of this attribution." Waite did make references to the Kabbalah in his book written to accompany the Rider-Waite deck, *The Pictorial*

Key to the Tarot, and Kabbalistic symbols are apparent in the images.

Many Jewish Kabbalists and scholars understandably frown on what they consider to be misrepresentations of the true Kabbalah, such as promulgated by the Hermetic Kabbalah occultists of the eighteenth century and later. One outspoken scholar was Gershom Scholem, who wrote in his book, *Kabbalah* (1974):

> The many books written on the subject in the nineteenth and twentieth centuries by various theosophists and mystics lacked any basic knowledge of the sources and very rarely contributed to the field, while at times they even hindered the development of a historical approach. Similarly, the activities of French and English occultists contributed nothing and only served to create considerable confusion between the teachings of the Kabbalah and their own totally unrelated inventions, such as the alleged kabbalistic origin of the Tarot-cards. To this category of supreme charlatanism belong the many and widely read books of Eliphas Lévi (actually Alphonse Louis Constant; 1810–1875), Papus (Gerard Encausse; 1868–1916), and Frater Perduabo (Aleister Crowley; 1875–1947), all of whom had infinitesimal knowledge of Kabbalah that did not prevent them from drawing freely on their imaginations instead.

Such criticisms, however, have not dampened study of the Kabbalistic Tarot, for the correspondences between the letters and the trumps do seem to have an interesting significance. Though Waite was not convinced of the validity of the associations, he did once allow, "The attempt to connect the symbols of the Tarot with the system of Kabalistic [sic] theosophy will seem in itself arbitrary, but it can, under certain circumstances, produce very curious results." Some will say these results are mere coincidence; others will say that hidden truths lie therein. At the very least, a parallel may be drawn between the Hermetic Kabbalah and the Tarot as different systems that express the same cosmic truths. The Tree of Life provides the road map for this avenue of study.

For detailed approaches to the Kabbalistic Tarot, see Case's *The Tarot: A Key to the Wisdom of the Ages* and *The Book of Tokens* (1934); *The Qabalistic Tarot* by Robert Wang (1987); and *A Practical Guide to Qabalistic Symbolism* (1978) by Gareth Knight. The latter book is a single-volume edition of two earlier works, *On the Spheres of the Tree of Life* and *On the Paths of the Tarot* (1965).

The Astrology Connection

An apparent connection between the Tarot and astrology is much less controversial. Astrology has been practiced the world over, and in the West was a science through the Renaissance and was readily accessible to the masses. In Western astrology, the Chaldeans, as early as the fifth century B.C., may have been the first to associate the positions of heavenly bodies with human birth times and personal destinies. The ancient Babylonians also practiced astrology, and either they or the Chaldeans codified the twelve constellations of the Zodiac around 3000 B.C. From these studies emerged the horoscope, though it was the Greeks who perfected it and made it available to the general public. The stars were believed to govern not only personal destiny, but all manner of decisions and the courses of events. Astrology was denounced by early Christians—in A.D. 333 the Emperor Constantine called it "demonic," and later St. Augustine opposed it as well—but it remained within popular belief. In the twelfth century, it enjoyed a comeback as a science, due in part, interestingly, to the work of Spanish Kabbalists (true Kabbalists), and did not fall out of favor as a science until after the mid-seventeenth century.

Thus, it is logical that popular cards originating in

medieval and Renaissance Europe would have some sort of astrological connotations. The cards alleged to have been painted by Jacquemin Gringonneur include one showing a crescent moon and two astrologers, clothed in long robes with hoods, holding a compass and a book bearing astrological symbols. The Tarocchi of Mantegna, from circa the late fifteenth century, include a card called "Astrology" in one of its five series, and ten cards in another series devoted to the order of the heavens.

→ Symbols in the Major Arcana of the Marseilles deck of 1790 do show some correspondence to celestial bodies. There are, of course, the cards titled for celestial bodies—The Moon, The Sun, and The Star. Aquarius is evoked in Temperance, in which a winged figure pours water between two vessels, as well as in The Star, in which a naked woman pours water from two vessels into a body of water. The Moon includes a scorpion (perhaps evocative of Scorpio or Cancer), Strength a lion (Leo), Justice scales (Libra), The Sun twin children (Gemini), and so on.

Occultists of the eighteenth and nineteenth centuries matched the Tarot to the heavens. No two agreed. Etteilla corresponded the trumps to the Zodiac and seven planets (which in astrology include the moon and sun), which totaled but nineteen—he solved the problem by leaving left three arcana unmatched. Oswald Wirth drew up a table corresponding the Major Arcana to both the letters of the Hebrew alphabet and the constellations (including the twelve signs of the Zodiac) and a few stars; he placed The Fool last. He gave some of the cards multiple celestial associations:

MAJOR ARCANA	CONSTELLATIONS/ STARS
The Juggler	Orion—the Bull (Taurus)
The High Priestess	Cassiopeia
The Empress	The Virgin (Virgo)

The Emperor	Hercules, Lyra, Boreal Crown (Corona Borealis)
The Pope	The Ram (Aries)
The Lovers	Eagle (Aquila), Antinous, Sagittarius
The Chariot	Great Bear (Ursa Major)
Justice	The Balance (Libra)
The Hermit	The Ox-Driver (Bootes)
The Wheel of Fortune	Capricorn (opposed to Sirius)
Strength	Lion (Leo), Virgin (Virgo)
The Hanged Man	Perseus
Death	Dragon of the Pole (Draco)
Temperance	Aquarius
The Devil	Goat (Capricorn), Coachman
Lightning-struck Tower	Scorpion (Scorpio), Ophiuchus
The Star	Andromeda, the Fishes (Pisces)
The Moon	Cancer, Sirius, Procion
The Sun	The Twins (Gemini)
Judgement	The Swan (Cygnus)
The Universe	Lesser Bear and Pole Star (Ursa Minor and Polàris)
The Foolish Man	Cepheus

Papus also applied his Tarot theories to astrology, stating in *The Tarot of the Bohemians* that such correspondence was necessary in order to prove the accuracy "of the principles upon which the construction of the Tarot is based." He based his analysis on the Egyptian year of four seasons, each with three months, and each month with three ten-day periods called *decani* (a five-day period was added to make a

365-day year). All of these things must be found in the Tarot, Papus said. He went on to correspond the suits of the Minor Arcana to the four seasons; the top three court cards of each suit to a figure of the Zodiac (the knaves were transition cards) and to a season; and each card in the Minor Arcana to a *decan*. The Zodiac signs and *decani* were in turn governed by planets. Papus also accepted Wirth's astrological correspondences to the Major Arcana. Upon this basis, Papus said, Tarot cards could be used to cast a horoscope.

Astrological correspondences became more overt after the turn of the twentieth century, when Waite reinterpreted the Tarot with his own deck and incorporated astrological symbols into his images. More recent decks also have incorporated astrological symbolisms, and spreads have been designed around the horoscope. However, there remains no definitive match between the Major Arcana and the signs of the Zodiac and planets; correspondences vary considerably.

New Directions

From the preceding, we can see that the history, development, and interpretation of the Tarot are by no means definite. Its known origins and history exist in the barest of fragments, and the precise meaning of it—assuming there is one—has been the subject of much guesswork and opinion.

During the twentieth century, the Tarot began to break free of rigid theories and assigned meanings, and to grow and flower in new incarnations. This has opened up exciting and challenging new ways to work with the cards.

THREE

From Waite to Jung and Beyond

In the early twentieth century, Arthur Edward Waite reinterpreted the Tarot cards according to what he believed were their original, lost mystical meanings. Waite, who was a Mason as well as a member of the Golden Dawn, drew upon *Book T* and his knowledge of the Hermetic Kabbalah in redesigning the card images. His version was executed by a fellow member of the Golden Dawn, Pamela Colman Smith, an artist with psychic abilities. Waite's stated purpose was to "produce a Tarot with an appeal in the world of art and a suggestion of significance beyond the Symbols which would put on them another construction than had ever been dreamed by those who, through many generations, had produced and used them for mere divinatory purposes." The card symbols, he said, were "gates which opened on realms of vision beyond occult dreams."

Published in 1910 by Rider & Company, the Rider-Waite deck, as it became known, established itself as the new, definitive Tarot, the standard against which all other Tarot interpretations were measured for the better part of the twentieth century. Despite the proliferation of Tarot decks, and the increasing latitude in their designs, the Rider-Waite deck remains the most popular. It is considered the best deck for learning the Tarot. While some Tarot practitioners move on to other decks and leave Rider-Waite behind, many more stay with it as the deck of choice. Still others make Rider-Waite their primary deck, and use other decks for occasional variation.

Although Waite did not believe Tarot cards to be older than the fourteenth century, he did believe their symbols were much older, of ancient origin, in fact, and that they contained universal ideas. The spurious history and theories concerning the Tarot, and the bad designs given the cards such as by Etteilla, prompted Waite to "restore and rectify" the cards. As for fortune-telling, the Tarot was never intended for such purpose, he said, but was adapted to it. The fact that nothing but divinatory meanings had ever been assigned the Minor Arcana indicated that the Tarot was a merger of two independently evolved decks. In his book, *The Pictorial Key to the Tarot*, written to accompany the deck, he said:

The true Tarot is symbolism; it speaks no other language and offers no other signs. Given the inward meaning of its emblems, they do become a kind of alphabet which is capable of indefinite combinations and makes true sense in all. On the highest plane it offers a key to the Mysteries, in a manner which is not arbitrary and has not been read in. But the wrong symbolical stories have been told concerning it, and the wrong history has been given in every published work which so far has dealt with the subject. . . .

[The Tarot] is not, by attribution or otherwise, a derivative of any one school of literature of occultism; it is not of Alchemy or Kabalism [sic] or Astrology or Ceremonial Magic; . . . it is a presentation of universal ideas by means of universal types, and it is in the combination of these types—if anywhere—that it presents Secret Doctrine.

In redesigning the cards, Waite said that he drew upon the "Secret Doctrine" (i.e., the Golden Dawn teachings) as much as he could within the confines of restrictions against revealing too much to noninitiates. He accepted sole responsibility for the variations in symbols from the Marseilles deck, the standard up to that time. He dramatically changed the Tarot forever by giving the pip cards of the Minor Arcana pictures instead of just designs of suit symbols in the number of each card. The pictures were interpretations of divinatory meanings, drawn from many sources but still somewhat arbitrary in nature.

It is sometimes erroneously reported in Tarot literature that he moved The Fool to the beginning of the pack. On the contrary, he left The Fool, numbered zero, between XX and XXI, where Lévi had placed it. He did so despite the fact that he believed that Court de Gébelin's placement of The Fool at the beginning of the pack made more sense, and that the efforts to correspond the cards to the Hebrew alphabet remained unsatisfactory. "The truth is that the real arrangement of the cards has never transpired," he said. The placement of The Fool was a source of disagreement between Waite and Smith; significantly, it is the only design she did not sign.

Waite also transposed two cards in the Major Arcana, Justice and Strength (or Fortitude), but gave no explanation for his reasons in doing so. In the Marseilles deck, Justice and Strength are XI and VIII, respectively. In the Rider-Waite deck, they trade places. The transposition is still debated. An argument is made on the one hand that Waite rectified a blind used to veil the true meaning of the cards, and an argument is made on the other hand that he deliberately created a blind. Paul Foster Case's theory was that Waite had changed the cards to fit astrological associations: the number VIII card should correspond to Leo, and thus Strength, the woman subduing the lion, is appropriate; the number XI card should correspond to Libra, and thus Justice, holding the scales, provides a match. Because Waite never made public his reasoning, this may or may not have been the case.

In the court cards, Waite replaced the Knave with the Page, a youth who is in servitude to the Knight, who in turn is the son of the Queen and King.

Waite's interpretation of the Tarot was nothing short of a revolution, especially concerning the pip cards, which became much more suggestive to divination and contemplation with the help of pictures. All images contain numerous occult symbolisms and provide rich terrain for advanced uses of the Tarot. In subsequent decades, the majority of new Tarot decks have taken their cue from Waite, or at least used his deck as a springboard. Most modern decks have Minor Arcana with pictures, follow similar suit designations, and have the transposed Strength and Justice. The Fool, however, most commonly—and most sensibly—is placed at the beginning of the deck. Some decks stay with the so-called French tradition, following the style of the Marseilles deck concerning Strength and Justice and nonpicture Minor Arcana. Other decks take off in completely new directions.

After Waite, another modern figure to greatly influence the Tarot was Case, an esteemed occultist who served as Praemonstrator General (Supreme Chief) of the Order of the Golden Dawn for United States and Canada. Case became fascinated by the Tarot in 1901, and devoted many years to its study. He resigned from the Golden Dawn in order to found the Builders of the Adytum, a Los Angeles-based organization devoted to the study of practical occultism. Case made his own interpretation of the Tarot, drawn by Jesse Burns Parker in the 1920s or 1930s. The deck is published by the Builders of the Adytum and is known as the BOTA deck. Some of the images are similar to Waite's but bear more and significantly different occult symbols; other images are very different altogether. Case's intent was to create cards that were explicit in their symbolism and not obscure, as he felt were Waite's cards. Case placed The Fool at the beginning and accepted Waite's transposition of Strength and Justice. His pip cards are not illustrated with pictures.

Case's cards are inscribed with a corresponding letter of the Hebrew alphabet. The cards are drawn in black and white, to be colored by the Tarot student according to instructions given, on the theory that the act of coloring imbues the cards with particular and personal energies. This is similar to the ceremonial magician's act of making his or her own magical tools, a concept that will be explored further in Chapter Seven, "Tarot Rituals." It is indeed an educational experience to participate in the creation of a Tarot deck, which serves to enhance its personal value and meaning.

There is not space here to discuss all the other interpretations of the Tarot, which made their appearance (some rather briefly) at about the time of Waite's and Case's studies. Of particular interest, however, are the Crowley ("Thoth") and Knapp-Hall versions.

Aleister Crowley's Thoth Tarot was the last great deck to come out of the original Golden Dawn. Crowley was indisputably the most colorful and notorious of the Golden Dawn initiates, the self-proclaimed "Beast of the Apocalypse" and "Lord of the New Aeon" whose ritual magic rites involving sex (much of it abusive), blood sacrifice, and the conjuring of demons earned him the media label of "The Wickedest Man in the World." There seems to be no middle ground when it comes to Crowley: he is either despised as a charlatan or revered as one of the most brilliant ritual magicians of modern times. He managed to destroy himself with dissipation and drugs, yet his writings of magical and mystical instruction survive with an ever-changing audience of formidable size.

Crowley's affiliation with the Golden Dawn was brief: he joined in 1898 and was expelled about a year later after engaging in ego battles with Mathers. He then joined the *Ordo Templi Orientis*, an occult order that he led for a while.

Crowley referred to the Tarot as "the Book of Thoth," and he gave his own interpretation of the Major Arcana—which he called the Atus of Tahuti—as a formula for initiation. "I have satisfied myself that these twenty-two cards compose a complete system of hieroglyphs representing the total energies of the universe," he said. He saw the cards as living entities that could only be understood by living and interacting with them daily over a long period of time.

He also used the Tarot for divination, and recorded at least one incident in which the Tarot passed "a very remarkable test" for that purpose. While in Shanghai, Crowley's hostess was visited by the postmaster, who was distraught over the loss of a packet of a large sum of money that had been mailed by a bank in Peking to its head office in Shanghai. The postmaster had placed the packet in a safe and found it missing less than an hour later. Crowley offered to investigate the situation via the Tarot. Laying out the cards, he was able to accurately describe two postal clerks who had access to the safe. One was reliable and conscientious, and the other, a junior clerk, was careless, a gambler who had an unsavory reputation. Naturally, the junior clerk was the likely suspect, which Crowley said was confirmed by the cards.

Then, however, the cards "went crazy," saying first that the junior clerk should not suffer for his act, and then saying that the postmaster's reputation would not suffer. To Crowley, it made no sense, in light of the loss of a large sum of money, for which the postmaster ultimately would be held responsible. The turn in the reading annoyed Crowley, and he wound up apologizing to the postmaster, saying, "Well, they [the cards] insist that it is all right for you."

Several days later, the reading bore out. The junior clerk had accidentally placed the parcel in the return mail pouch to Peking, and the bank eventually received it. It was all a mistake, and no one suffered any consequences.

Crowley applied the Trumps to astrology, Kabbalistic letter and numerical correspondences and the Tree of Life, and drew a relationship between the Tarot and Enochian magic, a system of magic developed in the sixteenth century by John Dee, the royal astrologer to Queen Elizabeth I, and his associate, Edward Kelly, for communicating with angels and spirits and traveling through various planes, or *aethyrs*, of consciousness.

Crowley set out to restore the cards to their "original form" and give complete explanations of their meanings. He admitted once in print that although he succeeded in doing so with some of the trumps, "[o]thers, however, I understand imperfectly, and of some few I have at present obtained no more than a general idea."

➤He renamed four of the Major Arcana: Justice became Adjustment, Strength became Lust, Temperance became Art, and Judgement became The Aeon. The suits of the Minor Arcana are associated with the four elements: Swords with air, Wands with fire, Cups with water, and Disks with earth. He named the court cards the Knight (father), Queen (mother), Prince (Son), and Princess (Daughter), based on the Hebrew concept of the Mother and Father, who issue the Son and Daughter.

In 1938, Crowley was asked by Lady Frieda Harris to work with her in painting a new deck. Harris's interest in the Tarot had been stimulated by P. D. Ouspensky's book, *The Model of the Universe*. The collaboration spanned five years, during which Harris and Crowley "endeavored to reinstate the cards in their original sacred, simple forms and, in addition, indicate the New Aeon of Horus, a terrifying apparition," according to Harris. Symbols were drawn from Freemasonry, alchemy, Rosicrucianism, Kabbalism, magic, geometry, gematria, mathematics, divination, numerology, the Druids, Spiritualism, psychology, philology, Buddhism, astrology, and heraldry, among others.

The images also are erotic in nature, which is not surprising, considering Crowley's sexual proclivities. Furthermore, the entire deck departs dramatically from the French and Waite traditions.

The first printing in 1944 was a meager quantity of 200 copies. A complete, color edition was not issued until 1969, and an improved edition appeared in 1979. Despite the unsettling, almost disturbed nature of the images, the Thoth deck is one of the most popular decks among the Tarot practitioners.

The Knapp-Hall deck is not widely known, but deserves much wider recognition. Designed by artist

J. A. Knapp in collaboration with philosopher Manly P. Hall, it was first published in 1929 as the "Revised, New Art Tarot Cards." Fifty years later, it was reissued as the Knapp-Hall deck. The classic Major Arcana images begin with The Fool and follow the French school sequence, with La Force (Strength) as 11 and La Justice as 8; influences from the Rider-Waite designs may also be seen, but with different interpretations and occult symbols, and with correspondences to Hebrew letters. The suits of the Minor Arcana as Scepters (enterprise and glory), Cups (love and happiness), Swords (hatred and misfortune), and Pentacles (money and material interests). The pip cards contain no pictures.

The most arresting feature of this unusual deck is that it joins Western and Eastern esoteric philosophies by using the mandala as its foundation. The mandala (a Sanskrit term for "circle") is a circular design used in Buddhist and Hindu religious practices, meditation, and art. In form, it is an ancient and universal symbol, and appears in Western religion and philosophy as well.

The symbolisms of mandalas are highly complex: they are instruments of contemplation, which take a meditator to higher and higher levels of consciousness. In Eastern religions, they are inhabited by innumerable deities, archetypal in nature. Essentially, the mandala represents an ultimate wholeness, and is the point at which macrocosm and microcosm meet—the "That which is above is like that which is below" axiom of the Hermetica. It symbolizes the mystic's journey through various layers of consciousness to the Center, the supreme union with the Divine. When applied to the Tarot, the mandala symbolizes The Fool's journey to wholeness—the spiritual quest of the Tarot student.

Each card in the Knapp-Hall deck features a meditational symbol of one of four levels of consciousness. The symbols, designed by Hall, have never been explained; rather, they are to be discovered and experienced by each Tarot practitioner through contemplation. Thus, the Knapp-Hall deck may be of particular interest to the Tarot practitioner in the pursuit of higher studies involving meditation, which are discussed in the final chapter of this book. Those who wish to delve into this area of study will find an enriching discussion of meditation symbols in Hall's book, *Meditation Symbols in Eastern & Western Mysticism: Mysteries of the Mandala* (1988).

The next great creative revolution in Tarot interpretations commenced in the 1970s, when artists pushed out Tarot boundaries and began exploring new territory. This new wave continues. All rules are off; all traditions subject to reinvention. At the very least, new names are given to the cards and suit signs in many new decks and, in some cases, substantial changes are made.

Tarot images have been interpreted in terms of culture, such as the Xultun (Mayan) deck, created by Peter Balin in 1972 and the Native American Indian deck, created by Magda Weck Gonzalez and J. A. Gonzalez and issued in 1982. Feminist decks, such as Motherpeace, Daughters of the Moon and Amazon, appeared in the 1980s. The first of these, the Motherpeace, created by Vicki Noble and Karen Vogel in 1981, seeks to reinterpret the traditional, patriarchal Tarot images by using Goddess imagery. The deck also broke away from the traditional rectangular shape of cards by using circles (symbolically female), a style also followed by the Daughters of the Moon.

Some Tarot decks seek parallels in other systems. The Mandala Astrological Tarot (1987), created by A. T. Mann, combines the Tarot with astrology. Furthermore, parallels are drawn to the mandala and to the alchemical symbol of squaring the circle. The cards are square in shape, and the images are contained within circles. The Merlin Tarot (1988), created by R. J. Stewart, draws on the ancient Celtic tradition based upon the *Vita Merlini* and *Prophecies of Merlin* set down by Geoffrey of Monmouth in the middle of the twelfth century. The Merlin Tarot also uses a simplified Tree of Life with different correspondents than those that are part of the Golden Dawn legacy. The Witches Tarot (1988), created by Ellen Cannon Reed, approaches the Tarot from the perspective of the Craft and Paganism, and the Hermetic Kabbalah.

Gerald and Betty Schueler's Enochian Tarot (1988) is based on Enochian magic, a system credited to John Dee, the royal astronomer to Elizabeth I, and his scalawag assistant, Edward Kelly. Following the deaths of Dee and Kelly, Enochian magic fell into obscurity for about two centuries, until the Golden Dawn revived practice of it. The magical system reportedly was revealed to Kelly by angels during scrying; Kelly encountered the angels when he traveled astrally to subtle regions called the Watchtowers and Aethyrs. According to Enochian magic, Divinity expresses itself from the spiritual world downward into time, space, and form in a series of planes and subplanes, the lowest of which is the earth plane. The five main planes are the four Watchtowers and the Tablet of Union, which connects them all together. Thirty Aethyrs exist separately but interpenetrate the main planes. The Enochian Tarot has eighty-six cards: the Major Arcana consists of thirty cards instead of twenty-two, one for each Aethyr.

Artist Bob Place draws a parallel between alchemy and the Tarot in The Alchemical Tarot. Place was inspired in 1987, while browsing through Emile Grillot de Givry's *Picture Museum of Alchemy and Magic* (first published 1929) [also reissued as *Witchcraft, Magic & Alchemy*]. He was struck by the similarity between an alchemical illustration of the philosophers' stone and The World card, and it dawned on him that the Tarot could be read as an alchemical text for the Great Work, the process of creating the philosophers' stone. Further research confirmed this.

"My basic hypothesis is that there is a common root to mysticism in Indo-European culture, perhaps all human culture, that is prehistoric, derived from shamanism and based on sexuality," Place explained in an interview. "It takes the form of various mystical teachings, such as the Tantra of India and Tibet and Taoism in China. Alchemy is part of it, and is related to Tantra and Taoism."

Alchemical symbols are found in traditional Tarot designs because they are influenced by the engravings that accompany alchemical texts and other allegorical Renaissance literature. Thanks largely to the work of Carl G. Jung, alchemy has had a revival of interest during the latter part of the twentieth century. Alchemy is the ancient art of transmutation, the precursor of modern chemistry, medicine, and metallurgy. It was practiced by the ancient Egyptians, Greeks, Persians, Indians, and Chinese. Different systems evolved in the East and West. Western alchemy was influenced by the Mysteries, Gnosticism, Neoplatonism, and Christianity. The Egyptians were responsible for one of the basic fundamentals of alchemy, that of "first matter," or *prima materia*, an imperceivable mass from which the divine force created four elements used to build the world of form. All things, then can be reduced to *prima materia* through *solve et coagula*, "dissolve and combine," which means to separate the masculine and feminine elements and recombine them in a spiritual sexual union so that they are transmuted to their most evolved state.

The alchemical process involves four major stages: (1) the *nigredo*, the blackening, which is the decay that precedes renewal; (2) the *albedo*, the whitening; (3) the *citrinitus*, the yellowing; and (4) the *rubedo*, the reddening, the end transformation.

Alchemy was reintroduced into Europe in the twelfth century through texts translated from Arabic. It spread and reached a zenith in the Renaissance. Surviving alchemical writings are obscure, and much of the science was couched in symbols. It began to decline in the seventeenth century. In the early nineteenth century, the discoveries of oxygen and the composition of water reduced alchemy to a pseudo-science and confined it to the realm of occultism.

Many alchemists pursued the philosophers' stone, a

mysterious substance never precisely or directly described, that would enable based metal to be turned into gold. It also was said to be the "Elixir of Life" that could bestow immortality and a panacea.

The great Swiss psychiatrist, Carl G. Jung (1875–1961) realized that alchemy was not just a metallurgical transmutation but a "spiritual process of redemption, the union and transformation of *Lumen Dei*, the light of the Godhead, and *Lumen Naurae*, the light of nature. *Solve et coagula* symbolized death and rebirth." The alchemist, as part of the process, transmuted his own consciousness into a higher state through symbolic death and rebirth. The ultimate goal: the philosophers' stone, a state of illumination or Gnosis. Early Christian alchemists used the philosphers' stone as a symbol of Christ, said Jung. In the highest mystical sense, then, alchemy represented the transformation of consciousness to love.

The alchemical process may be seen as mirrored in the Major Arcana: the Great Work of alchemy is the Great Journey of the Tarot. The philosophers' stone is expressed in The World. Additional information on alchemical symbols in relation to the Tarot is provided throughout this book, and in the Glossary of Symbols in Appendix A.

In designing the deck, Place drew upon alchemical symbols, illustrations, and texts; the Renaissance traditions of humanism and romanticism; the Visconti-Sforza deck allegedly drawn by Bonifacio Bembo (fifteenth century); various other early decks; the Marseilles and Rider-Waite decks; and the alchemical studies of Jung. Although the Alchemical Tarot can be used for divination as can any other Tarot deck, Place intended its primary purpose to be as a meditational tool. Figures 3 and 4 show two cards from The Alchemical Major Arcana—Temperance and The Devil.

Temperance is often called the alchemist, for it depicts the alchemical process. Place relates this card to the Matron or Mother aspect of the Triple Goddess of Pagan mythology (Virgin, Mother, and Crone, gov-

TEMPERANCE

Figure 3   THE ALCHEMICAL TAROT

THE **DEVIL**

Figure 4 THE ALCHEMICAL TAROT

erning all aspects of the cycle of life, death and rebirth), and to Maria Prophetessa, the mythical alchemist credited with discovering the process of distillation. He draws additional meaning from one of the definitions of the word *temper*, to toughen or make strong. The woman here is the Great Mother, She who maintains the ebb and flow of life. Duality is expressed in celestial-terrestrial imagery: the water of life flows down from the heavens into her cup and rises as steam in an ongoing process—one that the alchemist has copied from the natural cycle of evaporation and precipitation. The two streams form an opening shaped like a vagina, an ancient symbol for the portal of life. Within the opening can be seen a Tree of Life, with five branches bearing five-petaled flowers, representing humankind (five senses) and the four elements plus spirit. Thus the key meaning of the card is seen as renewal, a balancing of dual forces, and being in harmony with the life forces, which are beyond conscious control.

In The Devil, enslavement to lower nature and desires is represented here by the *nigredo*, shown as the blacker than black stone within the winged sphere, which, despite the darkness, still contains the light of spirit, the redeeming force. The Devil, seen as the mercurial dragon, sits astride the sphere, representing both poison and healing. The union of opposites is shown in the hermaphrodite. The card points to negative aspects of a situation, but in revealing them initiates the first step to renewal and recovery.

For inspiration, other Tarot artists have turned to modern psychology, particularly Jung's school of thought. Jungian archetypes (primordial images discussed here) and psychology are the basis for the Jungian Tarot (1988), created by Robert Wang, who also drew upon astrology and the Hermetic Kabbalah. James Wanless uses the archetype concept in his unique Voyager deck (1986), which has no drawings but utilizes composite photographs of cross-cultural and multilevel images. Wanless says that the New Age has brought a third evolution to the Tarot—the first occurring in the ancient Mystery schools when the Major Arcana symbols were created and the second in the Middle Ages when the Minor Arcana and Major Arcana were joined together. The unifying symbol of the Voyager deck, which appears on the backs of the cards, is the DNA—(deoxyribonucleic acid)—the genetic blueprint found in all living things. Wanless uses the DNA to symbolize the "Universe Self," an expression of the human as universe in microcosm.

One may apply Jungian concepts to virtually any Tarot deck, however. One of Jung's key concepts in relation to the Tarot is that of archetypes, universal and primordial images that exist in the collective unconscious. Jung did not originate the theory of archetypes, but elaborated upon it. The concept was known to the classical world, and is expressed, for example, in Plato's Theory of Forms, which holds that the essence of a thing or concept is its underlying form or idea.

The collective unconscious, Jung's term for the universal consciousness, is a realm deep below the personal unconscious (subconscious). It is not unique to each person, but is shared by all humankind, and consists of the memories of mental patterns.

Archetypes, Jung said, have been impressed upon this collective reservoir since an ancestral past that includes not only early humankind but prehuman and animal ancestors. They become like riverbeds: as long as they are reinforced through experience, they flow with life, but if experience changes, they dry up.

Archetypes are not easy to grasp; even Jung himself never offered a definitive meaning. They are not images, per se, or concepts, but are predispositions toward certain behaviors. They are patterns of psychological performance linked to instinct—for example, fear of the dark. Archetypes, which are endless in number, are continually created and shaped by repeated experiences by millions upon millions of beings. Virtually anything can become an archetype: God, birth, death, rebirth, power, magic, the sun, the moon, animals, the elements, and traits embodied in such figures as the hero, the sage, the judge, the child, the trickster, and the earth mother. All of these and more are portrayed in the Tarot.

Archetypes reach our consciousness through instinct and through symbols, as expressed in dreams. They must be taken seriously, Jung said, because if they are not recognized and reckoned with, they can cause neurotic and psychotic disorders.

Jung acknowledged the presence of archetypes in the Tarot. In *The Archetypes and the Collective Unconscious* (1968), a collection of essays written from 1933 on, Jung said:

> If one wants to form a picture of the symbolic process, the series of pictures found in alchemy are good examples, though the symbols they contain are for the most part traditional despite their often obscure origin and significance. An excellent Eastern example is the Tantric *chakra* system, or the mystical nerve system of Chinese yoga. It also seems as if the set of pictures in the Tarot cards was distantly descended from the archetypes of transformation . . .

> The symbolic process is an experience in *images and of images*. Its development . . . presents a rhythm of negative and positive, loss and gain, dark and light. Its beginning is almost invariably characterized by one's getting stuck in a blind alley or in some impossible situation; and its goal is, broadly speaking, illumination or higher consciousness, by means of which the initial situation is overcome on a higher level.

We see this symbolic process expressed aptly in the Major Arcana of the Tarot. The process begins with The Fool, "the spirit in search of experience," as Waite described him, in the impossible situation of being just about to plunge off a cliff. It ends with The World, which Waite described as "the perfection and end of the Cosmos, the secret which is within it, the rapture of the universe when it understands itself in God. It is further the state of the soul in the consciousness of the Divine Vision, reflected from the self-knowing spirit."

Jung said four major archetypes have a great influence on human personality and behavior. They are:

- *The persona.* The public mask a person adopts, according to the expectations of society. Most of us have a collection of personas for various situations.
- *The shadow.* The inferior, repressed and rejected aspects of a person that exist in the personal unconscious. The shadow is uncivilized and rebels against the persona. As long as it is repressed and rejected, it is split off from the rest of the psyche. Only when it is acknowledged and reintegrated can one become whole, a process Jung called individuation.
- *The anima and animus.* The male and female parts of the psyche, respectively, which exist in all persons. The anima and animus often are underdeveloped due to cultural conditioning that encourages certain behaviors in each sex.
- *The self.* The organizing principle of the personality and the central archetype of the collective unconsciousness. The self unites the conscious and unconscious, and fosters an awareness of the interconnectedness of all things in the universe.

In working with the Tarot, we come into contact with the archetypal realm through the images and symbols in the cards. This contact affects us consciously and unconsciously. We plumb our own depths and realize our relationship to the cosmos. We meet our personas, our shadow, our anima and animus. In the process, we begin to heal and grow, to take the journey of the Self to wholeness, which in the Tarot is the journey of The Fool.

FOUR

Symbols in the Tarot

The key to the metaphysical meanings of the Tarot lies in understanding symbols. Before language came symbols—pictures and designs that communicate thoughts, objects, concepts, and information. As written language developed, letters and words also became symbols.

Symbols speak directly to us. They imply something greater than their obvious, surface meaning, and thus elude precise description. In fact, a true symbol cannot be taken literally, but remains beyond rational comprehension, just out of reach. Symbols, said Jung, take the mind "to ideas beyond the grasp of reason."

Symbols take on a cosmological importance, and act upon our subconscious, and our collective unconscious, in ways that unlock powerful energies and creativity. Jung, who spent much of his life studying symbols, saw them as messengers to the psyche that connect us to the archetypes in the collective unconscious. William Butler Yeats, a member of the Hermetic Order of the Golden Dawn, termed symbols "the greatest of all powers," whether used consciously, such as in ceremonial magic, or drawn upon "half unconsciously" by those in the creative and performing arts.

Symbols fuel the vitality of culture. Whether we realize it or not, we react to and interact with symbols every day, either consciously or unconsciously. Everything around us—our art, architecture, ways of communication, and our mundane and sacred rites—make use of symbols. Without symbols, a culture is spiritually bereft, perhaps even dead.

It is impossible to pinpoint a time when symbols originated; they seem to be as old as mankind. They are evident in pictorial remains of the late Paleolithic Age, a time when humankind lived in caves and subsisted by hunting and gathering. These hunters and gatherers recorded their symbolic language on the walls of their caves. Cave paintings were discovered in France and Spain at the end of the nineteenth century, but it was not until later in the twentieth century that archaeologists began to comprehend the full, symbolic meanings of the pictures. Many of them depict wounded or dying animals, indicating belief in sympathetic magic for hunting. The most dramatic example is the cave at Trois Freres, France, which depicts scenes of successful hunting and perhaps some sort of shamanistic or magical rites, the focus of which is a dancing human figure with a stag head and bear paws.

The most universal and enduring symbols are man, stones, animals, and circles, all of which the ancients saw in terms of their relationship to the divine. Man was seen as the symbol of the universe, the microcosm that represents the macrocosm. Stones were animated with divine or supernatual spirits. The characteristics of animals were projected onto deities, who sometimes took animal forms. Animals also became culture heros. The circle, perhaps one of the most powerful symbols of all, came to represent the sun, the source of all light and life; the continuity of life through rebirth; and the totality of being.

Virtually anything can become a symbol. Besides man, animals, stones, and circles, there are symbols that are natural and manmade objects, numbers, shapes, the elements, the earth, the sky, the heavenly objects, and deities. Words and entire myths and folk tales can become symbols. A symbol's creation and its power depend upon the psychic energy invested in it, both at the moment of creation and over time. In some cases, symbols can arise quickly. Within a few years, the Nazis turned the swastika into the symbol of their ideology, probably destroying forever its original, pagan meaning of a solar symbol. The swastika resides now in the collective unconscious as a symbol of bigotry, hatred, greed, and abuse of power. Generally, however, symbols emerge over a long period of time as they are used over and over again in rites and customs. Not all symbols last—as civilizations rise and fall, their symbols perish if they are not absorbed into a succeeding society. Even within a culture, symbols can lose their potency over time, as beliefs and customs change.

In esoteric philosophy, symbols have the dual role of concealing information from the neophyte while revealing it to the initiate. Symbols are found in all esoteric philosophies and religions. In the East, the supreme symbol is the mandala. Symbolical devices are present in the Bible and in other scriptures. According to ancient scholars, the priests of the day devised a symbolic language called sacerdotal (which now means "priestly"), which they used to conceal information from the uninitiated masses. This language was made up of signs and symbols used in the everyday world, but which to the priests had entirely different meanings. The ancient Egyptians exhibited a wide use of symbols for philosophical purposes. Symbols became a veritable art under the Roman Empire, when numerous religious cults flourished, but had to conceal their true purposes with secular fronts as guilds, burial unions, literary societies, and the like. The cults, which included the early Christians, were forced to develop systems of symbols to communicate with members and spread their teachings. The symbolisms included images and signs borrowed from the building guilds, and sacred numbers borrowed from the Pythagoreans. In the Middle Ages, symbols formed the vital, secret language of alchemy and secret societies. The alchemists, who were engrossed in the mysteries of matter and spirit, created an impressive array of dreamlike symbols to express the process by which man could become whole in mind and body.

To the initiate, symbols are the means by which he or she can acquire or express the abilities or qualities embodied in the symbols. That is why it is so important to become thoroughly familiar with Tarot images, for they speak through symbols. Everything in the image, each element—including objects, people, animals, structures, nature, numbers, colors, and shapes—has a possible symbolic meaning. By understanding symbols, you can quickly comprehend the deeper meanings of the cards. The information conveyed by symbols will be received not as part of your rational thought process, but on an intuitive, knowing level. Deep within you, the messages will be absorbed; you will understand on a higher level of consciousness, without the need to put it into words.

Different interpretations of the Tarot use symbols to give unique and subtle shadings to the card meanings. For example, compare The Hermit from two different decks, and you will see that the essential meanings of the cards are the same, but approached differently through use of symbols. Knowing symbols will help you gain a better intuitive feel for the overall interpretation of a particular deck.

Not all decks follow the same traditions of symbols. The notable exceptions are some decks designed as art objects, or which use photo or drawing collages, or which are oriented to specific cultures or themes.

Jung said that symbols are capable of unleashing great redemptive power. The Tarot, then, offers an excellent opportunity to tap into powerful energies that can help one to heal and to grow. Jung also believed that modern Western society has lost touch with its own symbols. It is a mistake, he said, for Westerners to look to the East for meaningful symbols, for to do so is to take them out of context from the culture and way of life in which they arose. Appropriately, there has been a resurgence of interest in the Western occult tradition, with an accompanying rediscovery of the rich symbolisms it contains. The Tarot is a product of the Western tradition, and it contains symbols that are very old and that still have the ability to impact our psyches in profound ways.

The following sections discuss major symbolisms of numbers, colors, and shapes as they apply to the Tarot:

> ## Numbers

In occult philosophies, numbers are not quantities, but ideas or forms that constitute the building blocks of all things in the universe. Each number has its own character and attributes, which in turn influence all things physical that are associated with that number.

The mysticism of numbers appears in both Western and Eastern occultism and is of ancient origin. In ancient China, it was expressed in the *I Ching,* the Book of Changes, a means of consulting the divine through sixty-four hexagrams formed by six lines each. Traditionally, the hexagrams are formed by the tossing of forty-nine yarrow stalks. According to legend, the *I Ching* was created by ancient holy sages, who wished to communicate with suprahuman intelligence concerning matters of destiny. No direct communication was possible, so the sages used the established means of numbers and their symbolisms. The number 1 was not used because it was too abstract. The number 2, which issues from 1, was assigned to the earth, matter, and the feminine/passive principle. The number 3, which issues from 2 and includes it, was assigned to heaven, spirit, and the masculine/active principle. Thus, all even numbers corresponded to earth associations and all odd numbers to heavenly associations. The calculation of numerical values becomes quite complex.

More important to the Tarot is the development of numerical mysticism in the West. The ancient Greeks placed great importance on the significance of numbers. "The world is built upon the power of numbers," said Pythagoras, who believed that the entire universe could be expressed in combinations of the primary numbers 1 through 10. This stemmed from his discovery that the musical intervals known in his time could be expressed in ratios between the numbers 1, 2, 3, and 4, which, when added together, total 10. Ten then returns to 1, because its digits of 1 and 0, when added together, equal 1. Odd numbers were considered to be definite, masculine, and positive. Even numbers were indefinite, feminine, and negative.

The Hebrews, Gnostics, and early Christians applied numbers to letters, which enabled them to calculate the numerical value of words. The tallied numbers yielded secret meanings. For example, the number 888 represented the "Higher Mind" in the Greek Mysteries, because *Iesous* ("Jesus") adds up to 888. Both the Greeks and the Hebrews considered 10 the perfect number. The Hebrews most of all raised the numerical power of words to a high art—gematria—which, as we saw in Chapter Two, played a significant role in Kabbalism in the Middle Ages.

Numbers also were important in alchemy. One through 4 have primacy as the foundation of all things. In alchemical literature, the Hebrew prophetess, called Maria Prophetissa, states, "One becomes two, two becomes three, and out of the third comes the One as the fourth." Four is the number of the elements, which through a symbolic circular process of distillation and sublimation could be broken down and recombined in the higher unity of one.

In strict occult tradition, the system of ascertaining the numerical values of words works only when a word is spelled in its original Hebrew or Greek form; English does not agree closely enough with the Greek and Hebrew alphabets to work. Nonetheless, numerology—the reduction of names, words, and birth dates to their base numerical values—has become a popular modern form of this ancient practice. The letters in the alphabet are assigned values of one through nine. The base numerical values are one through nine and are obtained by adding together all digits assigned each letter until single digits remain. It is believed that one's fortunes may be changed by altering numerical values in names, for example, although the original Pythagorean philosophy offers nothing to substantiate this practice.

Numbers achieved a new significance in the psychology of Jung, especially the latter, who considered the importance of numbers and their unconscious roots in dreams. Jung attempted to find personal meanings behind numbers in dreams, yet recognized that their appearance also sometimes represented the presence of archetypal forces or qualities.

A grasp of number symbolism is essential in working with the Tarot. It is employed in the construction of images for the Major Arcana in many decks, especially the newer ones. This is expressed especially in backgrounds and objects, such as a pair of birds in the sky. All elements in a Major Arcana image should be examined with numerical considerations in mind. They should be interpreted in light of the essence of the card and its position, if applicable, in a spread. Number symbolism is of primary importance in deriving meaning from the Minor Arcana pip cards. The symbolism of the number of the card, plus the suit sign, determine the fundamental meaning of the card. Images, if they are used for the pip cards, give further shadings to the meaning, as does the placement of each card in a spread.

The following are the essential meanings of the ten primary numbers, plus zero and a few others that are likely to appear in Tarot images. Keep in mind that odd numbers (except the number one) have masculine properties, which essentially embody activity, creativity, logic, reason, and left-brain functions. Even numbers have feminine properties, which embody passivity, intuition, emotions, inspiration, fertility, and right-brain functions:

Zero. Before numbers, which represent creation and order, comes zero, the unmanifest, the nothingness that precedes all things. Zero also represents the Cosmic Egg, the container of all life. Symbols related to zero include the egg and the circle.

One. The Pythagoreans called one the Monad and equated it with God, the beginning and end of all things, and the Source. One is the Mystic Center. It is the spiritual unity that unites all beings. It is mind, which gives it stability, for mind is stable. Unlike other odd numbers, one is not masculine, but is hermaphroditic in nature, comprising both male and female principles, because one added to an even number makes an odd, and added to an odd number makes an even one. From one issues all other numbers; no number can exist without it.

The Pythagoreans associated one with the names of various deities, whose attributes reflected the qualities of one. Among them were Phoebus Apollo, the brilliant and shining god of the sun and the Python-slaying god consulted at the Oracle at Delphi; Prometheus, who brought man fire and light (illumination and creativity); Zeus, the primary father god; and Hestia (Vesta), goddess of the hearth and home fires.

Symbols related to one include the ship and the chariot.

One points to beginnings, creation, unity, divinity, light, and matters of spirit and mind. It is an auspicious number, holding promise and optimism.

Two. From one issues two, the number of duality. Plato said the number had no significance, since it implied the existence of a relationship, which introduces a third factor. In alchemy, two is the number of opposites, which must dissolve and recombine to form the philosophers' stone. Two is the number of balance. It is sometimes regarded as weak and sometimes evil, because of its associations with duality, opposition, and polarity, and therefore illusion. In fact, the Pythagoreans, who considered two the number of the divided terrestrial being, despised the number.

Two has passive, female properties. Its duality is symbolized by horns, which have associations with the crescent moon and with Mother Goddess. Thus, on a positive note, two embraces Her attributes. Goddess is primarily a symbol of fertility, She who brings forth all life, which cannot prosper without Her blessing. In mythology, She appears often in a triple aspect representing maiden, mother and crone, with such correspondences as youth, adulthood and old age, and virgin, nurturer and destroyer. In her many roles, Goddess rules over wisdom, truth, magical powers, nature, fate, the home, healing, justice, love, birth, death, time, and eternity. She also rules the inner self—one's emotion, intuition, psychic forces, and mysteries. In mythology, her consort, and thus another symbol of her, is the bull—again, the horns. She is also represented by the crescent moon, the source of magical, psychic, and fertilizing powers.

On a negative note, the horns of the number 2 signify the Devil, temptation, evil, weakness, and material preoccupations.

Two also represents ignorance, but even this cloud has a silver lining, for out of ignorance emerges wisdom. Two is the darkness before the light. In mythology, two often signifies the emergence of something into the consciousness.

In Christian symbolism two represents the dual nature of Christ (God and human). In Kabbalistic symbolism, it represents wisdom and self-consciousness.

Three. As the product of one and two, three symbolizes the generative force, creative power, multiplicity, and forward movement. It is spiritual synthesis, harmony, and sufficiency; also prudence, friendship, justice, peace, virtue, and temperance. Anatolius observed that three, "the first odd number, is called perfect by some, because it is the first number to signify the totality—beginning, middle, and end." Thus, we find in mythology, folklore, and fairy tales the recurrent motif of the triad: three wishes, three sisters, three brothers, three chances, blessings done in threes, and spells and charms done in threes.

Three is an important number in mysticism. It is expressed in the threefold nature of man: body, mind, and spirit. The name of the mythical author of the *Hermetica*, Hermes Trismegistus, means "Thrice-greatest Hermes." In Christianity, three is expressed in the Trinity. In the *Sefer Yetzirah (Book of Formation)* of the Kabbalah, three is expressed in the Three Mothers, Aleph, Mem, and Shin, which form the foundation of "all others." Aleph, Mem, and Shin are letters of the Hebrew alphabet which mean, respectively, "breath" or vital spirit; "seas," or water; and "life-breath of the Divine Ones" or "Holy Spirit." The Three Mothers resemble a balance, the guilty on one side, the purified on the other, and the tongue of the balance standing between them. The *Sefer Yetzirah* states:

The Three Mothers Aleph, Mem and Shin are a great Mystery very admirable and most recondite, and sealed with six rings; and from them proceed Air, Fire, and Water, which divide into male and female forces. The Three Mothers Aleph, Mem and Shin are the foundation, from them spring three Fathers, and from these have proceeded all things that are in the world.

The Three Mothers in the world are Aleph, Mem and Shin: the heavens were produced from Fire; the earth from Water; and the Air from the Spirit is as a reconciler between the Fire and the Water.

The Three Mothers Aleph, Mem and Shin, Fire, Water and Air are shown in the Year; from the fire was made heat, from the waters was made cold, and from the air was produced the temperate state, again the mediator between them. The Three Mothers, Aleph, Mem and Shin, Fire, Water and Air are found in Man: from the fire was formed the head; from the water the belly; and from the air was formed the chest, again placed as a mediator between the two.

In Wicca, three is expressed in the threefold aspect of Goddess as Virgin, Matron, and Crone, and in the waxing, full, and waning phases of the moon.

Three is also the number of wisdom and knowledge in its association with the Three Fates and the past, present, and future, and the ancient sciences of music, geometry, and arithmetic.

Among the shapes symbolized by three are the triangle, trident, and tripod. According to Pythagoras, Apollo gave his oracles from a tripod.

Four. The number of solidity, stability, foundations, hard work and toil, and tangible achievement. It also is the number of the earth, and of rational and logical thought and intellectualism. Pythagoras considered four the perfect number, the foundation of all things, connecting beings, elements, numbers, and seasons. To the Pythagoreans, four also symbolized God, because when added to the first three numbers, the total is ten, which returns to one. In addition, they believed that four represented the soul of man, which had the four powers of mind, science, opinion, and sense.

Many things can be associated with four: the four seasons, the four elements, the four cardinal points, the four basic functions of Jungian types (thinking, feeling, sensation, and intuition), the four suits of the Tarot, the four limbs of the human body, the four rivers that flow from the Garden of Eden.

When the number 4 occurs, it often indicates a stabilizing or ordering process taking place. In matters of hard work and toil, four can signify dullness.

Four is represented by the square and the cross (especially the equilateral cross); it also has associations with the cube. In alchemical symbolism, the element earth, which is associated with four, often takes the form of a dragon.

Five. Five essentially is the microcosm. This number symbolizes the physical man and his five senses, and

thus connotes sensuality and pleasure. It also reso-
nates with higher qualities: it is man with his four
limbs plus a head, the four cardinal points with the
Center, the four elements plus a fifth element of
ether, the universal vitalizing substance that permeates
all things. In this respect, five is the number of the
hierophant (appropriately, this is the number of The
Hierophant of the Major Arcana). Since five divides
the perfect number, 10, equally into two parts, it represents equilibrium.

Five is symbolized by the five-pointed star, the pentacle or pentagram, considered by the ancient Greeks
to symbolize light, health, and vitality. In occultism,
the pentacle is a powerful symbol of divine power,
and represents the dominion of mind over the lower
nature. Like the circle, the pentacle also symbolizes
wholeness. Another symbol for five is the pentagon,
which also has associations with the circle.

The number five is often represented by five-leaved
plants, such as the rose, lily, or vine.

The Kabbalistic meaning of five is fear.

Six. Also the number of equilibrium, as well as balance (as seen in scales), harmony, health, and time.
The six-sided figure, the hexad, is formed by the union
of two triangles. In addition, this union represents
marriage and the hermaphrodite, both of which are
the result of the union of the male and female. The
Pythagoreans considered six the form of forms, the
perfection of all the parts, and associated it with
immortality. In Christian symbolism, six also is the
number of perfection, because God created the world
in six days. In Kabbalism, six represents beauty and
creation. In shapes, six is represented by the hexagram, the symbol of the union of opposites.

Seven. Almost universally a sacred number, and the
number of mystical man, for it is the sum of three
(spirit) and four (material), thus making the perfect
order. Seven, then, represents the macrocosm. In

alchemy, seven metals make up the Work, the alchemical transformation to the philosophers' stone. Seven also is the number of religion, the psychic, magic, and luck. It is associated with clairvoyance and healing powers. In initiation, seven is the highest stage of illumination. In Hebrew symbolism, it is the number of occult intelligence.

The ancient Greeks associated seven with the seven known planets and their corresponding deities. There are seven notes in the musical scale, and seven colors in the spectrum (which in turn corresponds to a rainbow, the bridge between earth and heaven).

When the number seven occurs, it often indicates the search for wisdom, the growth of spirit, the need to rely upon intuition, or to meditate on what has been learned. It also indicates a fondness for, and harmony with, nature.

Eight. The number of regeneration and the spiritual goal of the initiate. Because of its association with regeneration, eight symbolized the waters of baptism during the Middle Ages.

On its side, the figure eight resembles an ellipse, which is the lemniscate, the symbol of eternity, infinity, the Alpha and Omega, infinite wisdom, and higher consciousness. Right side up, the eight is associated with the spiral, a shape representing evolution, growth, and flexibility. The serpents entwined in a spiral on the caduceus of Hermes represent transformed consciousness: spiritual illumination. Thus, it is not surprising that the number eight was important in the Eleusinian mysteries.

In the Hermetica, eight is the magical number of Hermes Trismegistus. In Kabbalism, it is the number of perfect intelligence, for eight is the numerical value of YHVH, Yahweh, the Tetragrammaton.

The octagon, the eight-sided figure, represents a transition between the square and the circle.

Eight also has strong associations with four, because it is comprised equally of two fours.

66

Nine. The number nine has polarized positive and negative associations. In its positive aspects, nine is the number of spiritual and mental achievement. The Hebrews considered it to be the number of truth, because when mulitiplied it reproduces itself. In Kabbalism, it represents the foundation. As the Triple Triad, it is the incorruptible number of fulfillment and attainment. In the Eleusinian mysteries, there were nine spheres through which the consciousness had to pass before it could be born anew. It is also a number of man, symbolizing the nine months of gestation before physical birth. Because of its composition of equal three's, nine has associations with the triangle.

The Pythagoreans regarded nine as an evil number because it is an inverted six, and also regarded it as the number of imperfection and failure, because it falls one short of the perfect ten. Within this context, nine is the number of limitations.

Ten. To the Pythagoreans, as well as the Greeks in general and the Hebrews, ten was the number of perfection. The Pythagoreans said it was the greatest number, the number of both heaven and earth, and associated it with memory, age, faith, power, and necessity. Ten also is a number of completion and wholeness, for it returns again to one. It is the number of the law.

In Christianity, it is the number of the Commandments. In Kabbalism, it is the number of the *sephirot* of the Tree of Life and the ten names of God.

Eleven. Because it exceeds ten, eleven is an unstable and imperfect number, and represents sin and transgression.

Twelve. This number represents the cosmic order and is expressed in many ways: the apostles of Christ, the months of the year, the hours of the day and night, the fruits of the Tree of Life, the signs of the Zodiac, the Tribes of Israel.

Thirteen. An unlucky number, also unstable because it exceeds twelve by one. In Christianity, it is associated with the betrayal of Christ, who had twelve disciples (himself making thirteen), one of whom betrayed him to the Romans. In some magical traditions, however, thirteen is a lucky number, representing the number of full moons in a year and the traditional number of the witches' coven.

Forty. There are numerous Biblical references to forty, the number of trial and initiation: the days Jesus spent in the wilderness, the elapsed time of the resurrection, the Deluge, the wandering of the Jews, the reign of David, the days Moses spent on Mt. Sinai.

666. A diabolical number which in Christianity signifies "the Beast," the Antichrist, and in Kabbalism signifies Sorath, the solar demon who opposes the archangel Michael.

888. In gematria, 888 represents the name of Jesus.

Colors

Colors are one of the most universal of symbols and have had esoteric significance since ancient times. In religion, heraldry, rank, occultism, alchemy, high magic, folklore, art, and architecture, colors are ascribed specific properties, attributes, symbolisms, or effects. Color lore was possessed by the ancient Indians, Chinese, Tibetans, Egyptians, Greeks, Persians, and Babylonians. The occult, healing, and protective powers of gems and stones were evaluated based on their colors and the logical associations made with them. Blue, for example, the color of the sky, naturally becomes associated with spirit and spiritual properties. The ancients corresponded colors to the planets, to musical notes, the seven major chakras, the seven virtues and vices, the days of the week, and the seven faculties of the soul. In the early Christian

Church, colors were used very carefully in the garments and implements of religious service. For example, the color of a saint's robe, and the ornaments upon it, indicated whether he had been martyred, and for what. The strict uses of color began to decline in the Middle Ages.

Colors are vibrations of light. White light—the Godhead in Pythagorean thought—can be broken down into the seven basic colors of the spectrum: red, orange, yellow, green, blue, indigo, and violet, which in turn can be combined to create secondary colors, shades, and hues. Edgar Cayce (1877–1945), the American psychic who gave medical diagnoses in trance, once noted that vibration is movement, and movement is activity that is either positive or negative. Thus, colors have an impact upon us emotionally, intellectually, physically, and intuitively.

In Tarot, colors are another element used to express hidden symbolic meanings. The color of an item of clothing, a flower, jewelry, a tool, an object in the background adds meaning to the card. This applies primarily to the Rider-Waite and post-Rider-Waite decks, although not all modern decks use color for occult meaning. The earliest known Tarot cards were created more as objects of art and were gilded. The Marseilles deck is colored entirely in red, yellow, and blue. The Egyptian Tarot, a modern deck, is done all in sepia tones, and the Aquarian deck, another modern design, is colored mostly in earth tones of green and brown. You will have to examine your cards and determine the extent of the role played by colors.

The following is a color symbol guide to help you interpret the Tarot. Some of the uses of color symbolisms in the Rider-Waite deck in particular are considered. Brief meanings of colors also are included in the Glossary of Symbols at the end of the book.

Red. As the color of blood, red has obvious associations with life, the life-force, the body, wounds, and death. It is also the color of animal life, and animal nature in man. It is the color of lust, passion, and materialism, and by extension, with evil, the Devil, and base energies.

Red is associated with fire. It is the color of activity, energy, courage, and willpower. It also is the color of creation, which links it to the Mother Goddess, who brings forth all life. Note that The Empress, a pregnant woman, wears a gown of white (the traditional feminine color) decorated with red and green fruit, the colors of life and fertility.

In medieval Christian art, red represents love and charity.

Red with white runs throughout mystical teachings. Red/white in alchemy is the conjunction of opposites, and is often represented by white lilies together with red roses, or red roses and white roses. Two-headed eagles and the Rebis, a two-headed hermaphrodite, are colored red and white to signify the sublimation of polarities. The foreground of The Magician card features red roses and white lilies, showing that The Magician is the interface and joiner of the macrocosm and microcosm. Also in alchemy, red is the color of the third and next-to-last stage in the creation of the philosophers' stone, which is the path of spiritual ascension, and it represents sublimation, suffering and love.

In Kabbalistic symbolism, red represents severity.

Orange. Pride and ambition, flames, egoism, cruelty, ferocity, luxury. These traits are amply represented in The Devil, in his orange skin and his chained man and woman. In the Strength card, the woman, who represents spiritual nature by the lemniscate above her head, subdues an orange lion, which may be seen as the animal nature in humankind. The Fool, though he wears boots of yellow, has orange in his garments—his pride, ambition, and egoism are leading him straight off the precipice. He will have many lessons to learn on his journey. The orange also signifies his health and vitality, thus his ability to weather the trials ahead. In Kabbalistic symbolism, orange represents splendor.

Yellow. The color of the sun, illumination, light, intellect, and generosity. The Fool, beginning his journey, wears yellow boots that will take him on the path of illumination. Death, the card of transition, bears a yellow sunrise in the background, and a bishop clad in yellow robes and miter, indicating that transition ends with the dawning of new light. In Kabbalistic symbolism, beauty.

Gold. Closely associated with yellow, gold in alchemy represents the attainment of the philosophers' stone—spiritual illumination—and glory. It also symbolizes the celestial.

Green. As the color of vegetation, green naturally symbolizes life, fertility, abundance, growing things, prosperity, youthfulness, and the earth. It also symbolizes sensation. Blue-green represents water. Spiritually, green is an intermediate, transitional color, the halfway point on the spectrum. Symbols of green vegetation decorate the garment of the King of Pentacles, signifying material abundance and prosperity.

Green also has associations with death: all growing things eventually die, but are reborn in another cycle of change, the budding of new growth. The Egyptians used green for Osiris, the god of both vegetation and the dead, and king of the underworld. Thus green can symbolize rebirth, regeneration, and renewal.

In Kabbalistic symbolism, green represents victory.

Blue. The color of the heavens, and therefore of a heavenly quality. Blue represents godliness, spiritual qualities, contemplation, inspiration, devotion, and truth. Water, the symbol of emotions and the unconscious, is blue. Mountains, the abodes of the gods and the symbols of the spiritual ascent, often are shown as blue. The High Priestess, wearing a gown of predominantly blue, holds spiritual wisdom, and her horned headdress connect her to the heavens to the Mother Goddess.

In Kabbalistic symbolism, blue represents mercy.

Indigo. Advanced spiritual qualities or wisdom, psychic faculties, intuition.

Purple. Royalty, imperial power, pomp, pride, justice, truth. In Christian symbolism, God, humility, and penitence. In pagan symbolism, the color of rites of chthonic deities.

Violet. Sanctity, religious devotion, knowledge, sorrow, temperance, grief, old age, mourning. In Christian symbolism, love and truth or passion and suffering, sacerdotal rule, and authority. In Kabbalistic symbolism, foundation.

White. Purity, holiness, sacredness, redemption, mystical illumination, timelessness, ecstasy, innocence, joy, light, and life. White is sometimes regarded as a purified yellow.

The combination of all colors, white is the opposite of black, the absence of color. White and black represent polarities of positive/negative, light/dark, feminine/masculine forces: the pillars of Boaz and Jachin, the sphinxes in The Chariot card, the twin duality of Gemini. In the alchemical process of the philosophers' stone, white marks the second stage, the beginning of the ascent up from darkness. In Kabbalistic symbolism, white represents the crown, a symbol of proximity to God and the highest spiritual attainment.

White with red and black symbolizes the three stages of initiation.

Black. The symbol of death, destruction, negation, and deterioration. It represents the underworld, and thus presages transition and resurrection. In alchemy, the process of the philosophers' stone begins with a stage of blackness, the necessary dissolution before the new and better can be created. In the Death card, Death wears armor of black and bears a black banner and a white mystic rose: death, or transition, preceding life, the new.

As the absence of color, black is the opposite of white, and is negativity, inertia, and lack of spiritual light. In Christianity, it is the symbol of the Devil, and thus sin, materialism, and ignorance. Thus, The Devil card is heavily black.

Brown. Renunciation of the world, spiritual death, and degradation. Also, the earth.

Gray. Mourning, humility, neutrality, penitence. In Christian symbolism, the death of the body and immortality of the spirit. In the Death card, the sun rises between pillars of gray, signifying death of the old and birth of the new, an ongoing process; in Kabbalistic symbolism, wisdom. The Rider-Waite pack makes extensive use of gray. The Hermit, for example, is clothed in gray, a robe of wisdom. In Judgment, gray bodies rise up out of their coffins. On the surface, this would appear to reflect the Christian symbolism of the resurrection and immortality of the spirit, and indeed it does work on this level. But on a deeper level, the gray signifies the transformation from material to spiritual.

Silver. The color of the moon, which gives it associations with magic, Goddess, psychic nature, emotions, and intuition. With gold, silver is the feminine aspect of duality of the cosmic reality. In alchemy, silver is Luna, "the affections purified."

Pink. A color often associated with love and the heart center. Pink is more likely to be found in newer Tarot decks.

Circle. One of the oldest and most universal of symbols, the circle represents wholeness, completion, perfection, unity, totality, eternity, and world without end. It is the wheel of life, the continuing renewal of life in cycles of birth-death-rebirth. The circle is the sun (intellect, light, and spiritual illumination) rolling through the heavens. It is also the psyche, the whole Self, a symbolism that dates back to the time of Plato, who described the psyche as a sphere.

A circle with a dot in the center is an alchemical symbol for the sun or gold, and corresponds to the divine circle of celestial unity of all.

Semicircle. The semicircle represents borrowed light. It is the spark, the hidden fire, which resides in the soul of man, waiting to be awakened.

Mandorla. A symbol of the divine and the holy, of Spirit and the soul, the mandorla resembles an oval with horned ends and is formed by the intersection of two equal circles, the circumference of which goes through the center of the other. It also represents virginity, the vulva, and a gateway; the interpenetration of heaven and earth and spirit and matter; and the perfect equilibrium between equal forces. Thus, it has associations with duality and the number two. It is also known as the *vesica piscis*, or "vessel of the fish," and *ichthus* ("fish") because of its shape. The mandorla appears often in sacred geometry, architecture, and art.

Mandala. Though used extensively in the East—*mandala* is Sanskrit for "circle"—in rituals of worship and contemplation, mandalas have appeared universally since the Paleolithic Age, in the circular spiral and the sun wheel. Mandalas appear in Gnosticism, Christianity, and other religions, and in alchemy (the Ouroboros, the dragon or serpent that bites its own tail, forming a circle), mythology, healing practices, art, and architecture. The association of the mandala with wholeness, individuation, and the structure of the psyche (a circle or sphere) has made it a useful therapeutic tool for integration in modern psychotherapies. Jung found that patients could begin to work out their inner chaos by drawing mandalas of their dreams.

The mandala is itself a symbol with form and meaning, but it symbolizes the formless: it is an expression of, and a means of communication with, the unknowable and the ineffable. It reaches a level of consciousness much deeper than conceptual thought.

A mandala has three main features of construction: a center, symmetry, and four cardinal points. All mandalas have a center, whereas their symmetries and orientation to the cardinal points vary considerably according to design.

The *center* of a mandala represents the Godhead, the Beginning and the Eternal Now, or the Self, which is the total psyche. *Symmetry* is expressed in concentric and counterbalanced geometric figures, with polarities often represented in terms of sexual tension. The purpose of the mandala then is to harmonize those polarities, to make order out of chaos. The circle may be *oriented* to the cardinal points, and this is done in several ways. The circle is squared—that is, placed within a square—or it can contain squares within its design. This orientation harkens back to Hindu and Buddhist creation myths. Before the Hindu god Brahma began creation, he stood on a thousand-petaled lotus (a mandala in itself) and looked to the four points of the compass. Similarly, Buddha, after being born, stepped onto an eight-rayed lotus flower that rose up from the earth, and looked into ten directions of space, one for each ray of the lotus, plus up and down. Jung associated the cardinal points with the four types that humans need to orient themselves to the world: thinking, feeling, intuiting, and sensing.

In studying the symbols of Tarot cards, virtually anything round can be viewed as a potential mandala

75

or component of a mandala: the sun, the moon, the earth itself, an equilateral cross, the Zodiac, the wheel, a rotunda, a halo, a flower, a maze, a labyrinth, a rose window of a cathedral, an octagon. Squares and triangles suggest mandalas, since circles may be drawn within squares and vice versa. Triangles appear often in circular mandalas.

Triangle. In its normal position with point up, the triangle represents the aspiration of all things toward a higher unity. It is a symbol of fire and the masculine, creative principle. In Christian symbolism, the equilateral triangle is a symbol of the Trinity. With its tip cut off, the triangle represents earth. Inverted, it is a symbol of water and the feminine, receptive principle. When two opposing triangles are joined together to form a hexagram, they represent the union of opposites, and also the human soul.

An inverted triangle contained with an upright triangle is a symbol for the number nine.

Square. The square, and sometimes the rectangle, represents earthbound matter and earthly existence, the body, the physical plane, the limited space of the terrestrial world. It gives the impression of solidity and firmness—it is a foundation, an anchor. It also indicates the process of becoming stabilized and secure. When squares are present, organization and cohesion are taking place; pieces are coming together. Squares also indicate organization in terms of fours, as in the four seasons, the four quarters and the four elements, all of which are part of the foundation of the natural world. In alchemy, the square represents salt, itself a symbol of the earth and of earthly matter.

The squared circle—a circle inside a square with its perimeter touching the sides—is one of the most important of alchemical symbols, and represents the transition from the material to wholeness.

In Masonry, the square or rectangle represents the lodge, the sacred temple.

Cube. Like the square, the cube represents earth, salt, and the fraternal lodge. In Kabbalistic teachings, the cube represents the manifest universe, with specific meanings ascribed to the six faces and the interior. In Masonic thought, the cube is analogous to the building block; each person should build a temple of the soul comparable to the physical temple of learning and worship. In another respect, the cube represents one's fundamental faith. Thrones and seats of power often are represented as cubes. The High Priestess sits on a cube, and the Hierophant rests his feet on a cube.

Cross. Like the circle, the cross is an ancient and universal symbol that appears in many different shapes. In general, it represents the world axis, uniting heaven, earth, and the underworld, and providing a means by which the human soul can access the upper and lower spheres. As a pagan symbol, the cross—customarily with equilateral arms—represented the sun. The cross with feet—a swastika—was a solar wheel. The Greek cross (equilateral) was a dominant shape until Carolingian times, and then was replaced by the Latin cross, a stake and crossbeam, which represents the elevation of man from earth to the heavens. The Latin cross is the central symbol of Christianity, representing the crucifixion of Christ and thus is the symbol of salvation and redemption. A cross with a serpent entwined upon it is a symbol of Christ. As a Rosicrucian symbol the cross represents the human body and spirit. Crosses are related to the number four.

Pentacle or Pentagram. A five-pointed star with tip upright. An inscribed pentacle is a pentagram. The pentacle was used as an esoteric symbol by followers of Pythagoras. It is an important symbol in the magical arts, and represents the five senses of man, the five elements (the fifth being spirit), and the five extremities of the human body (head plus limbs). "By means of the pentagram within his own soul, man not only may master and govern all creatures inferior to himself, but may demand consideration at the hands of those superior to himself," observed philosopher Manly P. Hall. The pentacle also symbolizes the dominion of mind over the lower forces.

Inverted, the pentacle represents the infernal.

Pentagon. A five-sided figure that is associated with the pentacle, and also with the circle as a symbol of wholeness.

Hexagram. A star formed by the interpenetration of upright and inverted triangles, which symbolizes the union of opposites, the philosophers' stone and the attainment of spiritual wisdom. It also represents the human soul.

Hexagon. A six-sided figure associated with the hexagram and the circle.

Octagon. The eight-sided figure carries the numerical meaning of eight, which is regeneration, renewal, and transition. It symbolizes the four cardinal points (the square) plus four intermediate points. In architecture, the octagon supports a dome, thus representing the squaring of the circle. Christian fonts, the receptacles for baptism, often are octagonal in shape.

Spiral. An ancient, widespread, and complex symbol that denotes emanation and the creative/destructive powers of the universe. The spiral represents waxing or waning, life or death, expansion or contraction, masculine or feminine, solar or lunar powers. In its perpetual unwinding, the spiral also represents the cyclic nature of the seasons and the cosmos. In Yoga, it is the coil of the kundalini force, a powerful, primal force that resides dormant at the box of the spine, and when aroused through Yoga spirals up the spine to the brain in a burst of enlightenment. As a whorl, the spiral is a symbol of Goddess, who weaves the web of

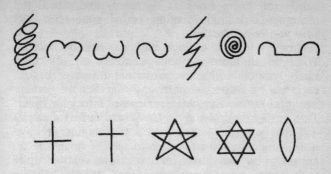

Figure 5   SHAPES
Top Row: Variations of the spiral
Bottom Row (l. to r.): Greek cross,
Latin cross, pentagram, hexagram, mandorla

life and controls all destiny. Lightning and spirals of
air are associated with fertility and generative forces,
as in the rainstorms that help to bring forth life on the
earth. The spiral also signifies change in an upward or
downward direction. Variations of the spiral are
shown in Figure 5.

These descriptions of primary symbols should help
you gain some understanding of the fundamentals of
the deep meanings in Tarot images. The more you use
the cards, the more you will become aware of symbols
on both conscious and intuitive levels. The symbols
will help shape your readings of the cards.

Exercise

To learn symbols, spend time studying them in your
Tarot deck. Examine each card individually for colors,
numbers, and shapes. In addition, look for other symbols represented by birds, animals, plants, tools, clothing, celestial objects, suit signs, shapes, and such. Use
the Glossary of Symbols at the end of this book as a

handy reference. Look at the cards and repeat the meanings out loud—making verbal statements will help you remember.

Now try to look at each card in a holistic fashion. What do all these symbolic elements say together? Each symbol is like an instrument in an orchestra: each has its individual part, and together they create beautiful music. Say whatever comes into your mind. Talk out loud. You may feel awkward at first, but you will find yourself getting into a stimulating, creative flow. Suddenly you will begin to see the images in an entirely new way, like fuzzy pictures that abruptly snap into a crystal-clear focus. Small, seemingly insignificant symbols will emerge into the forefront. Keep in mind that many symbols have multiple meanings, depending on the context in which they appear. As you practice, however, you will intuitively find the correct frames of reference. Discard whatever doesn't fit. Here is a sample stream-of-consciousness look at the Rider-Waite Magician:

The Magician stands with one arm raised toward heaven and one hand pointing to earth . . . a channel of energy from heaven to earth, spirit to matter . . . on an even greater scale, the macrocosm to microcosm . . . the lemniscate over his head represents eternity, infinity—better still, infinite wisdom and higher consciousness, the attainment of Spirit . . . the lemniscate has associations with the number 8, spirals and octagons: regeneration, alternating currents of opposites, transformation of consciousness . . . the table bears the objects that represent the suit signs of the Tarot . . . also the four elements, without which magic and transformation are not possible . . . four, the number of the square, the earth, matter, the building blocks of the spirit . . . the background is yellow, the color of the sun, intellect, spiritual wisdom. . . . The Magician wears red and white . . . red, the color of materialism, passions, life . . . white, the color of spirit and purity

. . . red and white together represent the union of opposites in alchemical transformation to achieve Unity and wholeness, the philosophers' stone . . . in his upraised hand he holds a white wand . . . wand, the conductor of supernatural force and power . . . drawing down Spirit into Matter, the macrocosm into the microcosm . . . around the Magician's waist is an Ouroborous, symbol of regeneration, immortality, the self-contained alchemical process . . . he stands framed in flowers, lilies and red roses . . . lilies, purity . . . roses, the mystic heart Center, the union of spirit and matter . . . the red-white theme again: the conjunction of opposites, the joining of the macrocosm and microcosm . . .

Thus you begin to see in a dramatic way how everything in the card's image works to reinforce the meaning of The Magician. You may know on an intellectual level that The Magician is the transformer, the interface between Spirit and Matter and macrocosm and microcosm; you can read that in a book and memorize it. But that's a one-dimensional understanding of Tarot. Now you see how much richer it is to understand on an intuitive level how symbols convey this message.

This exercise is important because it teaches you to listen to your intuition, a skill you will need in reading the cards. The exercise works best if you limit yourself to a few cards at a time. Don't move on until you feel you've fully absorbed each card (pip cards without images can be studied fairly quickly). Do the exercise daily. When you have gone through the entire pack, go through it again.

FIVE

The Major Arcana

The Major Arcana is the portion of the Tarot deck that offers the greatest depth of meaning and the most profound mysteries. Taken in sequence from The Fool to The World, the cards represent our journey through life, our spiritual Quest that begins in the Nothingness, the unmanifest, the Cosmic Egg, and moves through the trials and learning of the initiate to culminate in wholeness—the ultimate Oneness that is ever the striving of the human soul. The cards mirror different stages along the way. Each of the cards offers insight into a person's growth and development as the Wheel of Life turns.

The interpretations of the cards presented here, and in the following chapter on the Minor Arcana, are intended as a guide to prompt your own discoveries. They are designed as tools to give you insight into yourself and your own growth. They are handrails to hold during bumpy times and confirmation of the things you may have already come to know about yourself over the years.

The Rider-Waite deck, as the reigning standard in the field, is presented here. The meanings of the cards are given for their upright and reversed positions, and can be used for divination or personal growth work. (Chapter Twelve delves further into the Major Arcana for meditation work.) I have attempted to give a broad stroke to each card that can be applied to a variety of Tarot decks, not just the Rider-Waite. The order of the Major Arcana follows Waite's order, with

Strength as VIII and Justice as XI, except The Fool has been moved to its rightful and proper place at the beginning.

Read the meanings of the cards carefully. In a reading, try to draw parallels from the messages of the cards to changes you may be going through, or answers to questions that seem to elude you.

By no means do these descriptions do full justice to the cards. They are merely initial thoughts to help guide you. Every Tarot reader develops a unique relationship with the cards. Reflect on the descriptions and then meditate on what you think the cards are saying to you. Draw as much or as little from each description to help you.

There may be times when you'll think that, based on the descriptions provided, the cards seem to be saying something totally unrelated to your questions. Don't form such a judgment too quickly. Allow yourself time to reflect on both the message of the cards and your questions. The answers will eventually come.

In addition to using these descriptions in a reading, you might find it helpful to study both the cards and their meanings to learn more about yourself and in what direction your life is going. Are you like The Fool just beginning a journey? Or have you come to the end of one phase of your life and are waiting for Death to clear away the old to make way for the new? You might find the cards will help you answer those questions and many more.

O *The Fool*

Who but a fool would leap headlong into the void, seemingly uncaring about the potential dangers, trials, and challenges that lie ahead? The Fool's innocence is also his charm and what makes him so attractive. The Fool is untouched by life, but ready for the experience. He represents purity of action. There is no time for analysis or strategy. He doesn't look behind him. He only looks forward. The Fool needs no encouragement to begin the journey. He does not need to test the water. He'll find out when he steps in it whether it is warm or cold.

What about the rest of us? We all can think of thousands of reasons in any given situation why we should not take action or commit ourselves. Not The Fool. He stands poised on the precipice ready to jump without hesitation. He lives for the future—nothing holds him to the present.

His motives are pure. He seeks to discover. His quest is for life—and he is willing to give it a chance, come what may. The Fool lives to live.

Life has not left its marks or scars on The Fool. He is not yet connected to anything in this world. His few possessions are in a bag, tied to a wand, which rests against his shoulder. They do not weigh him down; they are behind him.

Unlike those of us who have been tested—and think we possess great wisdom from our experiences—The Fool cares not to hear the warnings. ("Don't be a fool.") The Fool frightens us a little because nothing frightens him. He is a liberated spirit.

The Fool is a believer in all things, especially the potential that life holds. But ask him to be elaborate, and he'll smile and say, "Find out for yourself."

His source of knowledge comes from inside. He trusts his instincts—he instinctively "knows."

The card tells us to take the plunge, follow our heart, listen to the inner call. We are being told to face the

THE FOOL.

risks, even tempt fate. The card also reminds us of the power of our imagination and our dreams. The message is simple: all things are possible.

Reversed Meaning: A thin line divides the act of The Fool from foolishness. The need to exercise caution, not to charge ahead foolishly. It also could mean that you are holding yourself back, not paying attention to your instincts. You say to yourself, "If in doubt, don't do it."

I The Magician

The Magician is one of the most practical of the Tarot symbols. He represents the powers we each possess to create meaning and purpose in our lives.

With one hand pointed to the heavens, the other pointing downward, The Magician tells us that this creative power resides both within and outside ourselves—but always within reach.

The Magician seems to be saying, "Open yourself to the forces surrounding you, the life-giving powers, the powers of creation—draw them to yourself, transform yourself into whatever you wish to be."

Unlike The Fool, who lives without order and approaches life with a randomness, The Magician represents a more structured way of life. He believes there is a formula for every given situation.

Although The Magician already possesses a great deal of knowledge, mostly what he has learned through trial and error, he seeks to learn more. He relies especially on his powers of observation to expand his awareness of how things work in the world. He is acutely interested in learning the basic structure underlying all things as well as the patterns, cycles, and rhythms that exist in the world.

The Magician believes in experimenting until he gets things right. For The Magician, failure means either the wrong formula was used or something was done incorrectly. Either way, there is always something to be learned, a piece of knowledge that can be used again later.

Not surprisingly, The Magician also is extremely self-reliant and self-confident. There's a bit of a showman in him as well. Notice in the card how he appears to be onstage, working his magic—he likes to show off what he's learned. He is not a teacher, however. He doesn't share his secrets, but he makes it clear that all of us can learn to do the same things.

The Magician is not intuitive. He does not commit

THE MAGICIAN.

to anything based on hunches or notions. He only believes in what he knows from past experience, or from what the formula suggests will be the outcome.

Reversed Meaning: You are blocking your creative energies. Or you are afraid to experiment, to try new things. Your self-confidence is lacking because you're unsure of yourself. At the same time, the card could be telling you not to be so self-assured, that what worked once may not be right this time.

II The High Priestess

The High Priestess symbolizes the power of unconscious forces in the world—the unseen powers that give the earth its form and purpose; the invisible thread that binds us together.

The High Priestess reveals little about herself the way she is pictured on the card. Her source of knowledge is kept hidden, yet she appears to know all. It is a depth we can hope to achieve during our lifetime or as we try to come to grips with a problem we face.

Her tranquility is also representative of her great powers. She is like a giant tree that stands tall but silent—or like still waters that run deep. The High Priestess also represents the invisible powers in nature that give life to all things. She is our link to the energy that turns a seed into a flowering plant, a sapling into a towering tree. In life, it's this same power that can nourish us on our journey.

She does not perform or ply her craft out in the open like The Magician, and does not jump from one place to the other like The Fool. Her silence exudes confidence. She is not seeking the truth we are. But she validates the search and encourages to look in earnest for it.

The High Priestess signals us to seek the answers from within—to look inside ourselves, to listen for the voices and to follow the prompting of our heart. From reflection, meditation, the answers will come. The High Priestess tells us to use our intuition as a guide.

Because The High Priestess does not reveal all to us, it is an indication that we must continue the journey for answers. Things will come if we are patient. What we don't know now will be revealed to us later. We should be open to the possibilities, especially things we haven't even considered. Life is a mystery. But it is with purpose. The High Priestess knows the secrets. And she lets us know that we can someday know those secrets ourselves. They could come to us in a flash, or after a lifetime of searching.

THE HIGH PRIESTESS

Reversed Meaning: You are ignoring your own impulses. Things don't feel right to you and you are afraid to follow your hunches. You want external validation. Your feelings are strong, but you are afraid or unwilling to act. You are distant from and not a part of the life process, still sitting on the sidelines watching. You want things revealed to you in advance before you will commit.

III The Empress

If The High Priestess represents the unseen forces in nature, then The Empress represents the visible manifestation of those forces. She is the fulfillment of the feminine or life-giving power in nature—she is the Earth Mother or Mother Nature. On one hand she represents fertility, creativity, and growth. She also symbolizes the passage from one stage to the next. She is the reason a seed planted in the soil will germinate and grow and why it will eventually wither away and die. She is the manifestation of the evolutionary process. She governs the eternal cycle of birth, death and rebirth.

The Empress is a very tangible power—something we can reach out and feel. We can sense The Empress in our daily lives when we look at the natural world that surrounds us. Although she is a material presence, she enriches our soul. Her presence fills our heart with joy when we watch a tree unfurl its blossoms in the spring. She also reminds us of the eternal process at work when we return in the fall to watch the leaves fall from the same tree.

In her dual roles as Earth Mother and Mother Nature, The Empress gives and she takes. She does so without prejudice, without judgment. She is the ebb and the flow. She stands for the process of life and its cyclical pattern.

The Empress makes our lives fertile so we can grow—in mind as well as body. As the symbol of motherhood, The Empress also stands for compassion and caring. When we welcome The Empress in our lives, she mothers us and looks out for us.

Because she represents growth, The Empress also reminds us that not all things stay the same, that the process of life is constant—that it is about growing and changing. The Empress can be telling us either to plant a seed or harvest the yield. The Empress can also be a sign of harmony and material satisfaction in

THE EMPRESS.

our lives that comes from a good solid grounding in the process of life itself.

Reversed Meaning: Refusing to accept change, to move to the next stage. Overly satisfied with the present, blind to the opportunities ahead. Seeing your material possessions as ends to themselves instead of momentary rewards. Also: not applying yourself to productive tasks, no growth, just stagnation. Need to get in touch with your creative forces.

IV The Emperor

The Emperor represents the external world that exists outside of the natural world. He stands for ties that bind us together as a society and civilization. He is the unity and order in our lives, the laws that guide us as well as the logic that dictates our actions. He represents the different controlling forces in our lives—"father," "ruler," "supreme being."

The Emperor lays it out straight for us, articulating the difference between right and wrong. He lets us know there will be consequences from deviating from the correct path. In The Emperor's world A leads to B and B leads to C. There is little room for deviation from the norm. In The Emperor's world—the secular side of our life—everything we need to know, every answer to every question is written down somewhere, all we have to do is look it up.

The Emperor and The High Priestess can sometimes symbolize the tension that exists between following the dictates of the heart and doing what logic says is right. Even so, The Emperor can only speak for what is right according to the external rules that govern our lives in general or the choices we face in every given situation. He cannot punish, only warn.

The Emperor can be a stabilizing influence as well. His firmness gives us something to hold on to in times of turbulence and change. His course of action is spelled out ahead of time, eliminating any ambiguity or decision about the correct actions to follow. His is the path of preservation, of protecting the status quo.

At the other end of the spectrum, The Emperor can represent the restraining influences in our lives—and the need for change. Instead of a path that leads to growth and fulfillment, the old, orderly ways can be restraining and stagnating. The Emperor could be telling us to turn our back on the comfortable and the known and that it is time to strike out into unfamiliar territory so that we can experience new growth and

THE EMPEROR.

make new rules as we go along. We can always return to the comfortable path—and we may eventually do so—wiser from the experiences of having tried something new.

Reversed Meaning: Your focus is too narrow. You use the rule of law to shield yourself from the truth. You say, "I know it's wrong, but it's the *law*." Or "I agree with you, but my hands are tied." You may need to listen more to your internal voice. Logic speaks only for the head, not the heart.

93

V *The Hierophant*

There are many ways of regarding The Hierophant, depending on your personal view of religion and its role in your life. According to classical interpretation, The Hierophant is the link between God and man—the high priest on earth. His are the ways of tradition.

Perhaps a more fitting interpretation for our modern age is to see him as the channel between divine or esoteric knowledge and ourselves. He is our spiritual guide who transcends the material world. He is our teacher. He can unlock the doors of hidden knowledge. He can help us get closer to the truth. He can help us see meaning in life. He can help us discover the God that exists within each of us.

Either way, The Hierophant can be an important element in our lives, particularly as a reminder that we cannot grow if we limit our pursuits to material satisfaction alone. Our spiritual side needs nurturing, too. The Hierophant will help us in this quest.

The path we choose on this quest is personal. It can be through avenues that traditional religion provides, such as prayer and following the tenets of our personal faith. For others, meditation, contemplation, may be the better way.

The Hierophant can also serve as a beacon in the night, guiding us toward the next level of evolution of our own consciousness.

On another level, The Hierophant represents our moral growth and development—the knowledge of true right and wrong, not that imposed by the rule of external law and order. But like The Emperor, The Hierophant reminds us that there are consequences from deviating from the "true" path. He suggests that there is a higher authority to whom we must answer.

The card may be a signal that we should take account of our spiritual stock, or perhaps, it's a reminder that we need to recognize the limitations when we are too grounded in the material world.

THE HIEROPHANT

In his guise as the keeper of the old ways, The Hierophant could be telling us we would be wiser to follow a more "orthodox" approach to a problem at hand or a question we're trying to answer.

Reversed Meaning: Too dogmatic in your interpretation of events. Allowing faith to be your guide, instead of questioning and seeking the answers. There is a higher truth to be discovered. You must open yourself up to new ways of thinking.

VI *The Lovers*

On its simplest level, The Lovers represents the act of union between the male and female spirits. Man and woman together are a potent creative force.

On another level, the card speaks to the next stage of a development—the point at which we move forward to begin building for the future with another.

A third meaning relates the male and female sides to a personality that exists within each of us—men and women alike. The male side represents the intellect, which is linked to the outer world, through conscious thought and reason, whereas the female is our connection to our unconscious self.

The card also acknowledges the emergence of sexuality within each of us—a change in our physical bodies and emotional and intellectual framework that both separates man from woman and at the same time creates the dynamic tension that draws us together. Similar tensions exist within ourselves as we try to live in both the external and unconscious worlds simultaneously.

Finally, man and woman united and, in the Rider-Waite image blessed by the angel Raphael, give a sense of harmony and balance. This could symbolize the harmony within ourselves, with both our emotions and intellect in balance, or a balanced relationship.

Even with these different meanings, there is a thread that binds them all together, and that is the power of love in our lives, both to create and to destroy. Both the love of ourselves and the love for another.

The card also speaks to the dichotomy that exists in our lives on different levels—and the constant choices we make. Do we follow our intellect or be guided by our inner thoughts? Is one side of our personality more dominant than the other and, if so, how do we find balance?

The card may be a recognition of the absence of

THE LOVERS.

love or another person in your life. Or that you need to turn to the person you love for help in resolving a problem. It can also be a sense of peace and harmony that reigns in your life. Or the need to put things in balance, with yourself or with another.

Reversed Meaning: Love can blind. A relationship could be out of balance. Not looking at both sides of an issue. Can't go it alone. The answers can't be found by looking on the outside alone.

VII The Chariot

A quick glance at this card reveals all: we can read the power, ambition, and determination in the face of the charioteer. But notice too that it is a youthful face. He is a young man driven by a burning desire to win, to dominate, to succeed.

The Chariot card reflects the innocent desire to charge ahead into the world when we are young. This is not the same innocence of The Fool. The Fool is just beginning his journey. He does not know what he wants. He is a free spirit who dashes to and fro, hither and yon. The charioteer has chosen his purpose. He has chosen his battlefield. He will emerge from the battlefield the victor. His successes will be a measure of how much he accumulates. It is only later in life that the charioteer—like the rest of us—recognizes that these possessions only bring limited happiness.

Clearly, there is nothing wrong with the drive for success, especially in the early stages of our lives. Ambition can serve us well. It can help us build the material foundation we all need. Our society depends on the charioteers who blaze new trails into the future.

On another level, the card reveals that there need to be no limits on our drive for success—no matter what our age. Of course, this is a particularly important strength to possess when we are young. If we feel we can conquer all, no task is too difficult. Only later when the stresses of life begin to take their toll, words like *burn-out* creep into our vocabulary. But if we can remember our past successes as we get older, we can rise above these stresses to confront new challenges. This is especially true when we begin new ventures; we need the determination of the charioteer to propel us forward and to prevent us from looking backwards.

This is also a card of discipline and control. The charioteer has his mind fixed on a single purpose. His emotions are under control. His path is laid out clearly and he has no desire to deviate. He feels he is the

THE CHARIOT.

master of his fate. He represents the power of the will. Too often in life we allow ourselves to get distracted. We lose sight of our goals. Not the charioteer. He charges ahead—and so should we.

Reversed Meaning: Too focused on material gain. Moving too fast, need to slow down. ("Pull back on the reins.") Need to temper your ambition. Time to take account of your success. Need to broaden your worldview.

VIII Strength

Just as The Chariot represents the outward manifestation of power and drive, the Strength card symbolizes the inner forces that help carry us forward throughout life. From the outset we learn that life will be filled with difficulties. Experience quickly teaches us that we must develop an inner strength if we are to persevere and enjoy life. It's also what helps define our personalities—distinguishing a strong person from a weak person.

With this inner strength we are able to face up to the questions in our lives, to cope with the changes, the positives and the negatives.

Strength is the belief we have in ourselves. A different kind of self-confidence than what The Chariot driver exudes. His is raw courage and might. This is the strength of wisdom and belief. The strength that comes from learning about ourselves and learning to trust ourselves. The more we believe in ourselves and our abilities, the more barriers that will fall.

A strong person also keeps his emotions in balance or—in the extreme—in check. Inner strength can be a calming influence. Think of the archetypal images of the strong, silent hero. You can read the strength in his face. He has proven himself to himself. He doesn't have to prove anything to anyone else. The same sense of serenity and strength combined is reflected on the Strength card. The woman silently strokes the lion. This is a representation that she has tamed the beast inside. Instead of fighting it, she draws from it. It is her source of inner power.

Strength also implies wisdom. A strong person believes in life. He recognizes that there is a reason for everything and from everything he can learn. He regards adversity and trouble as a test of will. He believes he can overcome. With this as his foundation he can never lose. Even in defeat, he can feel proud he stood his ground. By turning and running, we lose

STRENGTH.

more than the battle. We lose confidence in ourselves. We lay the foundation for defeat.

A strong person has hope. He faces life eagerly. "I am ready, willing and able."

Reversed Meaning: Lacking self-confidence. Questioning your abilities. ("Am I up for this?") Need to believe more in yourself. Don't look outside yourself for what exists within. Time to silence your fears.

IX The Hermit

As much as we need the company and counsel of others, there are times in life when we have to withdraw into ourselves and meditate upon the important questions we face. The Hermit, sometimes called the Wise Man, reflects this need.

On a simpler, more practical level, The Hermit underscores the need for peace and quiet, for contemplation, for meditation in our lives. Our minds are subjected to so much—especially in today's information age. We are bombarded with news, with opinion, with the stresses of daily life.

We need to become like The Hermit: in a contemplative or meditative state, withdrawn momentarily from the world, deep in thought and reflection. We need to seek the light of inner wisdom.

The act of gazing inward can accomplish many things. It can bring order to the chaos in our lives, helping us sift through the different signals we're receiving so we can put each in its proper place.

Meditation can also help us remove ourselves from our problems, to look at them objectively and weigh different solutions. The answers may not come immediately. But having prepared ourselves for this discovery the answers will eventually come.

Also, we occasionally need to look deep inside ourselves with no set purpose in mind other than to open our mind to new thoughts, new discoveries, new truths that reside in our unconscious self. We need to develop this link to our unconscious self; to build bridges to the higher reality, to those hidden forces that help determine our destiny. By spending this time alone, deep in thought and contemplation, we come to realize that we are not alone. That all of us are here for a purpose, that we are united in spirit, and that we all have access to the same truths. The Hermit lights the way for us to make these discoveries about the mysteries and meaning of life

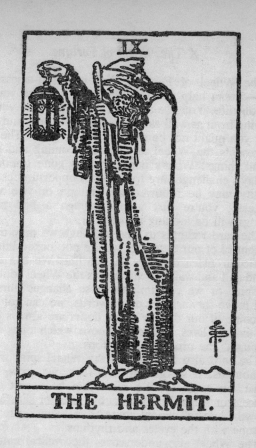

THE HERMIT.

Meditation also allows us to learn from our many past experiences. It provides the opportunity to glean the deeper lessons about what we've accomplished and how it relates to our true task.

Time spent alone gives us also a sense of peace. The memory of that serene feeling can be helpful in times of turbulence. It can help ease our anxieties.

Reversed Meaning: Closed off from others. Too self-absorbed. Need to connect with reality. Also: too externally focused. The answers are within yourself.

X The Wheel of Fortune

The Wheel of Fortune card is a self-assessment tool—it can help you take account of where you are in your life. You use it to get a fix on where you are coming from as well as where you are going, and even why you might not be making any progress. The card represents the Wheel of Life, the coming and going of all things. What's here today is gone tomorrow. Today's challenges are tomorrow's opportunities. Adversity may be followed by triumph or vice versa. ("Relax, you're just going through a bad phase. Things will be looking up soon.")

The card reminds us that although we may not be in control of our destinies, we are not locked into any particular place or stage in our life. We can either stand still and wait for changes as the Wheel continues to spin, or we can initiate those changes ourselves and move forward. In other words, we can color the outcome of our destiny. New doors are always opening in our lives. We can choose which ones to go through. The process never stops.

The card also tells us that the Wheel spins with or without us. If we go with the flow, we grow. If we resist, we stagnate. We can either be a part of the process or watch life pass us by. Greater satisfaction, growth, and fulfillment come from living a life that's in tune with the cycles and rhythms.

The Wheel also underscores the cyclical nature of our personal growth and development. We frequently relive the past by looking back over all the major changes in our lives as a way of measuring progress. The past is a part of our future. The Wheel card also warns that we are condemned to repeat the mistakes of the past if we don't learn. That's one reason why we often compare decisions we made in our youth with decisions we make years later. ("If I would have known what I know today, I would never have done that.") Just as important, the card tells us that we are

WHEEL of FORTUNE.

today because of what we did yesterday, and what we do tomorrow will depend on what we do today. At the same time, we must take responsibility for whatever comes around.

Reversed Meaning: You are stuck in a rut. Just spinning your wheels, or running on a treadmill. You know what happened the last time you did that. Things may take a turn for the worse before they get better. You are only in a phase, it won't last forever.

XI Justice

The Justice card is about bringing balance and harmony into our lives and what happens when we don't. The scales of Justice remain balanced as long as we maintain this proper equilibrium or harmony. When we tip the scales we pay the price. The cosmos operates on the principle of cause and effect, the law of Karma, punishment and reward.

By placing too much emphasis on work we can damage our family relationships. By finding balance, we enjoy the fruits of both worlds.

By placing too much focus on the secular side of our lives we leave ourselves spiritually deficient. By making time for material and spiritual pursuits, we feel wholesome and see purpose in everything we do.

By being too self-centered, we live life alone. By finding time for others, we benefit from their companionship, their counsel, their friendship.

By pushing ourselves too hard, we can damage our health. By knowing where to draw the line, we perform at peak capacity in all pursuits.

The list goes on and on. The choice is always ours.

Justice is nonjudgmental. When we are fair to ourselves and fair to others, we are rewarded. When we are out of balance, in our lives, in our relationships, in our pursuits, we are doing an injustice to ourselves, our friends, families, and associates. But because we are doing the injustice, we pay the price.

Life is give and take. We have to find that proper balance if we are to live life to its fullest. We must learn to compromise. We must learn to find where to draw the line between work and home, between the material and spiritual worlds, between drive and pleasure.

Justice implies living in harmony with nature.

An appreciation for justice also is a measure of our personal development. The more we understand the principle of justice, the more we practice it in our

XI

JUSTICE .

daily lives, the more we grow, the more we share in rewards, the more fulfilled we are. The more we as individuals believe in justice, the more it is practiced by our society, the more humankind will evolve.

Reversed Meaning: You are being unfair to yourself. You need to bring balance back into your life. Not looking at both sides of an issue. Weigh the pros and cons carefully before deciding what to do. You are getting what you "deserve," not what you want.

XII The Hanged Man

It takes a brave soul to hang upside down suspended from a tree—and by choice. Someone who has enough confidence in himself to risk injury, even scorn from others. But that is the essence of The Hanged Man card. It is a transitory card that represents a break with the past, a willingness to turn the world over, to take a fresh look at things from a new angle or vantage point. The card implies nonconformity.

Also the mere fact the card depicts someone hanging shows that things are in suspense, and that perhaps we are between stages in life—the known and the unknown—and ready to face what awaits us. In other words, we are willing to give up what we have because we believe we'll either grow or benefit in some important way by taking this dramatic step. Once suspended from the tree, there is no turning back.

The card also reminds us of the experience of the great mystics who plunge themselves into a spiritual crisis, hanging between reality and the unknown, hoping to emerge enlightened. Sometimes we must be willing to give up everything we know, cut ourselves off from our comforts and roots, and open ourselves up to the mysteries of the world.

Above all, The Hanged Man does what he thinks is right—not what others tell him. The Hanged Man represents a stage in our development when we have grown more sure of ourselves than ever before, when we know we can overcome the challenges we face and we willingly put ourselves to the test. There is a strong link to The Fool, who stands ready to jump headlong into the void. The difference is The Fool does so out of innocence at the start of his journey and without any idea of what awaits him. The Hanged Man has the experience of hindsight to guide his action.

This is also a card of faith and destiny, and a strong belief in both. The Hanged Man believes in the forces that rule our lives and because of his deep faith he

THE HANGED MAN.

has no fear about the eventual outcome. He believes he is fulfilling another step on the road to his eventual destiny. He is so immersed in the life process himself that he is giving himself to it entirely.

Reversed Meaning: Not willing—or able—to break with the past. Too comfortable with the way things are. Prefer the status quo over change. See yourself as the master of your fate.

XIII *Death*

The Death card strikes fear in the hearts of most people when it should be welcomed. It is not an evil card. It is a card of change, of transformation. It is the darkness that precedes the light, the death that is necessary for rebirth to take place. It is another turn on the Wheel of Life.

Death and life go hand in hand. Both are linked as part of the eternal process. Life ends in death. And from death comes new beginnings. Where The Hanged Man represents a suspension between two states, death symbolizes the end of the old and the start of something new.

Death takes many forms on the physical and mental planes. In nature, the four seasons are a graphic representation of the life-death process that we know well. From the end of winter comes the birth of spring, which leads to summer, then to fall, and back again to winter. Over and over and over again. For eternity.

Our lives are like that, too. From the moment of birth to our eventual death, we pass through different life stages. Each new stage follows from the death of the other. From childhood we grow to adolescence. From our teens we enter adulthood. Our middle age passes to our later years. The passage of each stage brings new beginnings, new challenges. Without the force of death, we would stagnate. The Wheel would stop turning. And then we might truly be dead.

Death is a revitalizing force. It is a cleansing, a clearing away of the old to make way for the new. Just as gardens have to be pruned of their dead growth, so do our lives. We have to cast off old ideas and old ways of doing things that are no longer valid or that apply. We have to embrace the new challenges, opportunities, cut our ties to the past.

The Death card symbolizes the immortality of our lives while we live them. We should take solace in the fact that nothing is forever, that new doors will always

DEATH.

open. We are not locked in place. We can grow in new directions, liberated from our past selves.

We should welcome the Death card and look forward to the changes in our lives. Death tells us to be open to new adventures about to begin.

Reversed Meaning: Fear of change, especially the future. Clinging to old ideas or values that are no longer relevant. Not a good time to make the break. Stop grieving for the old ways or what you've lost.

XIV *Temperance*

The Justice card tells us of the consequences of not living life in perfect harmony or balance; the Temperance card is a guide to living that harmony.

We know that life itself is a neutral process. The ebb and flow only lead to more of the same. How we live within the process—preferably in balance—is the key to fulfillment and happiness. The Temperance card suggests the need to recognize the need for limitations, to know how far to go and when to pull back on the reins. It is not a denial or sacrifice, but rather mixing or matching or weaving together what's right for you. Just as you have to keep mixing hot and cold water until the temperature feels right, you have to select the path that feels the best for you.

The Temperance card implies great self-knowledge. The more you know about yourself, the more able you are to find the balance between your wants and needs, strengths and weaknesses, likes and dislikes, as well as how you function in different situations. After all, we are not the same all the time. Our behavior changes as circumstances and environment changes.

The Temperance card also reminds us that to pursue anything in the extreme is a bad tactic. We would be wiser to choose the middle path and put together a plan that leaves room for accommodation, flexibility, and change along the way. By tilting too far in one direction we might topple over. Or by turning the flames up too high, we might get burned.

The Temperance card is a moderating force between the raw ("full speed ahead") determination of the chariot driver and the sword-wielding force of justice. Why live life on the edge when you don't have to? Draw from all that life has to offer. Compromise, accommodate, and be happy. Remember, you are in control and calling the shots. You can choose what's best for you.

TEMPERANCE.

By pursuing the path of Temperance you will also live a more fulfilling and enriching life in company with others. Your personality, your strengths and weaknesses, will be balanced against theirs. You will draw what you need for yourself and share from yourself what they need.

Reversed Meaning: Lack of control in your life. Close-minded. Not comfortable with what's facing you. ("It doesn't feel right.")

113

XV The Devil

The Devil is a card of darkness—the kind that limits our vision, that blocks reality from our view. In the dark, it's hard to find the path to happiness. The real evil that The Devil represents is being unable to enjoy life for what it is, but being misled by false notions, usually an attachment to material things.

The Devil also symbolizes the limitations we place on ourselves. Instead of facing challenges, The Devil urges us to turn and run, seek the path of lowest resistance. The Devil tells us to give in to our temptations, to do what we know is wrong, to be weak instead of strong.

In our modern age, The Devil is synonymous with the trap many of us build for ourselves—believing we can't make changes, we can't better ourselves, that our world is cold, cruel, uncaring. The Devil makes us believe it is our fate to suffer. The Devil would have us believe we cannot break free of a confining job or a stifling relationship. The Devil also would like us to believe that the Wheel of Fortune crushes us as it turns instead of carrying us to a higher plane.

In the same vein, when we feel so down, depressed, and mired in a sense of hopelessness, we're easy prey for The Devil. The key is not to give in but to plunge headlong into life's experiences with the innocence of The Fool, ambition of the Chariot driver, and draw on all our internal strength so that we can face the future with fearlessness of The Hanged Man.

The Devil also represents the fears we carry around and which limit our growth because we're afraid to confront them. For most of us, fear of change is the strongest and most crippling. Fear of making a commitment can grip us in an equally strong stranglehold. The fear that The Devil card represents is paralyzing. And The Devil would like us to think we can't do anything about it and that we have no control over our lives.

114

THE DEVIL .

We know the opposite is true. We didn't have this fear when we began the journey as The Fool. And we shouldn't succumb to it now, not after we've grown so much and learned to trust ourselves. We should recognize our fears, confront them, and get on with our lives. We must be strong and chase The Devil from our lives.

Reversed Meaning: In control of your fears. Letting go of the bonds.

XVI The Tower

The Tower card is about breaking free, knocking down the walls that imprison us. It is not a subtle change, but a major transformation in our lives. It's appropriate that it follows The Devil card. If The Devil card represents the darkness in our lives, The Tower card means we are ready to welcome some light in our lives—even if it descends upon us with the fury of a lightning bolt.

The Tower card is the process of transformation itself, not the steps leading up to it. This card says change is happening. A new door has opened in your life and you are going through it.

The walls of The Tower can symbolize many things: A relationship that has trapped you. A job that stifles you. A family relation that you can't get close to. Ideas or fears that imprison you. You are ready to break free.

The Tower card also reminds us that sometimes change is unexpected—even when we hope for it. Often this can be the best kind of change because we don't have to debate with ourselves about whether we should do something now or later. Like it or not, ready or not, change is happening right before your eyes. And the outcome is likely to be good because it's something you want.

Some see The Tower card as a final message that you can't hide from yourself or from life forever. No matter how thick the walls or how tall The Tower stands, it can be blown apart without warning. Maybe you'd be wiser to act first. It could be less traumatic or tumultuous that way.

The Tower card is also about inspiration. The way answers to tough questions that have eluded us suddenly break through our consciousness, usually when we least expect it. Sometimes after we've given up on finding those answers.

THE TOWER.

On yet another level, The Tower card represents sudden spiritual enlightenment—knowledge that comes to us from deep within, without warning, and opens our eyes to the wonders and mysteries of the world.

Reversed Meaning: The change is over and you'd better get used to doing things a new way. You are out in the open now, so don't try to hide. The old ways are gone forever. Better brace yourself for a bumpy ride.

XVII The Star

The Star is another card of balance and harmony— the kind that comes after a storm, a violent eruption or a major change, all the things represented by The Tower, the card that precedes The Star. The Star is a card of calm and peacefulness. Hope and joy. Comforts and pleasure. Things feel good. There is order in nature once again.

We can rest and reflect and turn our gaze to the heavens. The Star will guide us to our destination when we are ready to begin journeying again. The Star will illuminate the path for us. It will also protect us under the night sky.

When we look up to the starlit heavens we are left with a sense of awe and wonder. For a moment, we feel small in relation to the grand scheme of the cosmos. At the same time, we feel a part of this master plan. We recognize that all things have their purpose, all things their place. On the earthly plane, we are like the stars above. We light the path for our own lives and for others.

The Star's light is a soft light, not a blinding flash like the lightning that strikes The Tower. We want to look at it, not away from it. Although liberating, the lightning terrifies us. In contrast, The Star, which represents the light from the heavens, warms our soul and our inner self the way the sun warms our bodies. It nourishes our minds, and helps us think of the infinite possibilities—like the countless stars above—that life offers us. It is a card of inspiration.

The Star is another card of personal reflection, meditation, and contemplation. It's a reminder to turn our gaze inward and be guided by an inner light; to trust ourselves and our intuitions. We've come so far, learned so much, at last we are becoming enlightened.

The card also tells us to be at peace with ourselves, be true to ourselves, and bring love into our lives. The card encourages us to feel good about ourselves.

XVII

THE STAR.

On a spiritual level, The Star is our link to the higher plane. It tells us to open our minds and let the light shine in. To grow in spirit, awareness, and knowledge and to apply all we learn in pursuit of even higher knowledge.

Reversed Meaning: Eyes closed to future possibilities. Gaze focused downward instead of up to the heavens. Feelings of insecurity and disquiet. Need to latch onto your dreams again.

XVIII The Moon

The Moon glows, but it does not illuminate the earth below. It is not a guide like The Star and it does not warm or brighten. The light The Moon casts isn't even its own—it's a reflection of The Sun. The reality we know by day is now cloaked in an illusion.

When The Moon is high in the night, we enter the dreamworld. And in this netherworld, things are not as they always seem. The familiar shapes of the daytime hours take on different meanings. We must be on guard.

Even the Moon doesn't reveal all of itself to us. It grows from a little sliver to a full moon—another reminder that not everything has been revealed to us.

The Moon card suggests we are being tested. Can we remain true to the path, or will we be distracted by the shadows, the illusions, the mysteries of the night? Will we be able to tell our dreams from our realities? Will we be able to glean from our dreams what we need to apply to our waking hours?

Because we have only ourselves to rely on until morning comes, we must trust our instinct, follow our hunches, create an inner light. The night, ruled by The Moon, will teach us to trust our unconscious self.

The Moon also is a symbol of madness—or lunacy. Think of how often people's strange behavior is attributed to a full moon. The Moon is an unsettling influence. It looms overhead, appearing to threaten. The night of The Moon is an uneasy time. While it may be quiet outside, and seem peaceful, that is just another illusion. Inside we are churning. We are so close to completing our journey, so anxious to reach the end of the path, yet we must muster the courage to trudge onward in the dimly-lit night.

We must tread carefully during this period. We do not know what awaits us. But we have to have faith that we are up to the task. Our dreams will guide us.

THE MOON.

The Moon card warns us of the unknown, yet at the same time beckons us. It's that fear of the unknown that attracts. We don't know where the journey will lead and yet we're willing to take the risks, to venture out into the darkness. The Moon tugs on us, just as it pulls the tides.

Reversed Meaning: Not a time to venture out. Stay with the path you know best. Lacking in faith and in nerve. Going through a phase. In the dark about things.

XIX *The Sun*

The Sun is the source of life. Its rays nourish our bodies as well as our minds. Without it, existence would cease. When we see The Sun card, we should take a moment to reflect on all that is good in our lives.

In symbolic terms, a life without sun would be a life of total darkness. There would be no growth, no happiness. We would exist in limbo. Thankfully, The Sun on this card shines brightly. Our time in The Sun is our reward for passing through the trial of the night. We emerge into the warm rays of golden sunshine feeling reborn, renewed, and energized.

The Sun card exudes a satisfying, happy, and wholesome feeling. Contentment reigns in our lives again. Optimism is the word of the day. We are triumphant.

The Sun also means enlightenment and empowerment. With things so brightly lit, we can see clearly, which makes us feel positive about the future. We feel our creative juices at their highest. Because warmth is also synonymous with feeling secure, we feel more than able to tackle any and all challenges.

The Sun, which sits at the center of the solar system, means our lives are centered.

The Sun card depicts children at play. In the sunlight we are children of the earth. Innocent and happy, full of hope and promise, trusting in both life and in ourselves, and filled with a desire to live life to its fullest.

The Sun means a new day is dawning—another reason for the image of children on the card. The air is fresh, the sky blue, all is right and well. We are the masters of our fate.

In The Sun we are free. Free of our burdens, our material concerns. We have traveled far since beginning the journey as a Fool, and yet we come to this stop along the way even younger than when we began. That's because we are young in mind and spirit.

THE SUN .

Enriched by the past experiences of our lives, we begin a new stage in life on a higher plane, wiser and more confident. We have been reborn many times on this journey. And we will be reborn many times more.

Reversed Meaning: Unhappiness, emptiness. Lack of purpose. In the dark about things. Your mind is unclear. Clouds loom on the horizon. Too set in the old ways. Need to let some light, warmth into your life.

XX Judgement

Made pure by The Sun, we are now ready to face the challenges, tackle our problems, get on with new chapters in our lives. If the Death card meant the clearing away of the old to make way for the new, the Judgement card calls us to action. It tells us the time has come.

We are ready to assume a more meaningful existence, to live life on the higher plane. Not just as individuals, but united with all others. We have an appreciation of our role in the world. On our journey we have been seeking truth, enlightenment, hidden knowledge, self-awareness, and trying to bring balance, harmony, and a sense of peace and contentment to our lives. We now possess those things—and we can use them during the adventures to come.

The card tells us to look no further, wait no longer. New paths are opening. And as we travel along these new paths, we may be starting once again the cycle that brought us here in the first place. But as we've learned from the Wheel of Fortune, when we return again next time, we'll be even wiser.

The card itself draws on Biblical images of souls rising, awakened from the dead by Gabriel's trumpet. We can take this to mean that we, too, are being awakened, emerging from dormancy, lifting the obstacles that block our growth and development. We can also see ourselves rising above our problems, the mundane concerns that restrict us from achieving our potential and that leave us locked inside ourselves. We have been released.

By the time we reach this stage, we have changed—and we recognize the change. We now fully understand that our life's work is a combination of personal fulfillment and achieving some higher destiny. We understand our purpose for being here and how to integrate that purpose in everything we do.

The time for questioning is over. The real work—

JUDGEMENT.

our life's work—is just beginning. The next time we pass this point we will be able to show real progress.

Reversed Meaning: Unable to see the purpose in your life. The shackles have been broken, but you won't let go. Closing your mind to the new possibilities. Shunning responsibilities. Turning a deaf ear to a call to action.

XXI The World

The World card signals arrival. The journey's end. A coming together of all things. The joining of all the forces in the world. A wholeness, or oneness.

All is in balance. All is in motion. We have completed the cycle. And we are ready to move again. To dance the dance of life. And to go in any direction we choose.

It has been the journey of our lifetime—or the journey of an instant. Time is not the issue here, just what we've learned.

We have arrived at that stage in life when we have an appreciation for life and the world that comes from deep inside. The wisdom of the ages is now ours.

The card is also a reminder that life is infinite, not finite—that the world spins forever, and we with it. We must accept constant change in our lives, for that is the only constant of life. We must recognize this change as the life force itself. From change comes growth. From this growth we ascend to new heights. And someday, we'll start at the bottom all over again.

The World card is the ultimate goal for all of us. Total enlightenment. To see ourselves as part of the cosmic order. Not separate and distinct, and with our own value judgments about what's right and wrong with the world, but just as one piece of the puzzle that makes up the whole. In other words, we see our place in the universe.

The World card explains that there is a purpose for all things. We don't need to understand this process intellectually. We shouldn't stand at the sidelines and observe. Or put the world under a microscope. We only learn by being part of the process. By experiencing its wholeness. A Zen expression says that the danger of pointing your finger at the moon is that you might mistake your finger for the moon. We must not make the same mistake by thinking we know all

THE WORLD.

there is because we've watched the world in motion. Rather we'd be wiser to experience the truths for ourselves.

The World card is an affirmation of the life process itself—both its good and bad. It is nonjudgmental about either. The good and the bad are just elements of life. The card tells us to accept both and to recognize that they have a place in the grand scheme. The ups and downs, the wins and losses, the joys and sorrows—they are just different sides of the coin. They are part of life and they help us grow in equal measure.

Reversed Meaning: You are not there yet. Goals still elude you. Not committing yourself. Running in place, not moving forward.

SIX

The Minor Arcana

The meanings of the Minor Arcana are presented here with the same approach as that used with the Major Arcana. Once again, the Rider-Waite deck serves as the standard. If you use other decks, you will note that sometimes the names are different for the suit signs and court cards.

The four suits of the Minor Arcana correspond to the four basic elements of the universe: fire, water, air, and earth as Wands, Cups, Swords, and Pentacles, respectively.

Each suit has fourteen cards: ace to ten are the numbered (pip) cards; Page, Knight, Queen, and King are the court cards. Numbered cards represent events in our lives, their different stages of development, and possible courses of action open to us:

Ace: Beginning
Two: Formation, coming together of opposites
Three: Growth
Four: Practical attainment, tangible achievement
Five: New cycle, change, stability upset
Six: Finding equilibrium, harmony in the face of constant change
Seven: Facing complex choices, development of the soul
Eight: Setting priorities, putting things where they belong, balancing
Nine: Bringing things to an end, completion, conclusion

Ten: Over but not finished and about to begin
         again

Court cards reflect the influence of aspects of personality in our lives—from either ourselves or other people:

Page: Youthful innocence
Knight: Energy, drive
Queen: Understanding, awareness
King: Strength of will

The suit cards themselves represent different aspects of life and the forces surrounding it:

Wands: This suit stands for fire, the spark of life. It reflects enterprise, energy, and the constant renewal of all things. It is linked to our positive feelings about the future: hopeful, forward looking, and ambitious. Wands capture our desire for growth, how we strive for achievement and success, the inspiration that fuels us.

Cups: The Cups suit is about love, happiness, and the emotional pleasures of life. Like water, Cups go with the flow and relate to how we respond to emotional influences, impulses. Cups put the romances, relationships, and ups and downs of our lives into perspective.

Swords: Life is a constant struggle, and Swords represent the qualities necessary to survive: boldness and courage. It also is a suit of mental energies, reason, logic, judgment—all the things that stand separate and distinct from our emotions. Swords allow us to observe scenes from our life without emotion and somewhat detached.

Pentacles: This is the suit of the material world. Its images deal with attainment and the things you can feel and hold, the material aspects of life: money, wealth, and the acquisition of fortune. Pentacles represent the value of physical experience. They are also our connection to earth and nature.

The interpretations that follow are designed to guide you in your search for answers. They are not absolute and on the surface may seem unrelated to your questions. Ponder the meaning in the context of your question and where they fall in a reading. As always when using the cards, allow your mind to suggest fresh interpretations, new insights. After all, the Tarot is only a tool to help you make important discoveries about yourself, about life.

Ace of Wands

New beginnings. The birth of an idea that leads to action. The start of an enterprise or new challenges. You are filled with a sense of optimism, eagerness, enthusiasm, excitement, and boundless energy. You can sense the potential. You are looking forward to what's ahead.

Reversed: Difficulty in getting something started. False hopes. Misdirected energy. You are lacking motivation, ambition, or drive to face the challenges. You don't want to attempt anything new.

ACE of WANDS.

You have a grasp of what you are capable of accomplishing and know what needs to be done. You know your investments will pay off if you follow the plan you've laid out. You sense success, feel proud, and are looking forward to the outcome. You are moving in the right direction.

Reversed: Going in the wrong direction. Not paying proper attention to details. Receiving mixed signals. Tasks seem overwhelming, can't get a grip on what you must do. Not in touch with your energies.

Three of Wands

You are reaping success from your efforts. Like the ships on the card, the results are starting to come in. Now that you've proven what you can do on your own, it is time to form partnerships and alliances with others so you can seek their advice and work together as a team.

Reversed: Achievements may not last. Your alliances are not proving to be productive. Goals seem elusive. Control is slipping away. Best to take time to reassess and regroup. Be wary of advice from others.

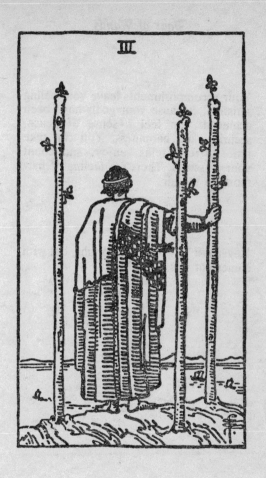

Your accomplishments leave you feeling satisfied. Because your goals have been achieved, you feel a sense of peace, security, and happiness. You can take time to rest, relax, enjoy, and count your blessings. There's a feeling of harmony in the air.

Reversed: The same as upright, but with somewhat less intensity.

Five of Wands

The calm is shattered. You face competition from others for the same thing. The outcome could be in your favor if you are careful, act forcefully, and don't give in. Be firm and stand your ground. Don't let anyone get the advantage over you.

Reversed: The conflict and disharmony are passing. New opportunities will be forthcoming. Positive change is in the air. Be ready for it. Also can indicate healthy competition.

Once again, through hard work, intelligence, and a clear understanding of the objectives, you achieve your goals. You have the drive, ambition, and desire—and a belief in your abilities—that lead to success. But even though you've earned your place, you'll have to work to keep it or someone might take it from you. Victory cannot last forever.

Reversed: Victory eludes you. Not strong enough for the challenge. Letting others beat you. Keep trying, you may be successful yet. Need to develop faith in yourself and a desire to win.

You are facing adversity and challenge—
and still holding your ground. You must
draw on your inner strength and personal faith to deal with this latest challenge. Something is coming to a head.
An unexpected confrontation looms on
the horizon, yet you are not afraid.

Reversed: Not willing to confront your
problems. Would prefer to turn and run.
Feeling a sense of anxiety. Uncomfortable about what's ahead. Disturbed by
choices facing you. Lacking willpower.

Eight of Wands

Things are moving fast, bringing you closer to your goal. Results are coming in quickly—and you must keep things in order. Sometimes indicates a journey.

Reversed: You can't handle the pace. Things are stacking up against you. Events may overtake you. Life is passing you by while you stand still.

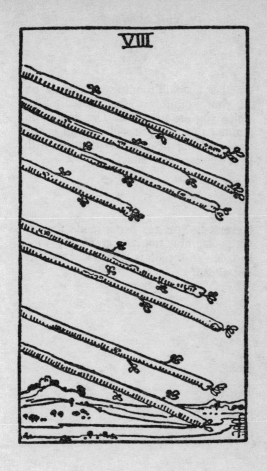

Nine of Wands

One last test will require you to draw on all your abilities; a final defense, for which you are prepared. The fight is on familiar turf and you will win out in the end, arriving at your destination with your achievement intact.

Reversed: You are being made to deal with something that you aren't yet ready to face. Your path is blocked. Adversity lies ahead.

You are carrying a heavy load—more than you can handle, more than you really want. Things weigh you down. You must share responsibility with others before continuing. Get rid of what you no longer need.

Reversed: Someone has made you responsible for their problems, or led you astray. You are near collapse.

Good news. Signal to proceed with something new, exciting. Time to tell the world about your plans, share your news with others.

Reversed: Don't know how to interpret the news. Information may upset you.

PAGE of WANDS.

Knight of Wands

A time of movement, journey. You are on your way to meet something or it is coming into your life. Things are in a state of transition. A stirring or turbulence in the air.

Reversed: Frustration. Knocked off track, derailed. Disruption in your life. Movement without purpose, no sense of destination. Running in place or moving in circles.

KNIGHT of WANDS.

An appreciation for life, relationships, friendships, family. Work, home life in harmony. All pursuits surrounded by a positive force.

Reversed: Under the influence of someone who is narrow-minded, self-centered, domineering. Must guard against feelings of jealousy.

QUEEN of WANDS.

Looking forward to challenges, new pursuits, healthy competition. Give to others and reap the rewards of self-fulfillment. Lead and others will follow. In a position of strength.

Reversed: Lack of tolerance. Opposition looms. May be necessary to bend to a stronger point of view.

KING of WANDS

A new outpouring of emotions: first love, new appreciation for life, a spiritual awakening. A journey that begins with special blessings. Good fortune shines on you. An acceptance of life and all the joys it brings. A sign of fertility.

Reversed: Emphasis on material over spiritual. Closed off from nurturing love or from your true feelings. Denying the wonders of life. Not ready for emotional involvement. Neither giving nor receiving love.

ACE ♣ CUPS.

The start of a relationship, love affair, a budding romance. A sharing of love, good feelings, ideas. A sense of harmony. The beginning of a partnership. Emotional balance. Give and take.

Reversed: Arguments, disputes, distrust. A relationship out of balance. Inequality among partners—one is putting in more than is being received. A relationship in jeopardy of coming undone.

Time to celebrate your accomplishments, reap the happiness you've achieved. Happiness in family relationships, friendships, work. A sense of joy envelops all you do. The cup of life tastes sweet.

Reversed: Anything enjoyed to excess can lose its value or worth. There's a price to pay for overindulgence. Happiness turns to sadness, joy to sorrow, pleasure to pain. Emphasis on the sensual instead of the spiritual.

Material pursuits no longer satisfy. Time to reassess, reevaluate, turn inward for answers. Looking for new, more fulfilling, satisfying challenges, pursuits. Answers to your questions are within reach.

Reversed: Ready for new challenges, relationships. A sense of excitement is in the air. Feeling revitalized, refreshed, and invigorated. Ready to resume past relationships, renew friendships.

Five of Cups

Unhappy endings, broken relationships. Time to pick up the pieces and start building again. See what you can learn from your losses. Turn your back on the past and look to the future. What's gone is gone. Hold on to what you have, no matter how little it is.

Reversed: Although a loss has been suffered, there's no reason to feel hopeless about the future. Things will start looking up again. An old friend may hold the key.

Six of Cups

Memories of good times fill you with happiness. The past is not lost, it can always be remembered. Also, past events can figure favorably in the present. Old friends may serve you well at this stage.

Reversed: Can't allow the past to cloud your emotions. Time to open yourself to the present. Need to find new friends, share new experiences. Leave the past in the past.

Seven of Cups

Feelings of indecision swirl around you. Choices must be made, but you're not giving yourself fully to the task at hand. You're spending too much time dreaming about the future when you should be acting on those dreams instead. Draw on those inner energies and begin moving from thought to action.

Reversed: Indecision is replaced with desire to take action, which will lead to positive outcome, sense of fulfillment. Time to pursue that dream, see where it leads.

The time has come to seek higher meaning and purpose from life. Also time to say goodbye to friendships and relationships you've outgrown. You may also want to follow the path of The Hermit and look inward for answers.

Reversed: Putting emotional pleasures ahead of spiritual needs. Hanging on to what no longer serves you or suits your needs. Not making an effort to grow or expand. Also, could mean that it is better for you to stay, not move on.

There's a place in our lives for material satisfaction, as well as spiritual happiness. Life should be enjoyed for its earthly pleasures, too. We should take steps to ensure our physical as well as mental well-being.

Reversed: What at first seemed like happiness leaves you feeling empty and unfulfilled. Spending too much time enjoying the sensual pleasures at the expense of spiritual growth and development. Living life in the shadow of false values.

Tranquillity reigns. Family relationships, friendships, home, and work are all under the sign of protection. Life itself means happiness. You've achieved what you've been seeking on both the material and spiritual planes. You feel complete—comfortable with yourself.

Reversed: Relationships in disharmony. Family quarrels. Loss of satisfaction. Unhappy, depressed, sad. Also, blind to the many wonders that surround you. No reason to be unhappy.

Page of Cups

A new idea will break through the surface. It may be delivered by a friend. It's a good time to apply your creativity, to try new methods, initiate new projects. Could also signal development of psychic ability.

Reversed: Acting on impulse could lead to trouble. Need to mature, become more thoughtful. Must learn to accept responsibility for self and actions. Ignoring ideas that may be beneficial.

PAGE of CUPS.

Following your dreams or traveling down your intuitive path could lead to fulfillment and satisfaction. A time for mental stimulation. Live your vision.

Reversed: Lost in a world of dreams, cut off from reality. Motives are insincere. Be on guard against duplicity, fraud, or trickery. Someone may tell you what you want to hear just to get the better of you.

KNIGHT of CUPS.

You are protected by love, warmth, and caring. Good time to pursue the creative arts—poetry, music, literature. Open yourself up to new visions, new possibilities. Follow the prompting of your heart.

Reversed: Emotions out of control, leading to self-deception, false hopes. Confusion reigns. Caught between the worlds of reality and illusion without knowing which way to turn. Be careful not to fall victim to deception by someone you think shares your best interests.

QUEEN of CUPS.

Seek out advice and counsel from trusted friend, a wise person. Follow your head and keep your emotions under control. Probe for the meaning in what you plan to do.

Reversed: Look beyond the facade—be careful someone isn't putting up a false front to hide insecurity, immaturity. Be careful of judgments rendered, advice offered from someone you don't know well.

KING _of_ CUPS.

The card indicates the unleashing of great mental energy. You must put this power to work to vanquish obstacles facing you. It may mean that you'll be able to think through a problem that has been troubling you. Set your mind to accomplishing your goals.

Reversed: Think carefully before taking action. Sort out all your options and consider each one carefully. Try to think more clearly. Instead of reality, your vision is clouded with illusions. Focus on the truth.

ACE of SWORDS.

You can't decide. Instead, you close your eyes to what faces you. You step back from the situation, taking time to get your emotions in check, to ponder things in silence. You can't remain aloof forever; soon you will have to decide.

Reversed: Although a decision has been made, and action has been taken, it is too early to tell if it was the right thing to do. Only time will tell. Either way, things are beginning to move.

It was necessary to remove what was causing you pain, trouble, or difficulty. And now you experience new pain. But it will soon pass. The new pain will cause you to sharpen your focus, to see new directions, to put the problems of the past behind you.

Reversed: Your pain will remain with you until you acknowledge the reason for the separation or change you had to make. You must put it behind you so you can get on with your life. Also, discord created by different points of view; can't seem to find a consensus with others.

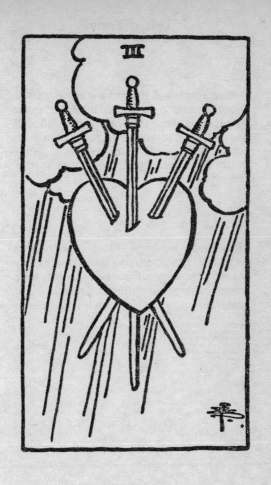

Once again it is time to back away from your troubles, to make time for quiet contemplation. Your problems will still be there when you return, but you'll be energized and able to approach things with a clearer head, wiser from your rest.

Reversed: No time to rest. Action is needed. You are being called back. Because you may not be ready to act, take care before committing yourself. Use caution.

All your emphasis is on winning. But victory itself may not be much of a reward. It could even be a loss in the long run. You must think of all the consequences that may arise—especially those who might get hurt, including yourself—before you come out swinging.

Reversed: Same as upright, but with stronger emphasis on likely defeat and feelings of pain, loss, and despair that follow.

You are able to navigate through your problems. And even though your difficulties still face you, you are learning how to deal with them, how to live your life in their presence. You are trying to look at things with a more open mind by putting distance between yourself and the past.

Reversed: You don't feel like you are making any progress. You are trying to paddle against the current. You aren't able to look at your problems afresh or put them behind you.

Your attempts to deal with your problems are feeble, incomplete, and not well-planned. In the process, you are hurting yourself. Trying to solve things alone may not be a wise decision. It may be more than you can handle by yourself.

Reversed: It's a good time to seek advice from someone else, to learn what you need to know, to do a little listening, seek constructive criticism. Good results may follow.

You've boxed yourself in and not allowed yourself any options. You are holding yourself back—and for no good reason. You need to cast off the blindfolds and cut yourself loose.

Reversed: You've removed the veil from your eyes and can see, think, and act without restriction. You can put your fears behind you and start moving forward again. You feel a great sense of release and relief.

The world is filled with pain and sorrow and somehow we must find a way to make our peace with it. You feel as though you want to take on the pain of the world yourself, to protect others from it. Pain and sorrow are only the other side of joy and happiness.

Reversed: A sense of hope fills you. The doom and gloom of the past are fading. The pain will be replaced with joy. You must have faith. Time will heal all wounds.

The card signifies an unexpected loss, the end to something on which you had been counting. The defeat could have been of your making or the result of circumstances beyond your control. As gloomy as things look, this too shall pass.

Reversed: Problems are beginning to wane. Blue skies appear on the horizon, signaling a change for the better. It's up to you to take advantage of this opportunity and move on before new problems crop up again.

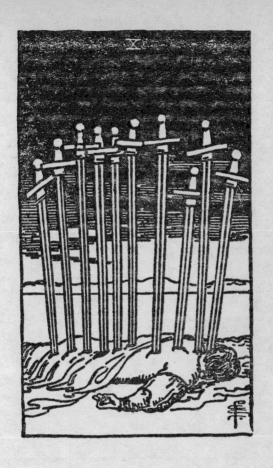

This card signifies a somewhat half-hearted approach to solving the problems facing you. Not taking things seriously enough or having a full understanding of the problem and what it means to you.

Reversed: Unexpected problems lurk in the distance.

PAGE of SWORDS.

Good time to apply your mental energies to solving problems, seeking solutions, developing plans. Time to evaluate results will come later.

Reversed: Thoughts are too scattered, coming too quickly. Need to focus, slow down. Be wary of anyone who suddenly presents you with unsolicited ideas for consideration.

KNIGHT of SWORDS .

Learn to rely on your mind; hone your intellectual abilities. Learn to see both sides of an issue, analyze carefully, free from emotions before deciding what action to take.

Reversed: Don't look at things from a narrow perspective. Don't shut yourself off from the truth by closing your ears to other points of view.

QUEEN of SWORDS.

Use your experiences of the past to guide your thinking. Be fair in making decisions that affect other people.

Reversed: Lack of compassion can cause hurt to other people. Don't be so strict that it borders on cruelty in your dealings with others. Don't allow prejudice to cloud your vision.

KING of SWORDS.

Ace of Pentacles

Good foundation for increasing money, perhaps through new venture or enterprise. Fertile soil in which to plant your ideas and come back later to harvest what grows. A chance to better your financial situation through promotion, career change.

Reversed: Move with caution before making major investments. Plan carefully, weigh the risks. Don't succumb to greed. Possible loss on the horizon. Material gain may not provide the answers you are seeking.

ACE of PENTACLES

What comes in goes out as well. New ventures may require you to adapt to changing circumstances. Check pros and cons before initiating new project. Keep home and work in proper balance.

Reversed: More than you can handle. Probably won't be able to hold things together. Something is out of balance. Things are up in the air. Misleading yourself into thinking you are happy in your pursuits.

You can apply your knowledge, skills, abilities to great advantage. A time of positive, measurable achievement that will win you reward, notice. Others will be happy to assist you and also will respond to your lead.

Reversed: Less than satisfactory efforts produce poor results. Disappointment. No gain. Not a good time to enlist others in your project or undertaking. There's a lot you need to learn. You're missing what you need to finish task.

Four of Pentacles

Seeking happiness exclusively from money. Putting material gain above all else. Also, solid financial foundation. Positive rewards are yours to enjoy. You'll work very hard in business to achieve your goals.

Reversed: Rewards are less than expected or less than fulfilling. Can't hold on to your money. Your goals are being blocked. Don't have the power or influence you require. Holding on to something when you should let go.

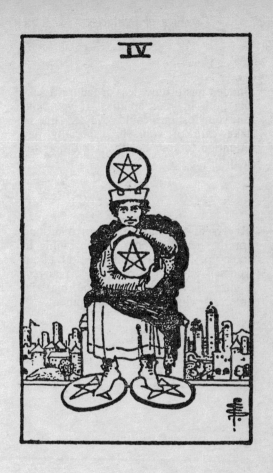

Sudden misfortune, loss or failure. Lacking faith in your abilities. If you hold on, your fortunes could reverse. Time to take care of yourself, especially pay attention to your health. Ask others for help.

Reversed: Situation has turned around for the better. Things are beginning to look up. You are feeling better about yourself and future prospects. You recognize the need to balance material interests with spiritual development.

Your hard work pays you dividends. A bonus is coming. Business pursuits prosper. You feel generous, want to share. Feeling satisfied, in harmony. Others around you appreciate what you do for them.

Reversed: Not getting your fair share. Someone is holding out on you. Not satisfied with the return on your investment. Possible debts. Not sharing with others, thinking only of yourself.

You have a lot to show for your efforts, but you are not sure if your achievements are what you want. Weighing your options about the future. Also, taking a moment to reflect on your gains.

Reversed: Difficult choices facing you about finances. In doubt about which way to turn. Afraid wrong choices could lead to loss or debts. Be careful not to make rash decisions. You want to abandon project, undertaking.

By applying yourself, you can build great success. Willing to learn new skills, trade to help improve your situation. Committed to project, venture, willing to invest time, effort, energy. Take great pride in what you do. The care shows.

Reversed: Interested in only short-term gains. Not willing to commit for the duration. Impatient. You mistakenly think shortcuts will produce desired results. Your heart is not in your work. Lack of quality shows.

You've earned great success and have much to enjoy. Skills honed in business world can help you manage your life overall. Your abilities can take you wherever you want to go; you're not dependent on others for success.

Reversed: Gains have been (or could be) lost. Bad decisions may be at fault. Didn't pay attention to what others were telling you. Expected yields aren't forthcoming.

You've achieved much of what you want, but you don't know if it's enough and you should seek more, or if it is as satisfying as you hoped it would be. At a minimum you are secure, have comfortable home, and sufficient wealth.

Reversed: Financial security in jeopardy. Not a good time to invest in new projects, gamble on possible return. You are facing a multitude of financial problems. You feel constrained, unable to do anything to improve your lot.

Approach new projects with a school-boy's wonder and enthusiasm. Study hard, apply what you learn and you'll reap positive rewards. Seek out solid, well-researched information before making any moves.

Reversed: Not using your intelligence to guide you. Your actions bespeak of ignorance, closed-mindedness. Should listen to the advice of others, learn from their experience. Don't allow your noncon-formity to lead to difficulties, losses.

PAGE of PENTACLES.

Knight of Pentacles

Hard work produces desired results. Stay on the path, don't deviate. Outline your goals ahead of time, then make a plan for achieving them. Don't leave things up to chance. Choose tasks in keeping with your abilities.

Reversed: Impatience will lead to failure. Be careful not to go in too many directions at the same time. Not applying yourself as you should. Don't narrow your pursuits so that you exclude opportunities as they arise.

KNIGHT of PENTACLES.

Time to enjoy what you've earned. Rest secure in the knowledge that your wealth, material comforts will continue to flower as long as you stay at it and apply your creative powers to tasks at hand.

Reversed: Not taking care of business or acting responsibly where your financial affairs are concerned. Depending on others to help you. This kind of behavior can cost you security and independence.

QUEEN of PENTACLES

You've reached the pinnacle. Your efforts have paid off and you have much to show for it. People know you as a reliable, hard-working person. It is no longer necessary to take risks. You concentrate on projects with reliable outcomes.

Reversed: Money is an all-consuming passion, and you are willing to do anything you can to accumulate more. Out of this stubbornness and your passion for gain, you put work ahead of everything else in your life, including family.

KING of PENTACLES.

Tarot Rituals

Working with the Tarot is richer, more powerful, and more fruitful if it is structured around ritual. In the modern West, the term *ritual* usually is associated with church worship or with the elaborate social and sacred ceremonies of tribal societies. Ritual, however, is much broader—it is any prescribed ceremony that is performed in order to accomplish a certain goal. Ritual is the means to come into contact with divine or supernatural will or forces. It helps the individual relate to the cosmos and mark progress through life and spiritual unfoldment.

Ritual raises energy. Even the smallest of daily routines is a ritual that puts in motion certain mental, psychic, and physical energies. When you work with the Tarot, you raise psychic energy, expand your consciousness, and heighten your intuitive ability. Ritual can help you do that most effectively.

Ritual essentially is symbolic behavior, consciously performed to discipline the mind, body, and spirit. Jung said that rituals "are an answer and reaction to the action of God upon man, and perhaps they are not only that, but are also intended to be 'activating,' a form of magic coercion." Hsun Tzu, a Chinese philosopher of the third century B.C., said rituals create harmony in the universe and bring out the best in human beings—they are the culmination of culture.

Mythologist Joseph Campbell once stated that the function of ritual "is to give form to human life, not in the way of a mere surface arrangement, but in depth." Ritual serves as a bridge between the conscious and

244

the unconscious: it releases psychic energies, opens psychic gateways, and allows the power of the inner world—where your intuition resides—to manifest in the physical. Ritual also works inward, causing changes to take place deep within the unconscious where attitudes and values are born and nurtured. The more a ritual is performed, the stronger it becomes, and the greater effect it has on consciousness.

Ritual has formed the backbone and structure of sacred and social occasions since the dawn of human history. The Paleolithic cave paintings in Trois Freres, France, depict rituals that appear to be aimed at ensuring successful hunts. A man with a stag's head, perhaps a shaman wearing an animal headdress, dances. Animals are shown bleeding and dying from spear wounds. Early man prepared for hunts by performing various rituals, which either were recorded by the cave artists, or which included the painting of such scenes as part of the rituals. The rituals helped the hunters visualize and expect a successful outcome. If the ritual was performed well, and energies raised were high, the outcome of the hunt undoubtedly was influenced in a positive way.

Throughout history, rituals have been central to all religions and all spiritual, mystical, and magical traditions. There are many types of rituals, such as worship or appeasement of divine or supernatural forces, or marking the transition from one major stage of life to another, such as puberty or marriage. Rituals performed over a long period of time accumulate great psychic power. Rituals can lose their potency, however, when the institution they serve deteriorates, or when the people performing the ritual lose sight of its original meaning. Unfortunately in the modern West, most rituals—the few that still exist—have lost much of their power. Campbell pinpoints the beginning of the decline of ritual in the West at 1914, the start of World War I, which profoundly changed European society. Since then, there has been an increasing disregard and even disdain for ritual, as though it has no place in a high-tech world but belongs to the outdated past or to less developed civilizations. People now attend church and go through the motions of moribund rituals without knowing their origins or true meanings, and thus receive little or no benefit from them. The machine has become a dominant god, replacing the need to propitiate the supernatural forces to aid us in our lives.

When we lose meaningful ritual, we cut ourselves off from our psychic roots, and from our deep sense of connectedness to each other, all life forms, the planet, and the cosmos. A strong sense of connectedness and harmony with the flow and flux of the universal energies is essential to good Tarot work.

There are no hard and fast rules or rituals for working with the Tarot, although there are some widely used practices, which will be described here. The beauty of the Tarot is that it is wonderfully adaptable to innovation. You decide what works best for you. This chapter will help you design your own rituals.

Tarot rituals need not be elaborate to be effective. If you enjoy ceremony, fine, but Tarot rituals that are short and simple can be equally good. In fact, sometimes the most powerful rituals are those that are simple.

Keep a Tarot Journal

Before you begin Tarot study, get a notebook to serve as a journal of your progress. Use this notebook to record your rituals, the spreads you use, meditations, and thoughts about readings. As your study progresses, you will get many ideas for creative ways to use the cards. Jot them down and allow them to grow.

When to Do Tarot Rituals

You should have a ritual to open your work session and one to close it. The opening ritual preps you, raises the energy, and opens you up psychically. The closing ritual helps you ground yourself and disconnect.

One opening and closing is sufficient and can serve as a general purpose for all kinds of Tarot work. You might wish to add new ones as you expand your work, however, so that you have different rituals for meditation, reading for yourself, reading for others, and such. The advantage of variety is that each ritual becomes a shorthand setup of sorts for work of a specific nature. The additional rituals need not be markedly different from your original ones—you can simply make small variations. The laying out of a spread is a ritual in itself, each unique unto itself, and so contributes to the overall procedure.

You also should have a ritual for breaking in a new pack of cards.

The Structure of a Ritual

Ritual is composed of concentration, intent and commitment, movement, and sound.

Concentration. The mind is stilled, focused, and relaxed—extraneous thoughts and mental chatter are pushed away. If you meditate, you will find it easy to center yourself quickly. Use the techniques described in Chapter Eleven, "Developing Your Intuition."

Intent and Commitment. Your intent and degree of commitment to the work influence the efficacy of the ritual, and in turn of the work. As you project, so shall you attract. A sincere desire to learn, to grow, and to help in turn attracts the appropriate energies.

Movement. The same things are done in the same way in the same order each time the ritual is performed. This establishes a pattern and rhythm, which help to raise energy and add to the ritual's cumulative power.

Sound. Parts of the ritual are spoken. Many Tarot users say their words silently, particularly if they are reading for others, but it's a good idea to include at least a few words that are spoken out loud. Sound carries power and contributes a great deal to the accumulation of psychic power of a ritual.

Sound in a ritual also includes background music or chanting, which many individuals find conducive to achieving an open, intuitive awareness in working with the cards. Others, however, find they work best in a quiet environment. Experiment with and without background sound. Choose something soothing and nonintrusive. A gentle chant, such as *Om Namah Shivayah* or *Hara Hara*, is conducive to a relaxed state of mind, as are many New Age recordings.

Ritual Objects and Tools

Ritual always involves ceremonial objects, the use of which fosters physical and psychological changes intended to help achieve the goal of the ritual. The more objects are used in ritual, the more they become imbued with power. For Tarot rituals, you will probably want:

1. A box for storage of your cards

2. A silk storage cloth

3. A silk reading cloth or a Tarot table

4. A candle or candles

5. Personal objects of significance

Storage Box. Your primary tool, of course, is your deck, and it should be well cared for. It's all right to keep the cards in the cardboard box they were purchased in, but they will be better protected and will acquire greater ritual significance if you store them in a special box. Buy one that's new—many greeting card, occult, and import shops carry inexpensive, hand-carved wooden boxes that are perfect for Tarot cards. Avoid used boxes because they contain the imprints of their previous owners, which will interfere with the cards. Objects pick up the energies of those who handle them, as your cards will of you. If they remain in a used box, they will absorb unwanted energies, which at best will interfere with your psychic attunement to the cards and at worst inject negative energy into your work, perhaps without you being aware of it.

Objects can yield amazing information to a psychically sensitive person merely through handling. Object reading is called *psychometry*, a term coined in 1840 by Joseph R. Buchanan, an American professor of physiology, from the Greek terms *psyche*, meaning "the soul," and *metron*, meaning "measure." Psychometry, said Buchanan, is a means to measure the soul of objects. He conducted experiments with students by having them hold vials of drugs to see if they could correctly name the contents. Buchanan's successful research interested others, most notably William F. Denton, a contemporary of Buchanan's and an American professor of geology. Denton conducted his own experiments and recorded his results in his now-classic book, *The Soul of Things*. Today, psychometry is used by many psychics, especially those involved in crime detection and missing persons work.

The longer an object is owned and the more it is handled, the stronger and more precise are the psychic impressions contained within it. If an object changes ownership or is handled by many people, it absorbs different impressions and will give a psychic an unclear or confusing picture. Since your Tarot cards are your personal tools and your link to your intuition and Higher Self, they must be indelibly *yours* and not clouded with the impressions of others.

Storage Cloth. In occult lore, colors have their own energies, too, and different colors have different effects and symbolisms. Your deck will benefit from being wrapped in a colored cloth while it is stored in the box. Many Tarot users prefer natural fibers—silk especially—and also cotton. More important are the cloth's newness—again for the absence of the impressions of others—and its color. You should steer clear of red, for example, because that is the color of the base passions, anger, sensuality, and materialism. Purple, gold (or yellow), and blue are best for the Tarot. Purple symbolizes the higher mind, deep affection, and spiritual power. It is the color of royalty and is associated with the crown chakra. Gold (or yellow) is the color of the sun's rays, the symbol of spiritual illumination, wisdom, intellect, and goodness. Blue represents spiritual qualities, such as inspiration, contemplation, and divinity. Furthermore, blue is a soothing, relaxing color that will augment the overall tone of Tarot work. Silver is another good choice, for it is the color of psychic powers, purity, and protection against negative forces. It has associations with the moon, and by extension with lunar powers of magic. Green is a balancing color that symbolizes youth, prosperity, harmony, well-being, and fecundity. Chapter Four, "Symbols in the Tarot," and the Glossary of Symbols in Appendix A provide additional information on the occult significance of various colors.

Reading Cloth. Some Tarot practitioners like to lay their spreads out on a cloth placed over a table instead of directly onto a table top. The purpose of the cloth is to protect the cards against unknown impressions stored within the table. This might be a concern for you if you travel with your cards and give readings in different locations, but if you always use your own table, a reading cloth is not essential. An attractive cloth, however, does have a pleasing effect and is a nice touch if you read for others. If you decide to use one, make sure it's a square big enough to contain the largest of your spreads, and choose the color as you would for the storage box cloth.

A Tarot Table. In lieu of a cloth or the bare kitchen table, you might want to consider purchasing or making a special Tarot table, which in effect becomes an altar. We generally think of altars only in connection with religious worship, but an altar also is a special table used as the center of a ritual, which is exactly what Tarot work is. If you have a table reserved only for Tarot work, it is transformed into a sacred space, a place where you connect with higher energies. Nothing else occurs in this space. If you are fortunate enough to be able to work in a space like this, you will find that the psychic atmosphere of it increases rapidly, because nothing from daily life will intrude upon it or diminish it.

If a Tarot table appeals to you and you are handy, it is preferable to make the table yourself. Whenever you make something with your hands, you imbue your own energies into the very substance of the object much more strongly than if you merely purchase it and use it. This is a traditional fundamental of ritual magic, which is why all magical textbooks advise the personal construction of ritual tools.

If you choose not to make a table, a purchased table will still serve the purpose quite adequately. Perhaps there is some decoration you can give it to make it more personal.

Candles. Candles should never be omitted from ritual work, for according to lore, their light illuminates the spiritual darkness, purifies the air, and attracts benevolent energy while repelling negative energy. Candles have a long history of use in religious, magical, and other types of ritual. Their origin is not known, but they appeared as early as 3000 B.C. in Egypt and Crete. By the fourth century A.D., they were part of early Christian ritual, and by the twelfth century they were given a place on Christian church altars.

White candles are customarily used in sacred ritual, because white symbolizes the spirit, purity, and protection. Both white and colored candles are used in magical work; the colors are selected for their specific occult meanings, and colored candles certainly are appropriate when working with the Tarot. Again, purple, gold, and blue are the best all-round choices, but choose according to your intuition and needs.

Personal Objects of Significance. If you wish, you can enhance your Tarot working space by putting out objects that have special significance to you, such as crystals, stones, good luck pieces, jewelry, or symbols of the four elements. The latter can be represented by small bits of wood or clay (earth); feathers (air); water in a small cup; and incense (fire). Incense is a staple in religious ritual because of old and widespread beliefs that it purifies the air of negativity.

A word about crystals: a great deal of spurious information has been written about their alleged mystical properties. Much of this information is channeled (supposedly from higher entities) and contains a lot of garbled material about the incredible array of powers said to be possessed by crystals because of their "vibrations," or assertions that crystals were implanted on earth by extraterrestrials. There is no scientific evidence to back up any of these claims. However, crystals do have a magical lore that has been projected onto them since ancient times, when people believed that they would act as amulets (protective forces) against bad luck, illness, and misfortune, or as talismans (active forces) to effect cures, enhance sexual powers and fertility, bring in riches, divine the future, and the like. There is no evidence to validate any of these ancient beliefs, either, but because the associations have existed for so long, they are deeply ingrained in our cultural folklore, which invests them with an archetypal energy of sorts. If you are attracted to crystals and believe they will work for you in meditation and divination, or even in luck, then use them. They will act as triggers to release creative energies at the conscious and subconscious levels. The ability of the mind to react to belief has been demonstrated repeatedly in the placebo effect, and in psycho-neuroimmunology, an emerging area of medicine that is revealing the enormous extent of how what we think influences our health. Similarly, if you have a lucky charm and truly believe it will bring you luck—no matter what the object is—then you undoubtedly will find yourself in propitious circumstances, because you will have put into motion the powers of thought, imagination, and will. Knowledge of this mental projection is age-old and universal, and has been called by various names. Norman Vincent Peale, for example, refers to it as "the power of positive thinking," whereas Shakti Gawain, an author popular with the New Age audience, calls it "creative visualization."

If you do choose to use crystals and stones, then stick with their time-honored, historical associations and avoid the outer space mumbo-jumbo. Even without the historical lore, crystals do make excellent meditation props. Their beautiful colors and ways of reflecting and refracting light help to focus attention and still the mind. The shiny surfaces of crystals and polished stones make them a natural for divination; since ancient times, the most common means of divination has been to gaze upon a reflective surface in expectation of seeing visions thereon. Crystal balls, of course, are the stereotype of fortune-telling parlors. True crystal balls, however, are very expensive. The small chunks of crystal you are likely to place on your Tarot table have facets too small to substitute for balls, or for mirrors or bowls of water, but they can help you expand to an altered state of consciousness in which your intuition and psychic faculties begin to function more freely.

Choose whatever crystals or stones "feel" right to you. Wear them, put them in your pocket, or place them on your Tarot table while you work. Appendix C, "Crystals, Stones, and Metals," features a list of items whose associations are especially relevant to the divination and meditation work with the Tarot.

After you've chosen and assembled the items you

wish to use in working with the Tarot, it's time to begin working with the cards themselves.

Breaking in a New Pack

A new pack of Tarot cards is fresh and virgin. With repeated handling, the cards become imbued with your own personal energies. Therefore, it's important that you be the first person to handle the cards, and that you be the only one to handle them during the break-in. This will ensure that the cards absorb the unique energies that constitute you.

After you've purchased your new cards, don't take them out of the box until you can set aside a time to work with them when you will be free from distraction and pressure. It is important that you be able to concentrate your full attention on the task at hand.

Take your cards to the place you have selected to conduct your Tarot work and readings. Unwrap your new pack and go through the cards, handling each one individually. Look at the images—even if you've used the same style of deck before and are thoroughly familiar with the designs—and absorb them into your consciousness. Take as much time with each card as you feel is necessary. Let your intuition guide you. Notice the feel, shape, and size of the cards. Observe the design on the backs of the cards.

Begin shuffling the cards. Notice how they feel in your hands. Turn some of the cards upside down and continue shuffling so that the deck gets well mixed. If you're an experienced Tarot reader and it feels appropriate to do so, lay some cards down in a spread. If you're a beginner, it's better to wait to lay down spreads until you're familiar with the card meanings.

When you feel you've shuffled and handled the cards enough, take the square of storage silk you've selected, wrap the cards, and place them in their box.

Many Tarot users like to place new packs under their pillow for a night or two, because they feel it quickens and improves the seasoning process. If you'd like to try this, keep the deck wrapped in its silk, and hold the cards in your thoughts as you fall asleep.

Once you've gone through an initial handling, get the cards out often to hold and shuffle, which strengthens the imprint of your vibrations. If you are a beginner or working with a new deck for the first time, take time to become thoroughly familiar with the symbolisms in the images. At some point, you will feel the time is right to begin working with the cards. Use an opening and closing ritual to frame the work.

Sample Opening and Closing Ritual

(Spread and smooth the work cloth. Place other working tools in their appropriate positions: candle, symbols of the elements, crystals, and such. Light the candle. Have a moment of quietude. Visualize your psychic protection.)

Say: "All the Powers around me, I give thanks for your assistance. Protect me from all negative energies. Only the positive may enter my presence." (Or, compose your own lines.)

(Take the Tarot deck from its container. Unwrap the cards and begin to shuffle them. When you have finished shuffling, place the cards on the table and tap them.)

Say: "All the Powers around me, I ask for your guidance. Let the Truth be revealed."

(Begin working with the deck. When you are finished, wrap the cards in their silk and return them to their box.)

Say: "All the Powers around me, I give thanks for the wisdom revealed."

(Blow out the candle. Put away whatever is to be stored.)

Exercise

Take a few moments of quiet time and compose your own Tarot ritual. Be as simple or as elaborate as you like. The only requirement is that the ritual works for *you*—that it makes you feel good to do it, and that it helps put you in a receptive state of mind to listen to your Higher Self.

Write down the spoken parts, which will reinforce the ritual in your consciousness.

Visualize the ritual, which will do the same.

Practice it. The more you practice and perform your ritual, the more it becomes part of you and unlocks creative energy. You can say the words silently to yourself or speak them out loud. As you polish your ritual, discard anything in it that makes you uncomfortable, awkward, or seems devoid of energy. Once you establish your ritual, it is important always to do it correctly and thoughtfully. Sloppy ritual is not effective.

As time passes, you will probably want to change your ritual to reflect the growth in your work. You may also want to add new rituals for particular kinds of work or readings.

Advanced Exercise

When your ritual has been performed enough so that it acquires its own power, you can augment it with *sigils*. A sigil is a shape or mental image that is linked to a particular idea or set of ideas. Concentrating on them can invoke higher energies.

For example, instead of going step-by-step through a visualization of protection, you can create a sigil that represents that protection, and accomplish the same thing by concentrating on the sigil. For example, use a crystalline egg as a symbol of the ideal protection. You visualize the egg, and in so doing automatically call upon whatever higher assistance you've chosen to work with. Another sigil can open the gates to the revelation of Truth in the cards. Still another sigil can close the work.

The effective use of sigils requires a certain amount of skill in mental imagery. If you're a beginner, it's best to work through each step in your ritual. The process of refining and condensing will occur naturally over time. You might also want to enlist the help of an experienced Tarot practitioner in guiding you with rituals.

EIGHT

Reading the Cards

The Tarot is a powerful tool for helping us answer life's questions and learn more about ourselves. Some Tarot practitioners believe that you should not read for yourself—only for others—and that you should have your own questions read by someone else. This is treated like a truism, but there is no reason why it should be so, nor is there any basis for believing that self-readings are going to be wrong or inadvisable. You can read for yourself just as well as for others. In fact, self-reading is one of the great benefits and joys of learning the Tarot.

The person who comes to you to seek a reading is, in some Tarot books, called a "querent," a curious term that is a nonword. Presumably, it is meant to be a derivative of "query," but the correct derivative for an inquirer or person who asks questions is "querist." "Seeker" is simpler and more than adequate.

Since Etteilla popularized the Tarot for fortune-telling, a variety of spreads has been developed to make the most meaningful readings of the cards. Many modern Tarot practitioners have developed their own spreads, and just about every new Tarot deck that's issued comes with its own unique spreads. The spreads in this book include some of the most familiar spreads, such as the Celtic Cross and Horoscope, as well as some new spreads and new variations of spreads. As you become comfortable with the Tarot, you can experiment with modifications and new spread designs. (Chapter Ten tells you how to design spreads.) Here are some general guidelines to keep in mind for your readings:

What to Ask the Cards

The Tarot functions best as a mirror and as an adviser. It reflects forces in motion, reveals directions, and shows possible and probable outcomes. It helps us to see when we are on a path that is straight and true, or when we have wandered off in an unprofitable direction. If asked, the Tarot will advise on a course of direction. Remember—and stress this to those who come to you for readings—that the ultimate outcome rests with the individual, who exercises the power of free will.

The Tarot also can be used to divine the future. For such questions, select a spread designed to give a yes/ no answer, or one that is intended to give answers according to specific time frames, such as seasons or months of the year. Individuals who have developed psychic talents will often get precognitive flashes when working with the cards.

Frankly, when it comes to fortune-telling, I prefer to exercise caution. Astrologer Dane Rudhyar once called astrology "the algebra of life"—it does not show predestination, but is a guide to help realize potential. The same is true for the Tarot.

Some people, however, place a great deal of faith in predictions of the future. Others place too much faith in them. They believe in predestination and that something is going to happen no matter what. The ancient Greeks and Romans, who were great diviners, believed that the future was immutable, and they constantly sought advance warnings through dreams, human oracles, and various divination procedures, such as examining the flights of birds and the markings of the livers of sacrificed animals.

But to believe that the future is immutable is to surrender free will. Numerous cases exist of persons using their free will to alter a future that was perceived psychically. When the ill-fated *Titanic* set sail on its maiden voyage in April 1912, it carried only 58 percent of its passenger load, despite the fact it was billed as the greatest luxury ship plying the popular Atlantic route, and was "iceberg-proof." The ship struck an iceberg and sank, killing 1,502 of the 2,207 persons on board. In a subsequent study by Dr. Ian Stevenson, a psychiatrist and parapsychologist, more than nineteen cases of precognitions of the disaster were identified. Most of the early warnings occurred to individuals two weeks prior to sailing. Some of the passengers scheduled to sail canceled their plans because they had dreams about the ship sinking, or because they had "feelings" that something disastrous would happen. Some may have canceled without really knowing why, or because other events intervened. J. Pierpont Morgan was among those who abruptly canceled, although it is not known whether it was because of premonition. It is impossible to say how many others had early warnings and did not record them, or who had warnings but ignored them, and died.

Other studies confirm that the future is alterable, at least in some cases. In the 1960s, researcher W. E. Cox studied rail passenger loads on American trains which had accidents between 1950 and 1955. He compared passenger loads on the same runs on the day of the accident, each of the preceding seven days, and the preceding fourteenth and twenty-eighth days. He found a marked drop-off in passenger counts on some, but not all, accident days. For example, the Chicago & East Illinois "Georgian" normally carried about sixty passengers on one particular run, but on the day of a fatal accident, June 15, 1952, it carried only nine passengers. Cox concluded that many people who had intended to travel on disaster-bound trains had altered their plans, perhaps unconsciously, or had missed the trains by being late, perhaps an intervention of fate.

Psychical researchers and parapsychologists have attempted to further define and quantify precognition, but it remains elusive and, ironically, unpredictable. The numerous cases of people altering perceived futures seems to support the theory that when we glimpse the future, we are seeing a *probable* future based on the present forces in motion, which, if unaltered, will continue to the event foreseen. In fact, psychical researchers estimate that one-third to one-half of all precognitive experiences may provide useful information to avert disasters.

Efforts to apply precognition have been largely unsuccessful, however, primarily due to inaccuracy. Either the disaster does not happen, or it does not happen at the predicted time. In 1967, a British Premonitions Bureau was established to collect and screen early warnings in an effort to avert disasters. The Central Premonitions Bureau was established in New York City for the same purpose a year later. Most of the tips received by both bureaus did not come to pass; those that did often were inaccurate in terms of time, rendering them equally useless. The British bureau ceased operation in the 1980s.

On the flip side is the question of self-fulfilling prophecy. That is, if one believes strongly that a certain event will transpire, how much does he or she bring it about? This question was studied in the 1960s by London psychiatrist J. A. Barker, who researched the effect of deaths foretold by fortune-tellers. In his book, *Scared to Death*, Barker concluded that some persons who were informed of the manner and/or date of their deaths, and believed in that inevitability, actually contributed to their own demise and fulfilled the predictions. They literally allowed themselves to be "scared to death."

So what does all this ultimately mean for the Tarot? It doesn't negate fortune-telling, but just requires a certain perspective. Above all, fortune-telling should not be undertaken as a lark or entertainment—you might be playing with powerful psychological forces. This applies to all work with the Tarot as well. One must approach the oracle with respect. Fortune-telling should be approached from the standpoint of possibilities based on present circumstances and forces, not as inevitabilities. I like to describe a reading as a "snapshot."

Be Very Careful About Delivering Bad News. In fact, most who work in the divining arts consider it unethical to disclose traumatic information such as foreseen deaths. Of course, one might argue that this information is desirable so that appropriate steps can be taken, if possible. As just discussed, however, the information could be wrong.

Some psychics will couch negative information, such as accidents or illness, in as positive a frame as possible. Some will discuss negatives only if the client specifically asks and seems prepared to deal with them. I do not know the best answers to these problems— they are quite delicate, and not for amateurs.

I once had the cards read by a woman who seemed to possess good psychic ability and could see beyond what appeared in the cards. My question concerned career matters, and many of the things she said seemed to be right on target. Then she stunned me by casually announcing that one of my two dogs was going to die. I had not mentioned I owned dogs, but she went on to deliver an accurate physical description of the dog in question, and said that she would be hit by a car and suffer a spinal injury, and that probably I was going to have to put her to sleep. She estimated that this would come to pass within six months, although she allowed that her sense of time could be a "little off." The shock of this unsolicited information was bad enough, but her manner of delivery, so cavalier, was downright cruel. I do not believe she did this deliberately; she was just thoughtless, and had no idea of the impact of what she was saying.

I cannot even begin to describe the devastation I felt. I could not fathom how such an accident could happen, because the dogs are not allowed to run loose. But, since the psychic had been so accurate about other things in the reading, I feared for the worst. I lived in absolute dread for six months. Nothing happened. More time went by. As of this writing, that reading was given almost six years ago, and the dog is quite healthy and has had no accidents. Nor has she had so much as a close call. This was the first and only time I have experienced a negative reading, and were it to happen again, I would not allow myself to be so influenced.

Later, I mentioned this incident to another psychic, who told me some of her clients came to her for "second opinions" because they had been told by this woman that their spouses or children were going to die (they, too, were probably given this information in an offhand fashion).

Naturally, *you* are not going to be so irresponsible!

So how do you handle negatives, even if they are far less traumatic? Other than stressing that the reading is a snapshot of possibilities given the present direction, you can ask questions to get the seeker to examine his or her true feelings or motives. For example, let's say a woman comes to a reading with the question, "Will I marry X?" It is obvious from her demeanor and remarks that she desires this outcome very much. The cards, however, say no or not likely. Depending on the spread you use, you may or may not get a reason for the answer. It's fair to assume that as much as the seeker professes to want the marriage, she has doubts about it coming to pass, or she wouldn't be asking the question. All of us from time to time harbor unrealistic expectations and then look for ways to convince ourselves that what we want will come to pass no matter what. By asking a few gentle questions, you may be able to bring inner doubts and fears to light where they can be acknowledged and dealt with. In this case, perhaps the seeker has projected a desire to get married onto the relationship. Or, perhaps she has fears that a marriage would not work out. Perhaps the relationship might well end in marriage, but hasn't progressed far enough. The important thing is that the seeker discover what lies deep within the heart—that she sees things in a fresh way and feels empowered to make positive changes. That is the greatest benefit of the Tarot.

How to Make the Most of a Reading

By the time you start giving readings, you should be familiar enough with the cards so that you do not have to rely upon descriptions of their meanings. You should know the cards well enough so that the information comes to you naturally and intuitively. In readings, you are considering much more than individual card meanings, however: you are also examining how the cards relate to each other in a spread, and their synergism, that is, the sum total of the spread that is greater than the individual parts. Thus, if you are a beginner in reading spreads, you might need a little help from time to time, so it won't hurt to refer to card descriptions when necessary. Never try to guess at their meanings, which will only muddy the quality of your reading.

Do not feel limited to the literal interpretations of the cards. Use your imagination and your intuition to draw deeper, more personal meanings from the cards. Look at them individually and collectively, and try to get a feel for the synergism of the reading. Tarot cards are like chemicals: each has its own properties, and when you put them together they react and combine to create something different. If a reading seems ambiguous or indefinite, don't be put off. There are many possibilities as to why, which will be considered in this chapter.

Remember, this book is only a guide to the Tarot. By working with the cards over and over again, they will begin to speak to you in their own way, especially as you grow more comfortable with them and learn how to listen to the inner voice the cards trigger.

After you have placed all the cards in their positions, analyze the spread carefully. Whether you are reading for yourself or another person, look for patterns in the spread as well as similarities or wide differences in the suits or arcana that you've laid out. Talk about what you see, what you feel. Is the reading a surprise? Does it suggest new directions that hadn't been considered before? Can you or the questioner make changes that will lead to another ending? Also, what does the reading tell you about you or the person seeking answers?

Make notes in your Tarot journal of the readings that you do for yourself. Record the date, the question that was asked, and a sketch of the spread. You can simplify the process by copying by hand diagrams of spreads onto pieces of tying paper. Number the card positions. Make photocopies. To record a layout, fill in the names of the cards that turn up in each position. Store them in a three-ring binder. It's interesting, and insightful as well, to compare readings over a long period of time, particularly if you have posed the same question at various intervals.

If you read for others, ask their permission to record their readings. You can either give them the records to keep, or store them yourself, provided you make certain that confidentiality will be secure. The records will be useful as a reference point in future consultations. If your client is knowledgeable about the Tarot, he may prefer to keep the records so that he can refer back to them for further contemplation. You might also consider having the client make the record on one of the forms you provide. This helps to personalize the reading and to stimulate the creative thought process.

Reading with a Partner

Solitary work with the Tarot is rewarding, but there's no need to limit yourself to that. Working with a partner adds a new dimension to study and readings. Two persons who are in tune with one another—close friends, lovers, or spouses—can spark off each other in interpreting cards. The result is often thought-provoking, lively discussion.

Working with the Spreads

Although the spreads differ, they all begin in much the same way. The seeker comes to the reading with a question. The question should be stated out loud, then written down. It is also acceptable—and preferable to some readers—to have the seeker concentrate silently on the question. When the question has been composed, shuffle the cards until you feel you should stop. Then pass the deck and ask the seeker to shuffle the cards. After doing so, the seeker then cuts the deck into three piles (they do not have to be uniform), placing the cards from right to left. After the deck has been cut, you reassemble the piles from right to left. Now you are ready to lay the cards down in the spread you've chosen. If you're giving a reading for another, always use a familiar spread—never try out a new spread. Tarot spreads are rituals, and require practice and repetition for maximum effectiveness. Practice spreads on yourself or on hypothetical situations before using them in readings for others.

In interpreting the cards, bear in mind that the Tarot should be consulted for insight, not for dictation. I do not recommend making any decision solely upon the Tarot—or upon any other divination method, for that matter. Tarot readings should be done with the intent of helping the seeker see a situation in a new light. If there are obstacles, the reading should help the seeker get fresh ideas for solutions. If a projected path appears clear, the reading should help crystallize and fortify resolve to push ahead. If you read for others, they should be counseled that the reading is but one way of gaining insight, and should be weighed along with other factors.

When More Information Is Needed

Occasionally the cards will seem incomplete and you'll wish the spread had one or two more positions to shed more light on the matter. It's perfectly acceptable to turn over extra cards for a little boost. Do so *after* the reading has been analyzed and discussed, and only if there is something unresolved that might be helped with more cards, or if the seeker seems to need extra assurance.

In these situations, I turn over one card and place it to the lower right of the spread. If necessary, I turn over two or three, working in a horizontal line left to right. However, you can place the extra cards wherever you like. Perhaps the spread you're using lends itself naturally to an extension.

Three extra cards is the limit. If you have to add more than that, something is wrong with the reading, and you should consider the possibilities discussed in the next section.

When Problems Arise

Every now and then a reading just won't gel. The cards don't add up or the message is confusing. Or, the cards seem to be talking about something else other than the question posed. When that happens, it's best to be honest and acknowledge that the cards are not clear. You won't do yourself or the seeker any favors by trying to fake your way through a reading. Instead, suggest that there's a good reason for this and then explore these possible explanations:

The Seeker Has Not Posed the Question Clearly. The seeker may be suffering from internal confusion or conflict that is preventing him or her from seeing the matter objectively. If this is the case, help the seeker reframe the question, and then do another reading.

The Real Question Has Not Been Posed. The cards may be saying that something else in the seeker's life is more pressing and needs attention. Perhaps it is something the seeker has been trying to avoid. Probe with a few gentle questions: "Is there another matter concerning you? "Is your question part of a larger issue?" The seeker may then be encouraged to open up and reexamine the question. If he or she insists there is nothing else to consider, use your intuition to decide whether or not to try another reading. First, consider some of the other possible reasons why the reading seems off-target.

The Question Cannot Be Resolved in One Reading. The question posed by the seeker may be like an onion—it has layers that must be peeled away one by one. This situation could be intertwined with the preceding two. Do not attempt to tackle all the layers in one sitting. Discuss the situation and decide how to approach it in a series of sittings. Use the initial reading as meditation material to help frame questions for the next readings. The meditation should be undertaken by the seeker in advance of the next readings. Use the tips in Chapter Twelve, which involves meditation and the Tarot, to help the seeker.

Your Ability to Tune In to the Seeker Is Impaired. This can happen for any number of reasons. Everyone has "off" days, and this can apply to either you or the seeker. You're out of sorts or out of harmonious flow. One of you is preoccupied with extraneous matters. Perhaps the seeker is unconsciously generating a great deal of pent-up anger, hostility, or anxiety that may have nothing to do with you, but nonetheless creates a barrier between the two of you. If you feel that's the case, the best thing to do is invite the seeker to come back at a later time. If you lay the cards out again, you're likely to come up with another unreadable spread. Tarot, like the *I Ching* and other systems of divination, has a way of telling you when it's not auspicious to consult the oracle. Listen and obey.

You're Projecting Expectations. Based upon the question and what you intuit about the seeker, you may begin a reading with expectations as to what the cards will—or should—say. You've allowed yourself to be attached to the outcome. In this situation, take a moment to re-center yourself and release the attachment. Look at the spread again and let it speak for itself.

Environmental Distractions Are Too Great. No matter how well you've learned to detach yourself in order to listen to the inner voice, there are going to be times when you're unable to overcome external distractions. If the distractions are not going to abate, you're in a no-win situation and should reschedule the reading. For example, for years I have had an annual reading given to me by a talented psychic with whom I share a good working rapport. One year, I showed up for my morning appointment to find that the neighbors in the upstairs apartment were doing substantial remodeling. It was impossible to ignore the thumping of hammers, the whine of saws, and the sounds of heavy objects being dragged across the floor. My friend was upset, because she had requested that they not work during the hour of our reading. The neighbors had agreed but did not honor the agreement. My friend stopped the reading to make a phone call, but the work continued. It was upsetting for both of us, and we should have rescheduled. Instead, we plowed on, but the concentration just wasn't there on either part.

Don't be afraid to suggest rescheduling a reading. Be judicious about when and how often you do so, of course, but recognize that a client would much rather come back for a reading than go away feeling dissatisfied. Wouldn't you if the tables were turned?

The Reading Is Beyond Your Present Ability. Yes, this does happen. It's more likely to happen in the beginning of your career as a Tarot reader, but even experienced practitioners occasionally find themselves stumped. If none of the other possible explanations bears out, then you've come up against a reading that outmatches your ability. Be gracious about it. Say that for reasons which are not clear, you are unable to read the cards. At this point, you must decide whether to pick up the cards and do a second spread in hopes that the oracle will smile upon you, or suggest a later time. There's no harm in asking the cards a second time in a situation like this, but if you're flustered and embarrassed, it may be better to wait.

How Often Should You Read?

You may have a client who wants a second reading right away to ask a follow-up question. It's difficult to demur when the person is stimulated by the first reading, but it's usually not wise to do otherwise. The Tarot is like a well of wisdom, and you should dip into it sparingly. The knowledge gained from a reading should be contemplated and absorbed. I have found the cards to be cranky when consulted again too quickly about the same thing. The oracle will tell you, "Enough is enough." Advise the seeker that he or she will get a much better reading if they allow some time to pass, during which they will have a chance to reflect upon the first reading. In all likelihood, they will find the answer to the follow-up question.

Other clients will not want an immediate next reading, but will want to come back too soon and too often for their own good. Some persons are oracle addicts, and bounce from reading to reading looking for someone—or something—to tell them how to live their lives. They defer all decisions to readings. You can help put a stop to this unhealthy habit by preventing it in the first place. Many Tarot practitioners have policies concerning how often a client may have a reading. One reader I know requires readings to be a minimum of eight weeks apart.

You might want to establish frequencies based upon the type of consultation being given. Someone who is using the Tarot to explore feelings in a life change, for example, may benefit from more frequent readings, say once a week, during a certain period of time.

Now try the spreads given in the following chapter.

NINE

Spreads

The Celtic Cross

This is one of the most popular spreads, and is usually the first one learned by beginners. It is particularly suited to divination readings. I use a wide variety of spreads, but the Celtic Cross remains my favorite. It's like a well-worn comfortable shoe. Because the spread is so popular and is a beginner's spread, however, many Tarot practitioners are tempted to leave it behind as their work advances. This is a mistake. The Celtic Cross remains a highly effective spread, because it benefits from the repeated overlays of collective psychic energy invested in it by untold numbers of Tarot practitioners. It is a ritual that has acquired a substantial amount of psychic power. As I mentioned in Chapter Seven, "Tarot Rituals," the more a ritual is performed, the more powerful and effective it becomes.

In the Celtic Cross, the cards are laid out in the form of an equilateral cross with a separate, vertical line of cards off to the right side (see Figure 6). The cards are placed on the table face up in front of the reader so they appear as either upright or reversed to that person. The exception is the first card, which is always turned upright even if it comes off the stack reversed.

Depending on personal preference, you can either recite the meanings of each of the positions of the cards out loud as you lay them down ("This is the cover . . ." "this is the foundation . . ." etc.) or you can wait until the spread is completed and you are ready to begin the reading.

It's traditional to have the seeker select a court card that represents him or her concerning the question at hand. This is done prior to shuffling and cutting. The court card is either placed to the left side, or is laid down in Position 1. I seldom do this, and I have never felt it to adversely affect a reading. There are legitimate reasons for omitting this step. The seeker may not wish to categorize herself within the bounds of the court cards. If the seeker is new to the Tarot and unfamiliar with the cards, making the choice can be confusing, off-putting, or onerous, and this can generate a tension that will interfere with the reading. Your ability to read for others is influenced not only by your rapport with the cards and your inner voice, but also by your rapport with the seeker—you want to "tune in" and be in harmony with him or her as much as possible. Use your own judgment as to whether to include this step, and do not hesitate to omit it if it feels appropriate.

You will find minor variations in the Celtic Cross spread from book to book, and the version presented here includes my own modifications.

Here is what each of the card positions represents:

1. **The Cover.** The forces covering, influencing, or surrounding the person asking the question.

2. **The Crossing.** The immediate obstacles, influences, or opposing forces that lie ahead. Influences may be positive or negative; the rest of the spread will indicate which applies. If the card has negative implications, try to interpret them in a positive way for the seeker. To fully interpret this card, it must be read not only in the context of the whole spread but also in its relation to the number 10 card, which represents the final outcome.

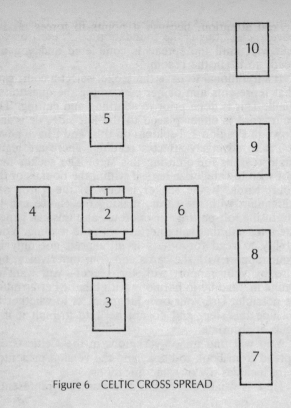

Figure 6   CELTIC CROSS SPREAD

3. **The Foundation.** The foundation or basis for the seeker's question. Things that existed in the past that have now become part of the present and are the reason for the question being asked.

4. **What has passed.** Influences on the seeker that are in the process of passing away or are already in the past.

5. **What may come to pass.** Some event that might take place in the future, perhaps influencing the outcome of the question. This card deserves spe-

cial attention, because it points to forces taking shape, which may or may not manifest, depending upon actions taken by the seeker. You will want to help the seeker make the most of potential opportunity or take steps to overcome obstacles. Again, look to card 10 for additional insight.

6. **What you must face.** Things that lie ahead, especially influences that the seeker will have to deal with. These are forces already in motion and manifesting in the life of the seeker. If changes are desirable, look to cards 3, 5, and 10 for inspiration.

7. **What you feel.** The emotions, including fears and apprehensions, the seeker has about his or herself or the question.

8. **What others think.** The opinions of others, especially family, about the questioner and the situation being examined.

9. **What you want.** What the seeker hopes will come to pass. Aspirations, goals, and dreams.

10. **The resolution.** Where events are leading, depending on what the other cards in the spread have to say.

For a deeper reading, try the Celtic Cross spread using only the Major Arcana. On some occasions, you will use the entire deck, but will see after you lay the cards out that a deeper reading is called for using only the Major Arcana. In that case, take the cards up, separate out the trumps, and do the spread again. See Appendix B for sample readings using this spread.

The Horoscope Spread

This spread is ideal for self readings as well as for others. It can help you gain valuable insight into how the various influences on your life and the different aspects of your personality are determining your future directions. In this reading, you interpret the meaning of the cards in relationship to where they fall in the horoscope. In these readings, you are not seeking specific yes or no answers, but are seeking answers to larger questions about the life process itself. A knowledge of astrology is essential to get the most out of this spread.

First shuffle the pack, then lay out twelve cards, counterclockwise in a circle in the fashion shown in Figure 7. Each of the positions corresponds to one of the twelve houses of the Zodiac. You may include an optional court card chosen by the seeker, to be placed in the center of the circle.

Here are the aspects of life governed by the houses, and the signs of the Zodiac that rule them:

First House (Aries): Personality, outward appearances, interests and attitudes

Second House (Taurus): Money matters, financial situation, material possessions

Third House (Gemini): Communication, relationships with brothers and sisters, travel

Fourth House (Cancer): Birth and death, home life, mother and father

Fifth House (Leo): Love, children, creativity

Sixth House (Virgo): Health, service

Seventh House (Libra): Relationships, partnerships, contracts, and agreements

Eighth House (Scorpio): Outside influences, death, inheritance

Ninth House (Sagittarius): Search for truth, long journeys, dreams, spiritual growth

Tenth House (Capricorn): Career, profession, ambitions

Eleventh House (Aquarius): Friends, associations, hopes, fears

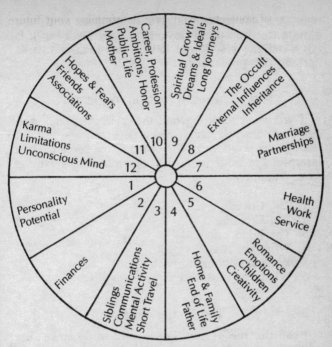

Figure 7   HOROSCOPE SPREAD

Twelfth House (Pisces): Unconscious mind, self-undoing, karma, limitations

Yes/No Spread

There are times when you want simple yes or no answers to questions. Here is a way to do that:

As you shuffle your cards, think of your question. Then count out the cards, stopping when you get to the thirteenth card. Turn that one face up. Repeat this until you reach the end of the deck and you have turned up six cards. Count the number of cards that are in upright positions. If four to six cards are upright, the answer is yes. If two to four cards are upright, the question is leaning in your favor but it is not a definite yes. If you have fewer than two cards upright, the answer is no.

Past ... Present ... Future Spread

If you want to go beyond the Yes/No spread, you can take those six cards, reshuffle them, and lay out the first six positions of the Celtic Cross spread. Then interpret the cards using the corresponding meanings from that spread.

1. The Cover
2. The Crossing
3. The Foundation
4. What has passed
5. What may come to pass
6. What you must face

The Trinity Spread

I call this the Trinity Spread because it makes use of the powerful mysticism of the number 3. As I observed in Chapter Four, "Symbols in the Tarot," the triad is a common motif in myth, legend, and fairytale, and we see trinities expressed in many things, especially in the triune nature of man: mind, body, and spirit. Three is a number of forward movement and the creative force—beneficial forces to harness in a Tarot reading.

The threefold elements that anchor this spread are Emotions, Thoughts, and Actions on one axis and Past, Present, and Future on a second axis. This spread is ideal for self-exploration and contemplation, because it gives you a good snapshot of sorts of your life's situation. Because three is the number of forward motion, the Trinity Spread reveals your progress through life.

Use only the Major Arcana and the court cards. Shuffle and lay the cards out from left to right in the order shown in Figure 8. Let them fall right side up or upside down. Vertically, the lines represent, from top to bottom, Future, Present, and Past. Horizontally, the cards are, from left to right, Emotions, Thoughts, and Actions. These are the primary forces that shape our lives. At the top, by itself, is the tenth card, which represents the Integration of the nine cards below it.

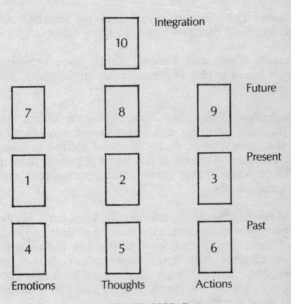

Figure 8   TRINITY SPREAD

Emotions. This category includes not only feelings, but impulses, inspirations, and intuitions, the things that bubble up from our unconscious or manifest in our dreams. Hopes and fears also belong here, as do creative urges and right-brain thinking. The cards that fall here give insight into the influences driving our emotions. If court cards turn up, consider whether they represent aspects of yourself or individuals with whom you are involved.

Thoughts. This category includes our rational, logical, analytical mental processes—the way we judge and assess, quantify, qualify, and justify. Our left-brain thinking fits here, which for most of us is the dominant means by which we make decisions.

Actions. This category reveals how we translate our emotions and thoughts into something tangible.

Present, Past, and Future. These lines represent major forces in play at the moment, on the wane, and emerging.

Integration. The crown card represents forces that could come into play and affect the picture revealed by the lower nine cards. It can reveal positive or negative energies. Remember that when negatives show in a Tarot reading, they provide an opportunity to correct and rectify.

In reading the cards, examine the lines horizontally, beginning with Present, then moving to Past and then to Future. Study each card in the line individually. Now integrate them into a single picture. When you have done that for each of the time lines, you are likely to get a new perspective on areas in your life that need attention.

Suppose you're feeling stalled about something. The cards might tell you, for example, that you're being too heavily influenced by a particular person or persons; that you're allowing rational thought processes to interfere with intuition or, conversely, that you're too impulsive; that unrealistic fears are holding you back; or even that you've been too lazy to act on your intentions. You'll get ideas for making changes.

The Eliphas Lévi Wheel Spread

Eliphas Lévi didn't invent this spread, but it is based on his Tarot wheel, shown as Figure 2 in Chapter Two, "The Kabbalah Connection." As you recall, Lévi laid out the letters T, A, R, and O (standing for Taro, rota) at the ends of the arms of an equilateral cross. The result is a wheel of sorts, representing the ever-changing cosmos revolving around an unchanging center, the Source.

To do this spread, compose a question. Take the Major Arcana only and shuffle. Draw five cards at random, one at a time, and lay them down as though on the axes of an equilateral cross. Start at the top with one and move clockwise with the next three cards. Place the fifth card in the center.

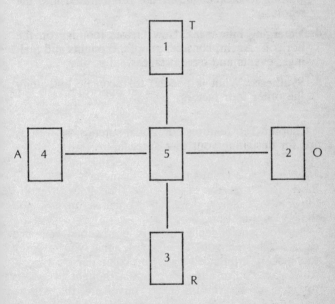

Figure 9   ELIPHAS LEVI WHEEL SPREAD

The cards represent the following:

1. **The present situation.** Forces and influences immediately affecting the question. Consider people, thoughts and feelings, events and circumstances.

2. **Waning influences.** Obstacles that have been overcome, aid that has come to an end, changes in emotion, energy, outlook, goals, and such.

3. **Hidden or unconscious influences.** What we repress or fail to recognize doesn't disappear, but finds other ways of expression. Here we find the stuff that usually surfaces in dreams: yearnings, fears, desires, our deepest and darkest secrets. These are fragments floating in the sea of our unconscious, waiting to be recognized and reintegrated into the whole.

4. **Emerging influences.** New factors looming on the horizon. Again, consider people, thoughts and feelings, events and circumstances.

5. **Synthesis.** What is needed to reconcile and unify the other four factors.

Chapter Ten features additional spreads, as well as tips for designing your own spreads.

Designing Your Own Spreads

After you've used a repertoire of spreads over a period of time, you'll begin to wish for changes in them—they won't quite fulfill all your needs. Perhaps you've made modifications here and there, but you still feel a need for something else—something new, something tailored exactly to your particular approach to the Tarot. The solution is to design your own spreads.

Spread design is easy once you grasp the basic blueprint. The building blocks of a spread are shapes, numbers, associations, and patterns. These must be assembled in a coherent and logical way so that a ritual can be performed with them, and so the end result is meaningful to you, the card reader. Like rituals, the complexity of spreads is not necessarily a mark of sophistication. Some of the most effective and useful spreads are the simplest. Laying out cards in a spread *is* a ritual, and the more you do it, the more ingrained it becomes in your consciousness and the more psychic power it acquires. If you design a spread that is so cumbersome you keep forgetting the correct card sequence or the meanings of the positions, it won't be of much use to you.

Here are the components of a spread, and the order in which you should put them together:

1. The purpose of the spread. What do you want the cards to reveal? Most traditional spreads are yes/no or are broad enough to cover a wide variety of situations. However, you may want to develop very specific spreads to use in certain circumstances. For example, you can design spreads solely to examine career matters, relationships, money issues, and such.

2. The time frame. What time period will the spread embrace? Will it cover past, present, and future, present and future, or present only? Spreads can be narrowed down further to seasons, months, and weeks.

3. The pattern. All Tarot spreads are organized according to lines and shapes. The cards are always laid out in a certain sequence, and each position in the pattern carries a certain meaning. Now you must decide how you want to elaborate the purpose and time frame. Start by drawing up a list of position designations, that is, what an individual card will represent in either purpose or time. You can, if you wish, use number and shape symbolisms to determine how many cards you will have in a spread. For example, a spread that deals with relationships might be expressed with six cards that are laid out according to the points of a hexagram, a shape that symbolizes the union of opposites.

Five to twelve or thirteen cards will give you plenty of options to explore. Beyond thirteen, spreads can become cumbersome. You can certainly tackle larger spreads, but in the beginning it's best to stick to simpler and smaller ones.

Experiment by arranging the cards in patterns. The simplest is a linear spread, a single line that moves horizontally or vertically. A little more complex is a multi-linear spread with two or more lines stacked one on top of another, like the Trinity Spread in the previous chapter. Perhaps you'd rather work with a geometric shape. One of the most effective shapes for spreads is the circle, which, as was noted in Chapter Four, "Symbols in the Tarot," is one of the oldest and most powerful symbols. It signifies unity, wholeness, completion, and regeneration, all of which are goals of Tarot work. Circle spreads are easy to work with, and can be big or small. Squares, triangles, pentagrams, and hexagrams also work well. You can make spreads more complex by combining shapes, such as placing squares or triangles within circles, or a circle within a circle, or a circle within a square, for example. Figure ten shows a variety of spread pattern shapes.

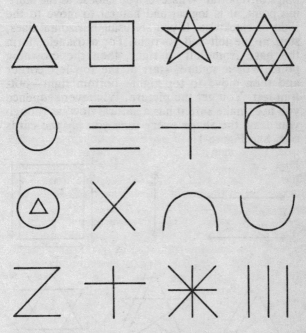

Figure 10   SIXTEEN BASIC SPREAD PATTERNS
Horizontal and vertical lines can vary in number

4. **The sequence of the layout.** You know the number of cards and the shape according to which you will organize them, but in what order will you place each card? The order will be governed by the

shape and the position designations. If you have chosen a circle, what determines the starting point? The twelve o'clock position, the top, is a logical point. Or, you may have divided the circle into quadrants according to cardinal points or seasons. Perhaps you'd rather start at three o'clock, which is the east, the direction of the rising of the sun and, symbolically, of illumination, spring, and the beginnings of renewal. Whatever you choose as the starting point, it is logical and natural to move to the right or clockwise. If you are using horizontal lines, start at the left and go right. For a triangle, form the base from left to right, then the crowning point. For a square, start at the top left corner and then move to top right—bottom right—bottom left. You get the picture. Whatever sequence you use, make sure it has a natural flow, as though you draw the shape every time you lay the cards out. See Figure 11.

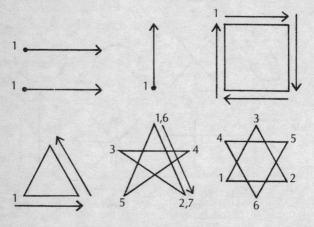

Figure 11   SEQUENCES

5. The position designators. Decide what each position in the spread sequence means. These should be

286

arranged in a progression of revelation that has meaning to the overall pattern.

As an example of how the design process works, consider again the Trinity Spread. Its purpose is to provide a mirror for contemplation, a picture of the Self based on three key aspects of Emotions, Thoughts, and Actions. Thus, the entire spread is then organized around the number 3. See Figure 12.

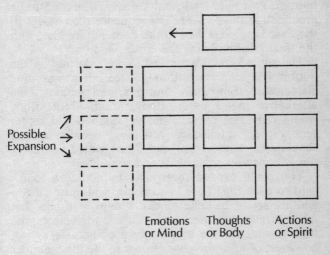

Possible Expansion

Emotions or Mind   Thoughts or Body   Actions or Spirit

Figure 12   TRINITY SPREAD VARIATIONS

The time frame divides neatly into three at Past, Present, and Future, a broad sweep that is desirable for the spread's purpose. Three times three gave me nine cards. These I arranged logically into three lines of three. I chose horizontal lines for the time frame, which fit our conception of linear time. Moving in natural sequence, I placed Past on the bottom, Present in the middle, and Future on top. Using the symbolism of numbers, I added a tenth for completeness, placing it in the center of a fourth and top line. This card signifies Integration, thus tying the other nine cards together.

For Emotions, Thoughts, and Actions, I decided their order in the sequence. Emotions-Thoughts-Actions has a progressive, left-to-right, forward motion, which also underscores the forward, creative motion of the number 3.

In choosing the starting point of the spread, I decided upon the middle, Present line rather than the bottom, Past line. I felt that the spread needed to be grounded in the present. The sequence then moves to the Past Line, and then to the third Future line, with the final position being the crown card.

The spread could work just as well starting on the bottom line, or by substituting three other organizing elements for Emotions, Thoughts, and Actions. One alternative that I use is Body, Mind, Spirit. Body would represent physical health; Mind would represent career, intellectual activities, decision-making capabilities, and so on; and Spirit would represent things concerning the heart and soul.

You could expand the spread by adding a fourth card to each time line. In so doing, you must shift to another set of building blocks, groups of things that fall naturally into fours, such as the four elements, the four seasons, or the four cardinal points. Be aware, however, of what this change does to the total number of cards. You now have thirteen in the spread, which many people would consider unlucky. I'm among those who consider thirteen an auspicious number (there are thirteen full moons in a year, and the moon in occult lore governs intuition, inspiration, the psychic, emotions, and the unconscious), and so use thirteen-card spreads often. If you read for others, you might not want to use a thirteen-card spread, in case they feel uneasy. One number I do avoid in designing spreads is eleven. It's awkward, and in occult lore is considered unstable.

The Trinity Spread can be expanded even more by

adding a fifth card to each time line (sixteen cards total). The other axis could represent the five senses.

Let's take a look at another spread that also has components that can be varied:

The Mandala Spread

As we saw in Chapter Four, "Symbols in the Tarot," the mandala is a powerful form for organizing and expressing the inner world. In Eastern meditation, the mandala expresses complex realms of higher consciousness, whereas in Western psychotherapy it helps people deal with forces welling up from the unconscious. In this spread, the mandala is used to examine the inner impulses that arise out of the self. This is a spread for contemplation.

The spread features nine cards. Nine is the number of man (nine months in gestation) and, as three times three, is the number of mental and spiritual achievement. The perimeter of the circle is formed with eight cards. Eight represents regeneration, renewal, and eternity, the Alpha and Omega, the beginning and the end, a meaning that is further reinforced by the circle itself as the symbol of unity and continuity. The ninth card is placed in the center as the Self.

In laying the cards out, begin with the Center. As you go around the circle, you will see how the cards build on each other progressively. See Figure 13.

1. **Self.** The unifying principle within the human psyche, the totality that embraces both conscious and unconscious. Through the Self, we make contact with our anima and animus, and confront our shadow, that part of us which is split off and repressed and needs to be reintegrated.

2. **Desires.** Our instinctive urges and basic needs.

3. **Dreams.** What we ideally want to be, accomplish, have, or give to be a human being in the fullest

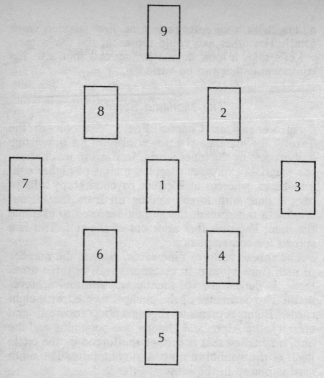

Figure 13   MANDALA SPREAD

sense: love, happiness, compassion, health, and so on.

4. **Pursuits.** Despite our dreams, the things we decide to pursue: careers, hobbies, volunteerism, and such. How do the pursuits match the dreams?

5. **Attachments.** Things we pursue that hold us back from achieving our true dreams. Attachments typically are to false values, such as money, prestige, fame, and possessions. How many pursuits are attachments? Do we name attachments as dreams?

6. **Qualities.** Our good points.

7. **Sorrows.** Our faults, areas that need improvement.

8. **Self-image.** Our overall view of ourselves. This card relates to the previous seven, and to the Self card. How does the self-image conform with what the cards in the other positions have to say? What areas need to be improved?

9. **Soul's urge.** Our true sense of purpose and destiny that transcends all else.

By adding another four cards (there's that number 13 again!) we can create the *Alchemical Spread*. You will need a large work area for this one. The four cards are placed on the outside of the circle forming a square around it and standing for the four elements. In alchemy, this represents the squaring of the circle, the great alchemical work, the philosophers' stone. The cards that comprise the square should be looked upon as clues to forces that can be tapped for positive change.

10. **Earth.** Darkness, mystery, the unknown, secrecy, the unenlightened state.

11. **Air.** Spiritual illumination, intuition, enlightenment, mysticism, the eternal.

12. **Fire.** Intellect, rational thought, will.

13. **Water.** Creativity, emotions, fertility, courage.

Adaptable Frameworks

Another technique in designing spreads is to look for things that can serve as a framework. The Horoscope Spread is an example of this, in which the spread is built around the circle of the houses of the Zodiac. For those who pursue Kabbalistic studies, the Tree of Life serves as a Tarot framework.

An easily adaptable framework that mixes East and West is the chakra system of Yoga:

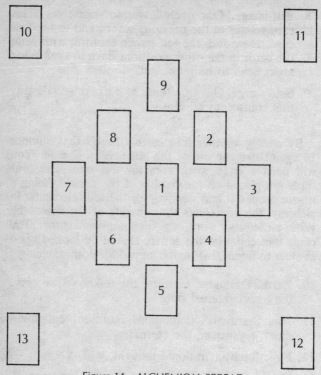

Figure 14   ALCHEMICAL SPREAD

The Chakra Spread

The Chakra Spread makes use of Tarot symbols as applied to the seven primary chakras. In Yoga, chakras are centers of energy that permeate the physical body and funnel *prana*, the universal vital force, throughout the body. Invisible to the ordinary eye, chakras are aligned along the spine and are shaped like wheels; *chakra* is Sanskrit for "circle." The chakras's rotation draws in *prana*, which influences physical, mental, and emotional health, and spiritual development. If the chakras rotate sluggishly, illness is believed to result. In various forms of Yoga, one seeks to refine and activate the chakras to rotate faster and more smoothly, thus drawing in more beneficial *prana*. The activation is done through ascetic discipline of meditation and diet.

For purposes with the Tarot, the chakras can be dealt cards in order to provide insights into one's state of being.

To do the spread, lay out seven cards in a straight, vertical line to symbolize the spine, moving from bottom to top. Each card represents a chakra, which has its own unique functions. The Tarot cards are interpreted in light of those functions. You can do this spread with the entire pack, but it is most powerful if limited to the Major Arcana. This is an excellent self-knowledge spread that lends itself well to contemplation. See Figures 15 and 16.

1. **Root chakra.** Located at the base of the spine, it is the seat of the kundalini, an intense and powerful force that is awakened in enlightenment. The root chakra governs self-preservation, one's animal nature, taste, and smell. It is orange-red.

2. **Sacral chakra.** Primarily red in color, this center is located near the genitals and governs sexuality and reproduction. (*Note:* In some Yogas, the sacral chakra is replaced by the spleen chakra, not considered here.)

3. **Solar plexus chakra.** Mostly green and light red, this center is just above the navel and is associated with the emotions. It governs the adrenal glands, pancreas, liver, and stomach.

4. **Heart chakra.** This center is located midway between the shoulder blades and is glowing gold in

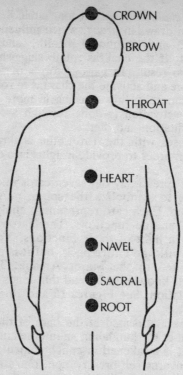

Figure 15   CHAKRA SYSTEM

color. It governs the thymus gland and influences immunity to disease, and is linked to higher consciousness and unconditioned love.

5. **Throat chakra.** Silvery blue, this chakra is associated with creativity, self-expression, and the search for truth. It is highly developed in artists in the musical profession and among public speakers. It influences the thyroid and parathyroid glands, and the metabolism, and is associated with certain states of expanded consciousness.

294

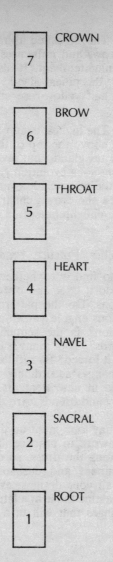

Figure 16 CHAKRA SPREAD

6. **Brow chakra.** The so-called third eye is located between the brows and influences psychic abilities and spiritual enlightenment. It also influences the pituitary gland, the pineal gland, intelligence, and intuition. It is half yellow-rose and half blue and purple.

7. **Crown chakra.** The highest center is glowing purple and whirls just above the top of the head. It is not associated with any glands, but reveals the individual's level of conscious evolution. It cannot be activated until all the other chakras are in balance and harmony. When the crown chakra is activated, it brings supreme enlightenment.

Practice, Practice, Practice

The only way to find out whether or not a spread is effective is to do it over and over again, posing a variety of questions. Do the pattern, sequence, and position designations enable you to arrive at a meaningful interpretation? Is the sequence natural? Are there enough cards? Too many? Does the spread "feel" right, or is it forced? Be ruthless in your evaluation and make changes accordingly. Throw out what doesn't work, add in new elements. Try the spread out on your family and friends. Are they satisfied with their readings?

Some spreads may look great on the drawing board but simply won't work in practice. There's bound to be some gold among the dross, so chalk it up to an interesting experiment and design another spread. Keep records of all your designs, even the ones that don't work. Reexamine those at a later date—you may get ideas for changes that will turn the spreads into winners.

ELEVEN

Developing Your Intuition

Intuition is another key to effective understanding of the Tarot and the ability to use it well for either divination or self-help. Intuition is a clear and direct knowing from within—that proverbial "gut feeling"—that comes suddenly and without explanation as to how or why. It is unerringly on target and accurate. It transcends time and space, which sometimes makes it seem paradoxical or puzzling, because it cannot be rationalized and may contradict what one thinks. At some point, circumstances bear it out.

We all know certain individuals who seem to be endowed with an abundance of intuition. These people are always having hunches that prove to be correct and, what's more, they have the courage to act on their hunches and use them to their advantage. They are always drawing an accurate bead on people the moment they meet them, and thus never seem to have the wool pulled over their eyes by deceptively charming persons. It's easy to assume that these intuitive types were just blessed at birth, but the truth is, *everyone* has intuition. Most of us merely have learned to repress it by overriding it with ego and analytical thinking. We get intuitive information every day, but most of it is lost in the shuffle of our busy minds. The intuition that reaches our awareness is usually shoved aside. How many times have you said to yourself, "I *knew* I should have done (or not done) that . . ." or "I had a feeling he was bad news, but . . ." or "I had a hunch that was going to happen but I didn't believe it . . ." Your intuition gave you guidance and you chose to ignore it because it contradicted the "shoulds" and "oughts" in your head.

Research has demonstrated that the right hemisphere of our brain processes emotions, creativity, and insights, whereas our left hemisphere processes logic. Thus, intuition is a right-brain function. Intuition is strongest in childhood, when imagination and emotions are given free reign without attachments. As we grow older and begin conforming to the expectations of society, intuition begins to fade in most of us. We base our decisions and actions on what we are told to do, what we have to do, and what we need to do in order to adapt and survive. We become attached to our decisions, emotions, attitudes, and desires, and we pay less and less attention to the hunches and gut feelings that tell us to behave otherwise. A fortunate few of us manage to stay in touch with this marvelous hot line to the inner voice—and tend to be more successful as a result. In 1962, a study of extrasensory perception among business executives undertaken by the Newark College of Engineering revealed that highly successful executives have a strong sense of intuition, believe in it, and rely upon it more than those who are less successful. Others who retain their intuition are persons who work in the arts, which requires fantasy and imagination.

You will find intuition to be an essential ally if you hope to progress far in your work with the Tarot. Intuition connects us to the Higher Self, a source of wisdom and illumination that knows precisely what is best for us. The Higher Self functions as an interface between the worlds of Spirit and Matter; it is ever ready to serve as a beacon, a guiding light. It is in touch with the collective unconscious, where archetypes reside as a form of inborn intuition. Accessing this source of wisdom will help you read the cards and go beyond what is apparent on their surfaces to probe their deep mysteries. Intuition will help you with insights in determining the message of a spread. In self-help, it will help you use the Tarot to plumb your own depths.

Don't despair if you feel hopelessly nonintuitive. No matter how distant you've become from your inner voice, it is possible to reclaim connection to it by cultivating it. Intuition is like a muscle: the more you exercise it and use it, the stronger it becomes. Intuition is elusive, however, because of its intangible nature. You can't see it, touch it, or isolate it—"aha, there's intuition!"—but when you get in touch with it, its impact upon you is unmistakable. Intuition functions holistically on physical, emotional, mental, spiritual, and environmental levels, and involves a wide variety of internal and external cues. It is often confused with, and mistaken for, wishful thinking or unreasonable fears, but through practice, trial, and error, you learn to sort out the wheat from the chaff.

Everyone experiences intuition in a unique way. For some, the cues may be mild, whereas for others, intuition grabs them and gives them a shaking. Intuition is not a psychic faculty per se, but can involve psychic phenomena. You may have physical sensations, such as a tingling of the skin or the feeling of leaden weights in the stomach. You may hear clairaudient or inner voices. You may feel seemingly inexplicable attractions or aversions to persons you've just met without knowing any facts about them. You may get inspirational solutions to problems, or get sudden creative ideas. You may suddenly feel close to the Divine. You may think of someone, without reason, just before they call or appear. You may have dreams that come true. You may have visions, either external or projected onto the screen of your mind.

In cultivating intuition, bear in mind that it does not, and should not, substitute for left-brain, rational thought. Rather, intuition should augment analysis. You need both left-brain and right-brain functions to be at your optimum. Jung saw intuition as a creative process with the capability to inspire. Without intuition, the intellect cannot achieve its fullest potential.

There are many simple exercises and other things you can do to strengthen your intuition, and the following material will help you get started. It's useful to keep a record of your intuitive experiences in your Tarot journal, noting whether or not they proved to be accurate. Over time, you will be better able to weed out the false signals and recognize that special quality that accompanies the real thing. For an in-depth discussion of intuition and additional suggestions, see *Awakening Intuition* (1979) by Frances E. Vaughan, an excellent, comprehensive and practical treatment of the subject.

Intuition Exercises

1. Be In the Moment. Most of us live nearly our entire lives somewhere else besides the present. We rehash the past and anticipate the future. Our thoughts are often not focused on where we are at the moment. All we ever have is *now*. The past is over and done with, and the future has yet to arrive and may not arrive as we anticipate. By not living in the now, by not giving ourselves fully to the moment, we are letting life pass us by.

This is not to say that you shouldn't daydream, or plan for the future, or analyze the past in order to help yourself. There are times when those mental diversions are appropriate. But intuition is a product of the now. It may provide a peek into the future, of a potential yet to be fulfilled, but unless you are present in the now you probably aren't going to get the message.

Make a commitment to living more in the moment. As you go about your daily affairs, invest yourself in them fully. Give them your total attention. You probably will be surprised at how much time you spend doing things you do not want to do, but feel obligated to do, or how much time you waste out of laziness. When you realize how precious the moment is, you will be more careful about how you spend your time, and will feel better about yourself. Being centered and in the moment creates conditions in which intuition can flourish.

2. Let Go of Attachments to Feelings. Attachments to emotions, especially negative ones such as anger, fear, and guilt, prevent us from having access to intuition, which has no emotion or bias. When strong feelings arise, try to detach yourself from them. Allow them to happen, and then let go of them. Be receptive to new feelings that arise—they may surprise you.

Many emotional attachments belong to events or circumstances long past. By living more in the moment, you will be less likely to carry a lot of emotional attachment baggage around with you.

3. Meditate. Meditation is by far the best way to cultivate intuition. In mystical meditation, intuition is the means by which to achieve direct and immediate truth, and knowledge of the most intimate secrets of life: the ineffable nature of the cosmos, the Divine Force, the soul, and the unity of all things.

Meditation is a discipline of the mind and body in which the body is stilled and the mind quieted. In mystical meditation, one seeks to transcend thought to higher realms of consciousness. On a more mundane level, meditation can be applied to any number of purposes, such as cultivating intuition, gaining self-knowledge, gaining spiritual insights, and improving health. Scientific studies from the 1960s to the present have demonstrated that meditation has a beneficial effect upon the body, by lowering the metabolism, blood pressure, and heart rate, and slowing brain waves to levels experienced in deep states of relaxation. Individuals who regularly practice meditation attest to an overall improvement in their lives, such as greater resistance to stress, improved personal relationships, greater self-confidence, and an overall enhanced sense of well-being.

Meditation is a universal and ancient practice that has evolved into different procedures within the context of spiritual and religious systems. Some of the procedures are quite exact. Taoist meditation techniques were developed during the fourth or fifth century B.C., and Yoga techniques were systematized between about 200 B.C. and A.D. 400. Here, our focus will be on relaxing the mind and body sufficiently to allow more intuitive insights to come through, rather than following precise procedures for spiritual transcendence. If you already practice a formal meditation system, such as one of the yogas or Zen, then stay with it. If you don't, some steps are provided here that will help you get started.

Meditation is best done early in the morning, before you are distracted with the day's activities, or at the end of the day, when you can put the day's activities behind you. Some people like to meditate in the middle of their day. Do whatever works best for you.

To get the benefits of meditation, you should make an effort to meditate daily, or at least frequently, for about fifteen to twenty minutes at a time. The more you meditate, the easier it will become, and the greater will be the results.

I like to meditate early in the morning. It puts me in a positive frame of mind and sets me up for the day. It has become so much an integral part of my daily ritual that if something should cause me to miss it, I feel my day is incomplete. My usual ritual includes first lighting a candle and some incense. However, I have also accustomed myself to meditating without these props so that I may do so effectively should they not be available.

The key to successful meditation is relaxation. Before you can center yourself, you must relax the body and get all the tension out of it. It's easy to hold a lot of tension in the body without being aware of it. When you begin to meditate, you will naturally release more of this tension so that you do not store it in the body.

1. Sit in a comfortable chair or couch, ideally one that allows you to keep your back fairly straight. Place both feet flat on the floor and let your hands rest in

your lap, either loosely folded or with your palms turned up. Close your eyes. It is appropriate here to petition and thank the Divine.

2. Allow your weight to sink fully into the cushions. Become conscious of every part of your body. Let the chair absorb all your tension, worries, and distractions.

3. Become conscious of your breathing. In formal meditation techniques, breathing and breath control are of paramount importance. For our purposes, we want to use breathing to relax. Breathe deeply and slowly, allowing the belly to expand with each intake of breath. Hold the breath for a moment, then release it slowly through the nostrils. Repeat this several times, then allow your breath to come naturally, still expanding the belly on intake.

4. Relax the parts of the body progressively. Begin with the feet. Feel all the tension drain away. Let it flow out through your feet into the earth. Move up to your ankles, then your calves, knees, thighs, and buttocks. One by one, release tension in each area and let it drain into the earth. Continue up your torso, relaxing the abdomen, stomach, chest, and shoulders. Relax your arms, wrists, and fingers, letting the tension flow out through the fingertips. Relax the neck, jaw, face, forehead, and top of your head, and send the tension down into the earth.

With practice, you will be able to relax and center yourself in seconds, without going through the individual steps and progression.

5. Now that you're physically relaxed, visualize a stream of glorious white and gold energy pouring down from the heavens, entering you through the top of your head. It flows to every part of your body, filling it with white-gold, energizing, healing light. It flows out your extremities, into space and into the earth, nourishing everything it comes into contact with. Surround yourself with the light. Allow yourself to feel good. You are light and buoyant, hardly aware of your body at all. You are protected from negative influences.

6. Quiet the chatter in the mind. Let go of thoughts and worries. Many people find this difficult, especially in the beginning, so don't be discouraged if you have trouble. One centering technique is to count your breaths. When you get to ten, start over again with one. If thoughts arise, don't be dismayed; just let them dissolve or disintegrate incomplete and continue counting your breaths. If emotions arise, allow them to happen, examine them without attachment, and let them go. Another centering technique is to think of an object, such as a pearl or diamond, and hold it in your mind. When thoughts arise, let them go and return to the image.

7. You are now in a meditative state, a state of altered consciousness. Stay with it. In the beginning, this may only be for a minute or two. The more you practice, the longer the meditative periods will last. The meditation will calm and center you, and clear obstacles to the intuition.

Don't necessarily expect thunderbolts of inspiration and insight to strike you as you meditate. You cannot make intuition happen; you can only provide a receptive awareness for it to occur. The purpose here is to learn how to quiet the mind and achieve a detached state of awareness. The centeredness that you achieve in meditation will carry over into your ordinary consciousness, especially after you have meditated regularly for some period of time. As a result, you will be better able to recognize intuition whenever it happens.

Visualize Geometric Shapes. The visualization of geometric shapes is a right-brain, intuition-enhancing exercise that you can do during meditation, or during a quiet moment. Imagine a white screen before you and project onto it a shape, such as an equilateral triangle. Hold it steady for as long as you can (this is not as easy as it may seem). Try a variety of shapes—circles, squares, pentagons, hexagrams, and so on. Make them increasingly complex: put a circle inside a square, a triangle inside a circle.

Manipulate Your Consciousness. If you had to locate your "consciousness," where would it be? Most people point to their head. That's an oversimplified answer, but it's a good starting point for this exercise, which will help you develop an awareness that extends beyond the physical senses. This works best in meditation.

Visualize your consciousness as a small sphere of light deep in the center of your head. What is it like? Is it sharply defined or soft and fuzzy? What color is it? Is it warm or cool? Gradually enlarge the sphere until it fills your entire cranium. Feel the light pressing gently against your skull. Now contract it to the size of a marble. Enlarge it again, but this time go beyond the bounds of your head and body. Fill the space around you. Now let your consciousness expand farther out until it fills the entire room with light.

You can also try moving the sphere around inside your body. Let the sphere drop to your heart center. Feel it expand in your chest. Move it down to the solar plexus. Now move it back up to your throat. Then let it return to the center of your head.

Free Associate. This exercise is done in psychotherapy, but the intent here is not to evaluate the associations, but to get you to loosen your thought processes so that you think spontaneously. Do this exercise with a partner. The partner throws out words. Say the first thoughts that come to your mind, no matter how bizarre they sound. If you hesitate, you are allowing your left brain to interfere, weighing and analyzing what you should say. Instead, don't judge. Be detached.

Absorb Your Environment. Most of us live in cities, which are filled with noise and distractions. As a consequence, we learn to shut out our environment. In the process, we also shut out environmental signals that may be part of our intuitive process.

Devote a quiet period to doing nothing but absorbing your environment. It doesn't matter if you are in a city or the country, indoors or outdoors. Relax and open your senses to the stimuli around you. Notice colors, shapes, textures, temperatures, breezes, smells, and sounds. Take note of people, animals, flora, machinery, objects, and vehicles. Look at the ceiling, the floor, the sky, the earth. Experience everything around as though you were just born and were sensing for the first time. Be fully in the moment. Be detached. Allow both pleasantries and unpleasantries to arise and fade without attachment or judgment.

The strengthening of your intuition will benefit you in all aspects of your life, not just in Tarot work. Lots of ideas and inspirations on all manner of things will come to you more easily. They won't always occur at the most convenient times, so it's a good idea to keep a small notebook handy wherever you go so that you can jot them down. Intuitions and inspirations often are like dreams—unless you write them down, they fade very quickly. If you record them, even a few key words, you can recover the ideas later when you have more time to devote to them.

You may find that psychic abilities open up. This is a natural part of the process and is one more skill that you can apply to the Tarot. The opening of the third eye, which brings awareness of a nonphysical reality, can be disconcerting to some people. If you find yourself unsettled by the manifestations of psychic ability, find someone who can offer you guidance. If you wish to cultivate your psychic ability, a good source for starters is *Develop Your Psychic Abilities* (1985) by Litany Burns.

For more information on meditation, one of the best guides is *How to Meditate* (1974; 1975; 1988) by Lawrence LeShan.

TWELVE

Meditation, Visualization, and Affirmations

Tarot Meditation

The Tarot provides a wonderful tool for meditation on matters of self-knowledge and personal growth. Two types of meditation are generally used in working with the Tarot. The first is contemplation, which essentially is thinking about the meaning of something: a word, a concept, an image, and so on. The second is concentration, which is the focusing of the mind on one thing, such as a mantra, a yantra (a geometric image used in Yoga meditation), a symbol, a candle flame, and such. In formal meditation practice, concentration seeks not to discover the meaning of the object of concentration, but to use the object as a means of transcending thought to an absence-of-thought state.

Contemplative meditation is best-suited to self-exploration with the Tarot. It's wise not to undertake meditation with the Tarot until you are thoroughly familiar with the card images and their meanings.

The Major Arcana, with its archetypal images and mystical symbols, provides the richest territory for meditation. When I meditate on the Tarot, I prefer to work primarily with these cards. They are seemingly endless in their potential and will take you deep within yourself. Certainly, you can include the entire deck in your meditation work. Meditation on the pip cards is most fruitful if they bear pictorial images rather than just numbers of patterns or single symbols.

Here are three ways to take a systematic approach to meditating with the Tarot:

1. Choose a card at random, knowing that the one you draw answers a need, perhaps not recognized consciously, within you.

2. Make a deliberate choice based on an analysis of what you need, or would like, to address.

3. Take the Fool's Journey and start at the beginning and work your way sequentially through the Arcana.

All three methods have their rewards, but number three, the Fool's Journey, is the most exciting. You never know exactly how the journey will go and what you will find along the way, and it's never the same twice. The Fool's Journey is best undertaken when you are fairly confident of being able to meditate on a daily basis for continuity until the Journey is completed.

You can spend months, even years, meditating upon the Tarot, with new territory continually unfolding before you. You may never want to venture beyond one deck, but if you do grow tired of one or feel you have learned as much as possible from it, then switch to another.

Include your meditation insights in your Tarot journal. By referring back to your records from time to time, you will be able to see changes and growth.

Treat Tarot meditation like a ritual: establish a routine and practice it, ideally on a daily basis. Refer back to Chapter Seven, "Tarot Rituals," for ideas. Environmental factors have been found to enhance or inhibit intuition. If possible, do your Tarot meditations in a room painted light green, light aqua, light blue, or light chartreuse, which is lit with natural sunlight. The ideal temperature should be between 70°

and 73° F with moderate humidity. Music also aids receptivity to intuition. Select something unobtrusive that will not engage you by triggering memories or strong emotions.

Before you begin your Tarot meditation ritual, draw the card you will work with. Get comfortable and enter a meditative state, using either your own procedures or the suggestions given in Chapter Eleven, "Developing Your Intuition."

When you feel centered and ready, begin your contemplation of the Tarot card. This is another appropriate moment to ask for guidance, inspiration, and the revelation of truth, and to give thanks in advance for receiving them. You can either keep your eyes closed and visualize the card, or open your eyes and gaze at it. Think of the card's symbols and meaning. What are its mysteries? What are its strengths? What are its weaknesses? How does it relate to you? Do you see yourself in the card?

Allow thoughts to rise freely. Don't dismiss anything, no matter how offbeat—it may prove to be a valuable piece in a jigsaw puzzle picture that emerges over time. Let the images in the card speak to you— let the birds, the animals, the plants, and the landscapes talk to you as well as the human figures. What are they trying to tell you about themselves? About you? If you were to go on a journey with them, where would they take you? Let mental pictures come to you.

If you have trouble getting the juices flowing or staying focused, re-center yourself on the card by examining its individual symbols and thinking about their meanings.

Every ritual must have a close. When you feel ready to end the exercise, give thanks for all you have learned.

While the exercise is still fresh in your mind, record your notes in your journal. What have you learned? What new questions have arisen for study?

Tarot Creative Visualizations and Affirmations

You may wish to act on what you have learned from your meditations. If so, creative visualization and affirmation exercises will help. Creative visualization, which also is called *positive imaging, creative imagination*, and other terms, is the use of positive thoughts and mental imagery to achieve desired goals. Thoughts and pictures of a desired result are held firmly and vividly in the mind, as if the result were already realized. Visualizations release energies in both the conscious and subconscious that will help you realize your goals. Norman Vincent Peale terms such imaging a "laser beam of the imagination." Shakti Gawain, author of the popular book, *Creative Visualization* (1979), calls creative visualization "magic" in the truest and highest sense of the word: the conscious mind connects with the Higher Self and aligns itself to the flow of cosmic forces in the universe, attracting the desired circumstances.

Affirmations are positive phrases and sentences that function in much the same way as creative visualizations. Typically, they begin, "I can . . ." "I am . . ." "I will . . ." Affirmations permeate the consciousness when they are written down and repeated often. However, mental pictures and positive words in and of themselves will not produce results. You must totally *believe* in them and in their eventual manifestation. You must invest in them your will to accomplish them. The more firmly you believe, the more likely you will reap what you believe. Doing the exercises once is not enough—they must be done repeatedly and frequently until the goal is attained.

These techniques have been around as long as the human race—every leader, every visionary, every highly accomplished person has used them, consciously or unconsciously.

How do you apply these techniques to the Tarot? Let's say that you wish to incorporate into your life some qualities expressed in a Tarot card, perhaps the

310

power of The Magician to create and influence his own destiny. Visualize yourself as The Magician, shaping your own destiny. See yourself as part of the card. See yourself as The Magician in the external world, going about your daily affairs. Now visualize yourself achieving the desired goal. The importance of this cannot be underestimated. *You must see yourself as having achieved the goal.* It is tangible and real, not something projected into a hazy future. Make the image as vivid and as detailed as possible. In your journal, write down an affirmation: "I have the power to create my own destiny. I use this power wisely and use it now to achieve _____. I give thanks now for my achievement." Say the affirmation out loud and repeat it several times while holding the image firmly in your mind.

Creative visualizations and affirmations are most effective when incorporated into meditation and journal writing. Because they require an investment of time and energy, choose them wisely and work on one or a few at a time. For more information, see Gawain's *Creative Visualization*, and two books by Peale, *The Power of Positive Thinking* (1952) and *Positive Imaging: the Powerful Way to Change Your Life* (1982). As a Christian minister, Peale also emphasizes prayer and a faith in God.

All of these exercises and procedures described in this chapter can be adapted to suit your own style and taste. It may take you awhile to settle on those that feel the most comfortable and productive.

The following are some of my own meditations on the Major Arcana. They are intended to give you a starting point, and ideas for your own meditations.

O *The Fool*

As the innocent, The Fool represents an open mind. In a meditation, this combination of innocence and an open-mind guides our search for deeper knowledge free of the judgments and biases we carry with us from our previous experiences. The ideal meditation with The Fool card is to become The Fool and seek the answers to our questions from the experience of life itself as someone who has yet to experience life. To become The Fool in a meditation brings a sense of excitement about the discoveries that await us and the adventures yet to begin. That's because we approach these meditations without attachments to any ideas or things and are willing to let our minds explore the unknown.

With The Fool as your guide, your meditation can take you to unexpected places and open doors you didn't even know existed. You have no fear of the unknown, only a thirst to learn.

In my meditations with The Fool, I begin with an image of myself surrounded by a golden aura as bright as the sun. I know that this golden light will protect me, even light my way, which is why I fear nothing even though I have no idea where my journey will lead. As I settle more deeply into my meditation, I feel myself fully transformed into The Fool, filled with a sense of happiness because I know there's much to learn on my journey.

Even though each journey as The Fool is different, they all begin with the same question: Where will my meditation lead me today and what will I learn about myself, about life, about the challenges ahead?

In these travels, I sometimes find myself in places that I know or in situations that are still unfolding as well as some from my past. In any event, I always feel like I am visiting these places or seeing these things for the first time. I become a neutral observer. This fresh look allows me to see things I've overlooked before when my eyes were clouded with preconceptions, false judgments, and an unwillingness to learn. At the same time, I frequently journey to places unknown and places that may not even exist. To my mind, this is a reminder that there is more to learn or experience about life than I can ever imagine.

I always emerge from these meditations with an

understanding that whatever path unfolds, it is mine to walk down. I also feel a renewed desire to plunge deeply into life and to experience all its different wonders. I yearn to discover. I do not fear the problems and obstacles that will block my path. Instead, I recognize that there is always a way to get where I am going—and not necessarily as The Fool. That's why it's essential to approach all meditations with this card with an open mind and a willingness to learn.

I. The Magician

When I select or draw The Magician card in a meditation, I always remember a basic truth: that it is within my powers to create my own destiny. Even if fate has its role to play, The Magician reminds me that I can influence its outcome.

Because The Magician symbolizes the ability to harness the creative forces that exist in the universe—both within and outside ourselves—I approach a meditation on this card with a great sense of awe and feeling charged with energy. This will not be a quiet or serene meditation, but one filled with purpose and determination. I will want to bring all the powers The Magician possesses to bear on whatever problems or challenges I face.

In a typical meditation, I lay out my problems or questions before me with a belief that I can solve them. While I try to be objective in understanding the problem or question confronting me, I let my mind suggest solutions based on past experiences that are similar or that seem like the best possible approach from the tools at my disposal.

Because the focus is on the solutions, not the problems themselves, in these meditations, I try to imagine the different outcomes that are likely to result from various approaches I could take. The Magician would never leave anything to chance—there always is a formula that can be applied—so the question becomes, "What works best?" The answers may not come automatically and the solutions may not present themselves immediately. But once you begin the process—with an eye toward resolution—the answers will come eventually.

In many respects, meditations as The Magician reflect the basic nature of the card itself—the ability to draw on forces that we can't see, but which surround us, and channel that power through ourselves. Meditation, after all, helps us draw on the hidden forces within and then provides a way to bring them to the surface so we can apply them to our lives.

When meditating with The Magician, it is also wise to keep in mind that reversed the card suggests you are blocking your creative energies and are fearful to experiment. These meditations can help you remove those blocks between you and your creative self. In a meditation you can allow your mind to suggest new possibilities that otherwise remain hidden in your subconscious. Over time, the walls will fall and you will be able to harness the creativity that exists within.

II. The High Priestess

It is only through meditation that you can truly appreciate the deeper meaning of The High Priestess. The symbol of the unseen, life-giving forces in nature, The High Priestess communicates without uttering a word or sound. She is pure thought and action. Through meditation we learn to speak her language—the language of silence and tranquility—and see the world as it really is. She will reveal to us the deeper mysteries of the universe.

When I pick up this card to meditate, my mind fills immediately with a sense of the power that flows through all things. It is not the same kind of power that The Magician represents, but rather the power The Magician taps into to create. I feel I am standing at a gateway to true knowledge, with The High Priestess beckoning me to walk through.

Because The High Priestess represents the invisible

314

in nature, I begin my meditation with a tangible image of some aspect of nature—perhaps a flowing river, or a flower unfolding in the morning sun. I try to become whatever image I visualize, allowing myself to experience the world as it does. If it is the river, I allow myself to merge into the water and flow along with it. As a flower, I let myself root deeply in the soil.

These experiences teach me that I am not separate from nature but a part of it and that all things are connected. These experiences also teach me that I will grow in life by becoming part of life, not standing to the side and watching, or thinking of myself as separate and distinct from everything that surrounds me.

Meditations with this card remind me to have trust in myself and be patient as I go through life. Also, the more I meditate on the symbolism of The High Priestess, the more I learn of the power of silence. By being quiet, I can hear so much more around me. Instead of seeing the void as empty, I see it filled with the mysteries of life.

III. The Empress

The Empress is the principle of creation. She is the merging of the invisible life forces into the visible. She gives life its myriad forms. In our meditations with The Empress we strive for the same. We want our ideas to be transformed from thought into reality. We want them to nurture and grow under her protection.

The Empress also represents the process of life itself, the ebb and flow of all things. As such, we must be willing to allow our ideas to come and go, to be born, grow, and then die. We cannot cling to that which we've outgrown.

The Empress can be a very comforting card for a meditation. Her mothering role appeals to our emotions, making us feel warm, secure, and whole.

In a meditation with this card, I always begin with a small prayer of thanks for all things in the world that spring from her. Then I ask for her guidance as

I meditate on questions about the directions my life is taking. Am I moving forward or standing still? Is this the right direction for me? Is it time to move on or stay a little longer?

In asking these and other questions, I am seeking emotional, not intellectual responses. I want to do what feels right in my heart. I want to know that the soil is fertile and it is a good place to plant the seeds of a new idea, thought, or plan.

Sometimes I meditate with The Empress card free of any questions. I seek instead to appreciate more fully the process of life, to better understand how things pass from one stage to the next and that nothing stays the same. I just want the comfort that comes from knowing that all is well and that things are unfolding as they are meant to. I also want to know that The Empress will look out for me. Like all mothers, The Empress will care for her children.

IV. The Emperor

Unlike The Empress who speaks through our hearts, The Emperor speaks to us in a meditation through our intellect. He is the manifestation of the constructs of the mind—rational thought, logic, and the order that man imposes on the natural world.

Meditations with The Emperor follow a more structured path than they do for any other cards of the Tarot with which we work. The questions are more basic and deal more with the form of our lives, rather than the substance—the how instead of the why. Questions are also less probing and deal only with surface issues of life. We don't try to understand what we are doing, but rather we want to be aware of the consequences of our actions, especially if they are wrong.

My meditations with The Emperor card have a stern, almost judgmental quality to them. I use these experiences to review my life or a particular situation that I am in. I seek to explain or justify my actions, particularly if they are contrary to the normal way of doing things. I also seek approval—I want The Emperor to tell what I am doing is right. If I am wrong, I want to know that as well.

A meditation with The Emperor can be a healthy exercise at the same time because it lets you outline things in a nonemotional, almost detached way. In other words, "Here is the problem or opportunity. This is the way logic says to handle it." Then if you act, you do so with the sense that you are proceeding properly. On the other hand, if you choose to go a different route, you've had the chance to consider the alternatives.

Similarly, a meditation with The Emperor can provide the impetus for making a break with the past, for changing directions. Because things are so clearly laid out in The Emperor's world and we know where they'll lead, a meditation can focus on the benefits of moving down an entirely new path. There are risks, of course, but at least we've been forewarned.

V. The Hierophant

The Hierophant is as complex a card in a meditation as it is in a reading. There is enormous room for latitude in interpreting its meaning and what you wish to draw from it for your meditation.

For some, it is a card of prayer and spiritual growth, with The Hierophant as the guide. For others, the card serves as a reminder that there is a higher authority and that The Hierophant is the link between you and that power.

For my meditation, I straddle both meanings and use the card to help me grow spiritually. I approach this card without any preconceived notions or particular beliefs in a divine power. Instead I start with the premise that there is some divine power at work in the universe—and The Hierophant serves as a visible symbol that it exists. Although I cannot define this power, I know that whatever is there, I will learn how

317

to integrate its presence into my life through meditation with The Hierophant. I recognize him as the link to this hidden mystery. I respect his ability to open doors to the unknown by giving myself to him.

My meditations with this card focus entirely on a desire to grow spiritually, and I accept The Hierophant as someone who knows how I can achieve this growth. In each meditation, I ask him to reveal the path I am seeking. Each time, of course, I receive the same answer: "I know the answers, but I cannot tell you. You must keep seeking them for yourself." In this way, The Hierophant becomes a constant reminder that the answers are not there just for the asking, but that someday they will come.

VI. The Lovers

The Lovers card symbolizes the combined forces of the male and female sides to our personalities—the male represents the intellect and the female the unconscious self—and the tension that exists between the two.

When I meditate with The Lovers card, I focus on the dynamics that these male and female forces create in my life and how they influence my decisions as well as my growth. Ultimately what I'm striving for is the same sense of harmony between the two that is represented on the card.

I usually meditate on a question I'm trying to resolve, perhaps a career change or some financial matter. First I try to see the possibilities from the two different perspectives: what my intellect says is right because of the way it adds up contrasted by what I feel emotionally is right. Because there is rarely agreement between the two, I continue my meditation and allow an answer to form that falls somewhere between the two halves—something that intellectually I can live with and that also feels right.

Not all my meditations with this card, however, are limited to solving problems or answering questions. I also use meditations with this card drawing on one of its other meanings: the importance of love in my life as a nurturing force. In these meditations, I ask myself some basic questions, such as "Am I a loving person?" or "Am I loved?" What I am ultimately striving for is an assurance that I am both giving and receiving love in my life, to myself and from myself, as well as to and from those within my life. Often from these meditations I realize that I cannot make all decisions alone no matter how personal they may be, but instead I need the help of my partner, the person I love.

VII. The Chariot

A meditation with The Chariot can be an exhilarating experience. That's because The Chariot represents the drive for success that exists within each of us. Although we hope that many of our other meditations with the Tarot will lead to a positive outcome, clear direction, or a better understanding about where we are going, The Chariot is about nothing else but winning. A meditation with The Chariot begins with a feeling of power and ends with a sense of accomplishment. It is a fulfilling experience.

Not surprisingly, I select this card for meditation whenever I am going to tackle a new challenge or begin a new task. I use this card to feel good about what I am about to undertake, to fill myself with a sense of power and accomplishment.

In a meditation I actually see myself as the charioteer. I see no obstacles in my path, just success. If I can, I try to adopt the single-mindedness that the charioteer wears on his face on the card. I begin my contemplation by visualizing the task or project that I'll be doing. The whole time, I envision its successful outcome.

You can also use this card to meditate when you feel blocked by a challenge. To begin, look deeply into the image on the card and, for the moment, try to forget the problem you face. Close your eyes and think only of the charioteer. As you feel yourself transformed, then begin thinking about the problem or obstacle. Ask yourself, "How would the charioteer handle this situation?" "What tactics would bring him success?" "How can I be like him?" This change in your attitude can help you see things in a whole new light, with the focus on success, instead of defeat or despair.

It is important when meditating with The Chariot to keep in mind that the successes it can help us achieve have to be put in perspective. Although the card is about power and accomplishment, this accomplishment is limited to material gain. Don't forget that our spiritual side needs nurturing too, and there are many other cards in the Tarot that will help us achieve that.

VIII. Strength

Most of us accept the fact that life is a struggle, that few things come easy to us, and that it is essential to be strong in all that we do. That's the message of the Strength card—and what we are looking for in our meditations with it.

Meditating with this card can give us the strength we need by showing us how to draw on the forces that exist within each of us and that we don't have to look beyond ourselves for help.

This is an entirely different force and sense of power than that which we draw from meditations with The Chariot card. That card is about outward strength. The power of this card is the strength of self-confidence, the strength that comes from accepting ourselves for what we are. Also, while the charioteer is singly-focused and thinks only about winning, this card is about strength in all situations, even defeat.

When I meditate with this card, I use these experiences as opportunities to assess myself. I'm especially interested in addressing my fears that are counterproductive to my growth and that I know have no place in my life.

Frequently when I meditate with this card, I start by imagining something that troubles me, something that I don't feel I can do. Then I begin to question myself, asking such things as why I really feel that way. I allow my mind to suggest other instances when I've faced odds that seemed just as difficult, yet I was able to overcome them. Over and over again, I watch as the negative is replaced with the positive until I feel I am firmly in control of myself and am ready to tackle what faces me.

There's more to be gained in these meditations than just a sense of strength. You can also develop a better appreciation for the process of life and its many challenges. But don't lose sight of the fact that whatever you do you must have faith in yourself. That way, win or lose, you can only progress.

IX. The Hermit

The Hermit card provides one of the deepest meditative experiences of the entire Tarot deck. That's because The Hermit card is a representation of the very essence of the meditative process itself—the withdrawal from our day-to-day existence to ponder the deeper truths of the universe.

While The Hermit himself represents the extreme and total withdrawal from daily affairs—something that few of us are prepared to do, or even want to—we can still borrow from his experience and enrich our lives, even for the briefest moments.

The Hermit has dedicated his life to breaking through to a higher plane of thought and consciousness. Just like the great mystics, he strives to reach the highest possible peak of knowledge.

When I meditate with this card, I try to become like The Hermit and push my mind as far as it will take me. I reach for the unknown, seeking just as The

Hermit does, to come face to face with the ultimate force that empowers the universe.

I begin by imagining a void, completely empty and without form. As I continue to meditate, I visualize myself drifting into this formless space. Eventually I feel cut loose from my earthly bonds, free to float deeper and deeper into this darkness. I never feel afraid, but rather, I'm drawn deeper and deeper into it, attracted by the unknown. Also, in this state, I no longer feel as though I am a physical being. In fact, I have no conception of myself—my individuality seems to disappear and I become a part of the void, without form of my own.

These meditations can be the most serene and peaceful of all. Because, like The Hermit, I leave all behind to experience the ultimate, to scale the highest peak of knowledge.

Meditations with The Hermit card are invigorating, too, because they open my mind to an awareness that there is far more to our universe than can ever be described in words. There are some things that you can only experience. And once experienced, you must lead the way for others to follow.

X. Wheel of Fortune

Throughout our lives we are constantly asking ourselves, "where are we going?" as well as "where are we coming from?" We spend a great deal of time in our meditations asking these same questions. The answers, although different for each of us, especially depending on when we ask the questions, all have a thread in common. That is, we are all spinning on The Wheel of Fortune—or wheel of life. Things come and things go. Our lives begin and they end over and over again.

We can meditate on this card in several ways. We can use the experience simply to get a focus on the many changes occurring in our lives—to assess where we've come from and to prepare ourselves for what's next. On a deeper level, we can use these meditations to measure our growth and to see if we've progressed in our development as the wheel has spun over and over again. We can also seek reassurance that, despite the turmoil that may be occurring in our lives, it too will pass. Finally, we can meditate on how our own actions have influenced the unfolding of events in our lives.

I try to approach a meditation with this card with a sense of neutrality. I come to learn, not to question, accepting the fact that the wheel spins with or without me. I just want to know if my life is in sync with the turning of the wheel. I find these meditations particularly helpful when I feel uneasy or if I'm stressed. By closing my eyes and allowing images to flood my mind of the many random events that have occurred over the days, months, and years of my life, I'm comforted by the fact that I can discern growth and positive change. I'm reminded that all things in life provide a lesson. And these lessons can be integrated into the next stage of the turning of the wheel.

XI. *Justice*

The world operates on the principle of justice—that is, when all is balanced, all is well. When things fall out of balance, when the scales of justice are tipped to one side, they must be righted once again. This is the message of the card and the key for our meditations with it.

I use these opportunities to meditate on the quality of my life, to find if I am living it in harmony or if things are out of balance and need correcting. I recognize that maintaining this balance is my responsibility and I am liable for the consequences when I allow disharmony to enter the picture.

I find that a meditation with this card—particularly when things are out of balance—allows me to put my life in perspective. When things need correcting, I can either make those corrections or risk the consequences. Either way, the decision rests in my hands.

In general, though, I appreciate the opportunities to head off trouble by meditating on the direction in which I am moving and looking for signs that danger might be coming my way. Typically, I start by focusing on the current state of affairs in my life, whether it be my work or my relationships. I allow scenes to play out in my mind and imagine where they will end up if they continue in their present direction. In a meditation, my mind presents different scenarios, allowing me to choose what I think will be the best course to follow in the long run.

Sometimes I just use meditations with this card to reflect on the meaning of justice, to make sure that I am practicing it sufficiently in my life. The more we show an understanding of justice in our dealings with others, the more we move closer as a society to living in equilibrium with one another.

XII. The Hanged Man

Life is a transitory process. Things come and go. Sometimes we are instruments of this change. Other times we are simply swept along. Major change usually entails a break with the past, often involving moving in new directions or doing things differently. Almost always, change concerns personal growth and development. The Hanged Man card represents ourselves in the early stages of this change, in a state of suspension, caught between the world we are leaving and the one we are about to enter.

This is an excellent card for meditation when we sense change coming and are looking for reassurance from ourselves that this change is right for us. By essentially becoming The Hanged Man we thrust ourselves into the unfamiliar and begin the process of integrating new things and experiences into our lives.

In a meditation, I literally feel myself in a state of suspension. Instead of hanging from a tree, I imagine

324

myself walking through a door into a dark room. I tell myself that once I walk through that door I cannot return from where I came. I know I must walk through a new door and welcome the experiences that await me.

These meditations are especially helpful when I feel apprehensive about what I will face. I find that if I can use this meditation simply to convince myself that the decision has been made and there is no turning back, the feelings of discomforts ease considerably and I am well on my way toward the new direction.

Also, meditations involving The Hanged Man card fill me with a great sense of purpose in my life. As long as I know there is movement, I know there will always be growth.

XIII. *Death*

The Wheel of Life could not spin, The Hanged Man would have no reason to be suspended between the known and unknown, we would have no growth in our lives without the power represented by the Death card. Death, in Tarot symbolism, is not something to be feared. Rather it is an empowering force that clears away the old to make way for the new.

Meditations with this card can be both useful and enriching. They're useful because they help us move on. Similarly, they're enriching because they open our eyes to the underlying dynamics of change at work in the universe, reminding us that nothing stays the same forever.

I welcomed these meditations with the Death card, seeing them as opportunities to tap into the life force that guides my destiny. I begin by looking back over my life at the big and little changes I've made. I review the different events that seem relevant to me at the time of my meditation. I let the images come and go at their own will. I am more an observer and less the participant, watching these comings and goings. All I want from a meditation with the Death card is a sense of the unfolding of the new from the passage of the old. I do not seek any answers to questions about the current direction in my life. Those can be answered with other cards from the deck.

I always find a meditation with the Death card a liberating experience. Too much time is spent clinging to old ideas, thoughts, and values long after their usefulness has gone from our lives. Yet we are always afraid to let go, thinking it's fine to hold on to them for just a little longer. "Who knows," we tell ourselves, "we might need them again." The Death card stands in opposition to that belief, reminding us that the old can only stand in the way of progress, of growth, of true learning.

XIV. Temperance

The Temperance card is more a state of mind and thought than anything else. It is a symbolic representation of a merging of all the forces in our lives that influence our daily activities—our likes and dislikes, our successes and failures, what we want and what we have.

By meditating with the Temperance card, we have the chance to see our life from its total perspective. We see all the forces that come into play and how they affect us. How they define our personalities and how they color our thoughts. How they make us what we are or prevent us from becoming what we want to be.

A meditation with the Temperance card is a passive experience. We do not use these opportunities to judge ourselves or make conclusions. Rather we are only interested in taking the temperature of our inner self. We want to know if all the ingredients are there to ensure that we are in harmony, that equilibrium reigns in our life.

I usually meditate on an image of myself as I think I appear to others. I accept this image with all its negatives as well as positives. I try to visualize myself functioning in different situations—at home, at work, when I'm happy, and when I'm sad. I want to learn about my strengths and identify my weaknesses. I am seeking knowledge about myself that I can apply to making myself a better person.

Ultimately, if I can apply what I learn from these meditations, I can make changes that will help me grow and become the person I want to be. I'll have a better understanding of life and how to live it in harmony. I'll be able to make wiser choices, because I'll know myself better and have a stronger fix on what's right for me.

Also, meditations with this card can remind us of the basic virtue of temperance: Living in equilibrium brings peace and a greater sense of self-worth to our lives. Living in disharmony causes pain, discomfort, and self-doubt.

XV. The Devil

Despite its ominous look and sense of evil foreboding, The Devil card can help us deal with our fears, with our weaknesses and the other restraints we place on ourselves. We should welcome a meditation with this card because it can help us purge ourselves of all the obstacles we've placed in our path, the things that block our growth and cloud our vision and leave us feeling without hope or sense of purpose.

Each of us carries our personal devils around with us. Fear of change. Fear of commitment. The fear that we can't progress or that we can't better ourselves. All these are illusions—just like The Devil. He doesn't exist. We only invent him as an excuse to explain our failures and fears.

A meditation with The Devil card can help us get beyond all that and see reality for what it is and to appreciate all that life has to offer.

When I meditate with this card, I ask myself questions such as "Am I making progress with my life or is there something holding me back?" "What is it that

I'm afraid of?" "Is it really as bad as I imagine?" I should know the answers to these questions—the fact is I do because they're with me every day of my life. But until I meditate on them—and see them as the Devils they are—I keep them alive and with me. I do nothing to get rid of them.

By confronting these fears and doubts in a meditation, I put them in their proper perspective and recognize that they have no place in my life. I see how they prevent me from growing spiritually, from enjoying life. I learn through meditation that I have the power to rend them powerless, to exorcise them from my thoughts, to be rid of them.

Once I recognize I have this power, I can go much further in my mediation and shift my focus from the negatives in my life to the infinite possibilities that await me.

XVI. The Tower

Try as we may to protect ourselves from change, there comes a moment when it is unavoidable, and ready or not, it descends upon us with the fury of the heavens. With a flash of lightning from above, The Tower that we thought was impregnable, comes crashing to the ground.

Is this something to fear? No. Because from the ruins of The Tower can emerge a sense of liberation. Without walls to hold you, you are free to grow.

In meditations with The Tower card, there are three ways to apply the symbolism.

First is the idea that we must break free of the walls we've built around ourselves. By seeking inner guidance, we can find a way to shatter the artificial barriers holding us in.

On another level, The Tower is a metaphor for sudden enlightenment that meditation can bring. The image of a lightning bolt destroying our image of reality is more than appropriate.

Finally, the image of the lightning bolt exploding

across the sky can symbolize the way sudden inspiration comes to us after a meditation.

You can choose any or all of these different approaches to meditating with The Tower card to suit your personal situation and needs.

When I meditate with this card, I don't distinguish among the different meanings. I allow the experience of the meditation itself to determine that.

In general, though, I find that I start with a series of questions about my life. These questions often relate to a specific situation that I'm in, and I'll ask, "Am I trapped or am I free to make changes?" At other times, the questions can be more broadly focused and I might ask myself, "Is my outlook toward life open or is it narrow and hemmed in?" From there, the meditation takes its own course and the answers flow from within, providing the direction I am seeking.

Sometimes these answers explode across my mind, other times they come long after the meditation. Either way, the experience brings me a greater self-awareness and sense of purpose.

XVII. The Star

The Star is our link to higher knowledge and enlightenment. Its light pierces deep into our unconsciousness, illuminating the hidden truths that we seek in our journey through life. Thus, when we meditate on the symbolism expressed by the card, we are merging our minds with the universe as a whole, opening ourselves to an infinite number of possible experiences and new directions. The Star also symbolizes the world of our imagination, the world of the unseen that we can only experience by looking deep inside ourselves.

Meditating on The Star has the same effect as looking upward to the night sky and being dazzled by the light of the heavens. We know there is so much more there than we can see. What we can't see, we imagine.

In my meditations with the card, I use the light from The Star to guide me in new directions. I allow it to bring me in touch with the unknown thoughts that reside deep inside. I close my eyes and let the light from The Star flood through me and illuminate the darkest regions of my mind. I say to myself, "I am ready to learn, to explore the unknown. Please take me where I have never been. I am open, I am ready."

Often I feel myself transported out of my body, floating in the heavens far above the earth. When I look down, I see the earth as I've never seen it. New paths appear before me. I see new opportunities for growth. I also feel I'm a little closer to understanding the cosmic order and the reason for all things. It's an experience that leaves me inspired.

XVIII. The Moon

The Moon is a card of dark secrets and illusions, of dreams and shadows, of images not fully formed and phantoms of the night that make us feel uneasy. The card provides the chance to meditate on some of the things in our life that unsettle us, that chip away at our strength. A meditation with The Moon card can be a test of faith and a demonstration of strength.

We must be willing to plunge ourselves into the darkness, using the eerie reflection from the moon to light our way. We must prepare ourselves to be confronted by illusions that seem as large as life. And we must use these experiences to prove to ourselves that we are strong, that we have faith, that we can continue the journey.

A meditation with this card can be like a dream in which all things seem real, but yet you know they're not—or so you want to think.

I find meditations with this card an ideal time to confront those hidden fears, those self-doubts that I carry with me but don't want to deal with openly. I let these images come into my mind, as they would in a dream. But unlike a dream, this time I am in control and can direct the outcome. I show myself that there is really nothing to fear—the things that frighten me don't exist in the real world, they only live in my mind. I remind myself that if I am strong and have faith, I can overcome all my fears and doubts.

Almost always I find that I had little to fear in the first place, but I am glad I had the opportunity to be reminded of this truth once again.

XIX. The Sun

The Sun is one of the most joyous cards of the Tarot deck, a quality that carries into meditations with it. It is a card of warmth, happiness, hope, and enrichment. Its image is one of boundless energy and a fulfilling life. The Sun is also the symbol of the life-giving powers of the universe. Under the light of The Sun, things are constantly being reborn. By gazing deeply into this card, we can feel the revitalizing powers of The Sun, how its energy lights up our soul, giving life to our deepest wishes and dreams.

The card also exudes a sense of innocence and freedom. This is not the same as The Fool, whose innocence comes from a state of not knowing anything. Rather, this is the innocence of a new day and new beginnings. We have traveled quite a distance on the road of life and reached another level of development and consciousness.

Our meditations with this card should give us the chance to examine our life and the progress we've made. We should use these meditations to say a prayer of thanks for the richness of the experiences we've had. We should also meditate on the new experiences that await us.

Knowing that I am going to meditate with The Sun card, I instantly feel good. I know it will be a rich experience and that I will feel as free as the young children pictured on the card at play.

I call these my "thanksgiving" meditations. It's my chance to feel grateful for the wonderful bounty of my life, for the richness of my discoveries, for the growth I've experienced and for my freedom to grow more. I'm also thankful for all that awaits me as my journey continues. We should all be blessed with the sun to light our path, to warm our soul, and to fill us with the same energy that courses through the universe.

XX. Judgement

The Judgement card reflects the coming together of our life's experiences. We use this card to meditate on the myriad events that have passed before our eyes and receded into our memories, to take account of what we've accomplished and apply it to understanding the purpose of our existence on this planet.

Despite the title "Judgement," the card is nonjudgmental. Similarly, our meditations are not judgmental either. Instead we should use the experience to understand that all that we've done has been leading somewhere, that we have been fulfilling our individual destiny, even if its true meaning has been kept hidden from us.

When we meditate with this card, we can feel the stirring in our soul from the trumpet's blast. We are being called—and we must answer that call. Our life has reached the point at which we are ready for answers to our deepest questions. It's important, however, to keep in mind that this does not imply an end to one's life. Instead, the Judgement card usually implies that you've reached the end of a cycle or the passage from one stage to the next, when we begin The Fool's journey again. Meditation with the Judgement card helps us prepare for this new stage. It provides a chance to see how things have led to where we are and where we are going next.

To meditate with this card, I look for a common thread that binds my life's experiences. I look for some acknowledgment that I have been moving in a direction leading to a sense of purpose. I try to take from these meditations a feeling of fulfillment and self-satisfaction. I also prepare myself for changes that may be on the horizon. I say, "This is what I have done. I am ready and waiting for what comes next."

XXI. The World

The World card symbolizes the essence of life—how all things come together to form the whole and how we are one part of that larger picture. If we lived a thousand lifetimes, the one thing we'd see in common as we passed from one to the other is that the life process is eternal. We do not make life, we live life. We flow with it. All the forces we encounter on our journey through time, all our experiences, all the knowledge we gain, we draw from life. Our lives spin forever just as The World spins round and round.

When we meditate with this card, we try to tap into the cosmic flow. We try to see our lives as part of the world, not as unique or distinct. We allow our minds to separate from our bodies and become a part of the eternal process, to experience the coming and going of all things, to see how the ebb and flow comprise the whole.

To meditate with this card, I picture a river flowing endlessly. I become part of this river and flow with it. It leads me nowhere, and I seek nowhere to go. I just want to experience the flow. From it comes an appreciation of the eternal flow of life itself.

I find these meditations help me put things in perspective. They teach me to be humble and not to think of myself as particularly important, but one of the many living things on this planet. I seek no answers to any questions. Rather I use the experience to affirm the life process, to get a sense of the purpose in my life and to feel connected to the greater whole. These meditations leave me feeling grateful for the time that has been afforded to experience life and learn all the lessons it has to offer.

APPENDIX A

Glossary of Symbols

The following is a glossary of symbols used in the design of various Tarot decks that generally follow the Western occult tradition. Some of the symbols presented are complex with multiple meanings. In such cases, meanings most appropriate to the Tarot have been selected. Use the Glossary to enrich and deepen your understanding of individual cards. There are 163 entries.

Anchor. An early Christian symbol of salvation that was substituted for the cross when necessary. The anchor also symbolizes stability, security, hope, and good luck. *See* **Cross**.

Androgyne. *See* **Rebis**.

Animals. In general, animals represent mankind's animal nature, instincts, and subconscious self. Qualities they symbolize are true to their own natures, such as gentleness, loyalty, ferocity, and so on.

Ankh. Egyptian name for a looped cross meaning "life" or "hand mirror." The ankh symbolizes life, the universe, regeneration, resurrection, and immortality. Also, the union of the male principle (the staff) and the female principle (the closed loop). *See* **Cross**.

Apple. Forbidden knowledge, earthly desires, evil. Untransformed power. Also, the apple has associations with magic (the fruit of eternal life), witchcraft, and fairies. *See* **Fruit**.

Arrow. Energy, solar rays, divine power. Also, a phallic symbol of creative energy.

Bag (also Sack). Related to the vessel, and thus a container of wisdom, inspiration, and transformation. *See* **Vessel.**

Banner. Freedom from material bondage, victory, self-assertion. The banner heightens spiritual significance.

Barley. Fruitfulness, fertility.

Bee. Industry, diligence, creative activity, productivity, orderliness, discipline. Bees' honey symbolizes sweetness and religious eloquence.

Beehive. A pious and unified community. Center of industriousness and creativity.

Birds (general). The soul. Messengers to the gods. Thoughts and aspirations in flight.

Black. Death, destruction, humiliation. Also, beginnings. When paired with white, black represents the polarity of negation, inertia, and darkness.

Blue. Heaven, contemplation, godliness, spiritual qualities, numinosity, inspiration. The unconscious. Darkness made visible. Devotion and religious feeling. Kabbalistic meaning: mercy.

Boat. *See* **Ship.**

Brown. The earth. Also, spiritual death, degradation, and renunciation of the world.

Bull. Fecundity, regeneration. Also brute strength.

Butterfly. Resurrection and rebirth, and the attraction to light. The ancients regarded the butterfly as a symbol of the soul.

Caduceus. A wand or staff entwined by two snakes and topped by wings, a winged helmet, a ball of light or a tip of fire, which symbolizes spiritual enlightenment and illumination, the transformation of consciousness. It also is a symbol of healing, and has been the emblem of physicians for centuries. The Greek messenger god, Hermes, who also escorted souls of the dead to Hades, carried an olive wood caduceus of immortality, the shaft of which represented power, the serpents wisdom or prudence, the wings diligence, and the helmet high thoughts. Overall, the caduceus symbolizes immortality. To the Romans, the caduceus symbolized moral conduct and equilibrium. The components of the caduceus also represent the four elements: the wand (earth), the serpents (air and water), and the wings (air). In Freemasonry, the caduceus represents the balance between negative and positive, the fixed and the volatile, and the continuity and decay of life.

Cave. The womb, containment, the unconscious, the center. Embryonic development, inner transformation. Jung saw caves as the security and impregnability of the unconscious.

Chariot. Solar symbol of divine power in motion. Triumph, glory. Plato saw the chariot as a symbol of the human soul; one horse was of good stock and one was of bad stock. The good horse represented the higher elements in humankind's mind, whereas the bad horse represented vice. By working with the good horse, the charioteer could subdue the bad horse.

In Jungian psychology, the chariot represents the Self: the chariot is the body, the reins willpower and intelligence, and the horses the life force.

Cherub. Youth, life, the innocence of childhood.

Chimney. Chimneys, stovepipes, and smoke holes in the roof, especially of a tipi or temple, symbolize access to heaven.

Circle. Oneness, completion, perfection, the cosmos, eternity, the ever-renewing cycle of life, and the sun. Also, the Self, the totality of the psyche, the process of individuation. Sacred circles offer protection against evil or negative forces or beings: that within is protected from that without. *See* **Wheel.**

Clouds. The unseen God. Divine Omnipotence.

Cone. *See* **Pine cone.**

Cord. Incarnate life, that which binds the soul to the body. Tied around the waist, the cord has associations with the circle and the Ouroboros. *See* **Circle; Ouroboros.**

Crab. Creature of dreams, existing both in the waters of the unconscious to the land of consciousness.

Crocodile. As an inhabitant of both land and water, the crocodile is associated with fecundity (earth) and power of the unconscious (water). Generally, it represents destruction and fury, but can also represent knowledge.

Cross. Like the Tree of Life, the cross is a world axis at the mystic Center, and its predominant meaning is that of conjunction of opposites: the binding together of heaven and earth, spirit and matter. Also as the world axis, it is the means by which the soul reaches God. Thus, it often represents suffering and agony. The Christian cross is the symbol of the Passion of Christ and His sacrifice for humankind.

The cross is one of the oldest and most universal of symbols, and since ancient times has served as an amulet against evil, the forces of darkness, misfortune, illness, and bewitchment. The ancients also associated the cross with the sun, and so it signifies light, creative powers, intellect, and illumination. The Rosicrucians see the cross as representing dual aspects of the human being, body, and spirit.

Crosses have hundreds of shapes. The swastika is one of the oldest, and is a solar wheel. The Egyptian ankh, with a closed loop, signifies resurrection. (*See* **Ankh.**) The Greek cross, with four equal arms, symbolizes the Church; in esoteric philosophy, it represents the equilibrium of opposing forces. The T-shaped cross, also belonging to ancient Egypt, represents the near-equilibrium of opposing forces. It is also the Old Testament cross, which Moses used to lift up the serpent (wisdom) in the wilderness, a foreshadow of the crucifixion of Christ, whose crossbar-shaped cross is called the Latin cross. In the hierarchy of the Church, a double cross, a cross with two crossbars, is used by patriarchs and archbishops, whereas the triple cross is used only by the Pope.

Crossroads. Like the cross, crossroads is a symbol of the union of opposites. According to Jung, this makes a crossroads a mother symbol, for the "mother" is the object of all union.

Crow. Prophetic vision, creative power, spiritual strength. Also, beginnings, solitude.

Crown. Preeminence, divinity, spiritual illumination, and light. Victory over sin and death. Proximity to God, the highest spiritual achievement. According to Jung, the radiant crown is the quintessential symbol of reaching the highest goal of eternal life; thus it signifies victory over the self and the material.

Cube. In alchemy, salt, a symbol of the earth. In Kabbalism, the manifest universe. Also, a symbol of the fraternal lodge. *See* **Square.**

Dog. Fidelity, guardianship, obedience. Companion to humans. Guide to the underworld.

Dolphin. Resurrection, salvation, especially of Christian soul.

Dove. The soul, the Holy Ghost. Purity and peace. Also, a symbol of Sophia, the Gnostic Wisdom. In Hebrew thought, Wisdom forms the triune nature of God, together with the Father and the Word.

Dragon. Evil, the Devil, dark forces, temptation. Also, the element of earth. *See* **Serpent.**

Eagle. Renewal, regeneration. The spirit in the sun's full light. Imagination. In alchemy, the volatile spirit.

Egg. The cosmos, the earth, the seat of the soul, life. The archetypal, feminine symbol of world creation. The cosmic egg is the container of opposites, light and dark, life and death, heaven and earth, and is represented by a black-and-white egg or an egg entwined by a snake. The Easter egg is a Christian symbol of immortality.

Eight. Regeneration, spiritual illumination, never-ending cycles of cosmos. Kabbalistic meaning: perfect intelligence, the numerical value of the Tetragrammaton. *See* **Lemniscate; Spiral.**

Eleven. Sin, transgression, excess, instability, imperfection.

Eye. A solar symbol denoting divine, all-seeing attributes. Protection against dark forces, disease, misfortune. The Egyptians used a highly stylized eye of the god Horus, called the *udjat* eye, as an amulet against evil and to ensure rebirth in the underworld.

Fire. Spiritual energy. Purification. In its good attributes, imitative of the illumination and vital energy of the sun. In its negative attributes, destroyer. (Passing through fire symbolizes transcendence from the mundane to the spiritual.)

Fish. The unconscious, the spirit, the life-force, fecundity. In Christianity, a symbol of Christ and the Christ spirit.

Five. The microcosm. In alchemy, the quintessence. Kabbalistic meaning: fear. *See* **Pentacle; Pentagon.**

Flag. *See* **Banner.**

Forest. The unconscious. Dark, mysterious, unknown territory, inhabited by unfamiliar and possibly dangerous beings. Unfettered, wild growth.

Forty. Initiation, trial, especially in a spiritual sense.

Four. Foundation, stability, solidity. The square, the elements of nature, the earth, the four parts of the cross. Rational and logical achievement, hard work. The human body. Kabbalistic meaning: the Four Worlds, the four directions of space, the four levels of heirarchy in the Torah. *See* **Cross; Cube; Square.**

Fox. Cunning, shrewdness, guile. A Christian symbol of the Devil.

Fruit. Generally, fruit signifies fertility and the abundance of nature. Fruit is a symbol of Goddess and Her blessings upon growing things.

Garden. The conscious. Controlled, orderly growth in the sun's light.

Goat. Sinners, the damned. A symbol of the Devil.

Gold. *See* **Yellow.**

Goose. Descent into hell, the soul of the dead in flight to the underworld. The universal aspect of the soul, able to go anywhere. Bird of Hermes, quicksilver messenger to the gods and escort of the souls of the dead. Companion to witches, who represent magic and nature. Also, a symbol of providence and vigilance.

Grapes. Fertility. If red or purple, grapes represent sacrifice, as a symbol of blood. As the source of wine, grapes also represent pleasure. *See* **Fruit.**

Gray. Mourning, neutrality, penitence, humility. Christian meaning: the death of the body and immortality of the spirit. Kabbalistic meaning: wisdom.

Green. Fecundity, fruitfulness, harmony, youthfulness, prosperity, energy. Green also has associations with magic and the supernatural. In terms of the spiritual journey, it marks the halfway point. Kabbalistic meaning: victory.

Hands. The right hand symbolizes masculine, positive, and active forces (including intellect, reason, and creativity), whereas the left hand symbolizes feminine, negative, and passive forces (including intuition, emotion, psychic nature, and fecundity). Thus, which hand holds an object in a Tarot image has much to contribute to the card's meaning.

Hare. An animal with many symbolisms. Generally, the hare is a symbol of fecundity and procreation, and a frequent companion of Goddess; this is how it is most often found in the Tarot. The Gnostics and Algonquins were among those who considered the hare a demiurge, the creator of the material world. According to the Egyptians, the hare defined the concept of being. The Hebrews regarded the hare as unclean. In Christian symbolism, the hare is degraded to a symbol of lust, but also represents those who surrender themselves to Christ. In medieval allegory, the hare was portrayed as a symbol of fleetness and diligent service.

Harp (also Lyre). Instrument of divine music, a bridge between heaven and earth. *See* **Swan.**

Heart. The center of the body, the mystic Center of love and illumination, the center of eternity. The source of emotions, courage, understanding, sorrow, and happiness. The heart has deep and profound religious significance. A flaming heart symbolizes religious fervor, whereas a heart pierced by an arrow symbolizes contrition, repentance, and devotion under extreme trial. Both flaming and pierced hearts also represent God's guidance. A heart carried by a saint indicates love and piety. A heart with a cross represents the replacement of one's heart with that of Christ, as happened to St. Catherine of Siena in response to her prayers.

In alchemy, the heart is the sun center of man, and thus has solar attributes of light and intellect. The ancients regarded the heart as the seat of intelligence.

Hermaphrodite. *See* **Rebis.**

Heron. Generation of life. Patience, silence, speed, secrecy, solitude.

Hexagon. A six-sided figure with associations of the circle and with the hexagram, which represents the union of opposites. *See* **Circle; Hexagram.**

Hexagram. A six-pointed star formed by the union of two triangles, which symbolizes the union of opposites, specifically, the mystical union of male and female principles. The hexagram—sometimes called the Seal of Solomon—is also a symbol of the human soul.

Horse. Instinct, intense desires, lust. Uncontrollable instinctual drives arising from the unconscious. The physical body, especially in terms of health. Powers of clairvoyance. The power and motion of solar energies. Omen of death, carrier of souls of the dead to the underworld. Winged horse: vehicle of consciousness, especially in flights to higher levels.

Indigo. Advanced spiritual qualities or wisdom, psychic faculties, intuition.

Iris. Purity. *See* **Lily.**

Ivy. Fidelity, immortality, attachment, undying affection. Also, a force in need of protection.

Key. Passport to knowledge, the unconscious, spiritual realms, immortality. The act of discovery.

Labyrinth. Death and rebirth. Also, the mystical Center. The labyrinth is an ancient and complex symbol. There are two basic types of labyrinths: unicursal, in which there is only one path in and out without retreading the same ground, and multicursal, which are mazes filled with choices of paths intended to confuse and mislead; thus it can represent secrecy. At the heart of the labyrinth lies the Grail or the Absolute; death is experienced on the way in and rebirth on the way out. *See* **Spiral.**

Ladder. A means of access between planes of being or levels of consciousness, by which the human soul can transcend physical reality and reach the Absolute. Ladders also offer communication between humanity and the Divine, allowing the Divine to descend to earth as well as mankind to reach upward. In initiations, the rungs of the ladder, which are always seven or twelve, represent degrees of initiation or the increasing powers of consciousness, attained through knowledge and realization.

Ladders also provide passage between earth and the underworld.

Leaf. Fertility and regeneration. Green and lush leaves indicate prosperity, abundance, and well-being, whereas dry, brittle, dying, or dead leaves represent diminution and withering away. The number of leaves on a plant can carry number symbolisms. *See* **Pentacle; Rose.**

Lemniscate. A figure eight lying on its side, the lemniscate symbolizes eternity, infinity, regeneration, the Holy Spirit, infinite wisdom, and higher consciousness. It is the alpha and omega, with no beginning and no end. Its serpentine shape represents the endless spiraling and balancing of opposing forces in the universe.

Light. Spirit, spiritual strength, morality.

Lightning. Divine power, revelation. Lightning is a type of spiral that represents fertility and the generative force. *See* **Spiral.**

Lily. Purity. Also, sweetness and virginity. In Christianity, a symbol of the Virgin Mary.

Lion. Majestic strength and courage. Solar light. Occasionally, a symbol of Christ. In Jung's view, latent passions. The kundalini force. *See* **Serpent; Sun.**

Mandorla (also *vesica piscis* or *ichthus*). An oval with pointed ends formed by two intersecting, equal circles, which represents the equilibrium between equal forces, and the interpenetration of heaven and earth, or spirit and matter. The mandorla also represents the divine and the sacred, and is a symbol of virginity and the vulva. Concerning the latter, it has associations with Goddess, and is a gateway, as the vulva is a gateway to the mysteries of sex, life, and birth.

Mask. Outward appearance or persona. Masks both conceal and transform. In concealing, they hide flaws. In transforming, they connect one to the powers residing within the collective unconscious. In sacred ritual, masks represent spirits, deities, archetypal figures, or the souls of the dead. The wearer becomes magically transformed by donning the mask and is able to invoke the powers represented by image.

Maze. *See* **Labyrinth.**

Moon. Intuition, the emotions, fecundity, the psychic, magical powers. A female symbol and representative of Goddess. A crescent and waxing moon (C-shaped) signifies beginnings, endeavor, energy, promise, and growth. A full moon signifies fruition, fulfillment, boon, maximum potential. A waning moon (reversed C-shape) signifies deterioration and diminution. (*Note:* Some crescent moons may not be drawn to true waxing–waning meanings.) In Western occultism, the crescent moon also symbolizes borrowed light, for the moon has no light of its own, but reflects the light of the sun.

Mountains. Dwelling places of the gods. The ascent of the spirit.

Narcissus. Self-love, self-contemplation, introversion, indifference, coldness.

Nine. The Triple Triad, attainment, fulfillment, truth, incorruptibility. Kabbalistic meaning: foundation. *See* **Triangle.**

344

Octagon. Rebirth, regeneration, transition from matter to spirit.

One. God, Spirit, creation, unity, light, beginnings.

Orange. Pride, ambition, egoism, flames, luxury. Also cruelty and ferocity. In good aspects, health and vitality. Kabbalistic meaning: splendor.

Ouroboros. A serpent, snake, or dragon biting its own tail. A Gnostic symbol, the Ouroboros represents eternity, the self-sufficient and endless cycle of Nature, and the continuity of life and time. In alchemy, it is sometimes depicted as half dark and half light, denoting the opposites of the female and male principles, or earth and heaven. The Ouroboros is a symbol of the alchemical process as circular and self-contained. In Rosicrucianism, it is a symbol for the solution to the mystery of eternal life. *See* **Circle; Serpent.**

Owl. Death, the forces of darkness, night, passivity. Also wisdom.

Ox. The earth, self-sacrifice, patience, submissiveness. Also, cosmic forces. The ox has lunar associations. *See* **Moon.**

Palm. Triumph, victory, and in Christian symbolism, a martyr's victory over death. Fecundity. The anima.

Path. *See* **Road.**

Pentacle. A five-pointed star with a single point upright, symbolizing the dominion of intelligence and mind over the forces of man's lower nature. The pentacle has numerous other meanings, including the five senses of man; the four elements plus spirit; the five points of man (head plus limbs); and the five wounds of Christ suffered on the cross. The pentacle is a powerful occult tool with both protective and creative powers attributed to it. Inverted, with single point downward, it represents the infernal and man's lower nature. *See* **Rose.**

Pentagon. A five-sided figure which, like the circle, is endless and thus represents wholeness. The pentagon also is a symbol of the microcosm. *See* **Circle; Five; Pentacle.**

Pentagram. An inscribed pentacle.

Pig. Companion and guide to the archetypal figures of hero, king, and magician, the link between earth (body) and air (mind).

Pillars. A single pillar symbolizes the world axis or World Tree, the central pole that runs through and connects the three worlds of heaven, earth, and underworld. Twin pillars of white and black symbolize the Kabbalistic Jachin and Boaz. Jachin, the white, is the positive principle of life and light. Boaz, the black, in the negative principle of passivity and darkness. Pillars also symbolize the ceremonial chamber.

Pine cone. A phallic symbol. The creative, generative force, fecundity, good fortune. The cone may be interpreted as a type of spiral. *See* **Spiral.**

Pink. The mystic heart Center. Love.

Pomegranate. The symbol of Proserpine, who in Greek mythology emerged from Hades every spring to return to earth for six months. The pomegranate represents rejuvenation, resurrection, and fertility. The many seeds within the whole represent multiplicity contained within Oneness.

Purple. Royalty, imperial power, pomp, pride, truth, justice. In pagan rites, used for underworld deities. Christian meaning: humility and penitence.

Rain. Fertilizing forces, purification. The descent of spiritual forces to earth. *See* **Water.**

Rainbow. Bridge between heaven and earth. A symbol of Goddess, specifically, of the Greek goddess Iris, messenger to Hera, wife of Zeus.

Ram. Strength. Victory over obstacles, dark or negative forces.

Rebis. In alchemy, the Androgyne, represented as a two-headed human being. The Rebis symbolizes the union of opposites to attain unity or wholeness; thus it is the philosophers' stone, the attainment of enlightenment.

Red. Blood, life-force, lust, eroticism, anger, passion, sensuality, materialism, animal life, human animalistic nature. Red is also associated with courage, willpower, and strength. Kabbalistic meaning: severity.

River. The passage of time. Loss and oblivion.

Road. The spiritual journey. *See* **Crossroads.**

Rocks. Solidity, firmness.

Rose. Victory, pride, triumphant love, erotic love, the mystic center of the heart. A single rose signifies consummate achievement, a white rose purity or victory, a red rose blood or martyrdom. Dante used the white rose as a symbol of joy and regeneration. In Rosicrucianism, the rose is a symbol of the unity between the dualistic principles of the physical and the spirit in humankind. The rose also is a symbol of the pentacle. *See* **Pentacle.**

Salamander. A mythical lizard that lives in fire and has powers of alchemical transmutation.

Scales. Equilibrium, balance, immanent justice.

Scorpion. Evil, treachery.

Serpent. Wisdom, resurrection, and guardian of the spirit and great mysteries. Transformational energy for spiritual illumination. "Serpent power" is another name for the kundalini force that resides at the base of the spine, and can be activated spontaneously or through Yoga to rise up the spine to the crown chakra, bringing enlightenment.

Also, serpents represent viciousness, aggression,

forces of destruction. In Christianity, they represent matter, evil, temptation, and the Devil; however, a serpent entwined upon a Latin cross is a symbol of Christ.

The serpent is the enemy of the lion, eagle and stag. *See* **Caduceus; Dragon; Ouroboros.**

Seven. Mystical man, the perfect order, the macrocosm. The highest stage of illumination. Also, the psychic, luck, and religion. Hebrew meaning: occult intelligence.

Shell. The feminine principle, the unconscious, fertility, the moon.

Shield. Spiritual defense and protection. Also, the protection of the feminine principle. Round shields may be compared to the **Circle.**

Ship. Vehicle of the soul through the waters of the unconscious. Carrier of the souls of the dead. In the mystic journey, the key vehicle that transports the old (dead) spirit to the land of rebirth. *See* **Harp; Swan.**

Sickle. Mortality and death.

Silver. Psychic qualities. Lunar power and magic. Luna, "the affections purified," of alchemy. The feminine principle of the cosmos. Protection against dark forces.

Six. Equilibrium, harmony, balance, and health. Union of opposites. Christian meaning: perfection, for God created the world in six days. Kabbalistic meaning: creation and beauty. *See* **Hexagram.**

Snow. Purity, spiritual qualities.

Sphinx. The sphinx, a creature with the body parts of four different animals (and sometimes man), symbolizes power, the mysterious and enigmatic, wisdom, vigilance, strength, and royal dignity. To the Egyptians, the sphinx represented the four elements, and the combined physical, intellectual, natural, and spiritual powers incarnate in the pharaoh. A human-headed sphinx represents the union of physical and intellectual powers, and the human spirit subduing animal instincts.

Spider. Skill, creativity, aggression. The ceaseless alternation of building and destroying, life and death. The weaver of time and space, the spider sits in the center of the web of the universe. In Christian symbolism, spiders are misers, evildoers, and the Devil, and their webs represent human frailty.

Spiral. The waxing/waning, cyclical powers of the cosmos. Growth, evolution, flexibility. The need for change. *See* **Labyrinth; Lightning.**

Square. Firmness, solidity, organization. Becoming whole, secured, stabilized. The four elements, four seasons, four quarters.

Staff. Support. A branch of the Tree of Life.

Stag. Regeneration, renewal (as symbolized by the cyclical shedding and growing of antlers). The Tree of Life. Messenger of the gods. Like the lion and eagle, the stag has associations with heaven and spiritual light. In Christianity, solitude, piety, and purity of life.

Stairs. Connections between different worlds or different levels of consciousness. Descending stairs provide access to the underworld or unconscious. Ascending stairs reach heaven or higher, spiritual consciousness.

Standard. *See* **Banner.**

Star. The spirit, especially the spirit in its struggle against dark forces. A light in the darkness, or the light within. The celestial realms.

Stork. Herald of good news, birth, spring. Emblem of travelers.

Storm. The creative power, especially sacred. Fertilization. *See* **Lightning.**

Sun. Spiritual illumination. A male symbol, also denoting heroic and courageous forces, the creative principle.

Swan (white). Essential symbol, together with the harp and death ship, of the mystic journey. The mystic Center. Self-sacrifice (as in the sweet swan song sung to bring about the swan's own death), the complete satisfaction of desire, the union of opposites. In Greek mythology, the companion of Apollo, god of music. In alchemy, the volatile spirit. *See* **Harp; Ship.**

Ten. The number of perfection, the cosmos, the law. The container of all things. Kabbalistic meaning: divine support, the mystic return to unity.

Thirteen. Christian meaning: unlucky, the betrayal of Christ. Pagan meaning: lucky, the number of full moons in a year and the traditional number of a witches' coven.

Three. The generative force, creative power, forward movement. The totality of beginning, middle, and end. Multiplicity. Christian meaning: the Trinity of God, Son, and Holy Ghost. Kabbalistic meaning: the trinity of male, female, and uniting intelligence. *See* **Triangle; Tripod.**

Tiger. Cruelty, wrath, darkness of the soul. Also, the defender against the forces of chaos.

Tower. The process of ascent, or the construction of the World of Forms. The height and integrity of the structure depend on its foundation.

Tree. The inexhaustible life of the cosmos, the center of the world and universe. The tree links the three spheres of all creation: its branches reach into heaven, its trunk represents the earth, its roots reach into the underworld. As the provider of shelter and the home of various creatures, the tree also can symbolize Goddess or Mother Nature. From a Christian perspective, the tree also represents the Cross of Redemption.

Triangle. With one tip pointing up, the triangle symbolizes fire, the masculine principle, the Trinity, and the upward aspiration of all things to the Source. It is associated with vision, seeking, and planning. Inverted, it represents water and the feminine principle. Inverted with the tip cut off, it represents earth. *See* **Hexagram.**

Trident. Threefold sin or hostility, the infernal opposite of the Holy Trinity. Symbol of Neptune, Greek god of the sea, which represents the unconscious.

Twelve. The cosmic order.

Two. Duality, opposites, balance. The dawning of something new in the consciousness. Alchemical meaning: the conjunction of opposites. Kabbalistic meaning: wisdom and self-consciousness. Christian meaning: dual God-human nature of Christ. Also, the horns of the Devil. *See* **Scales.**

Unicorn. Purity (especially in the face of great temptation). Female chastity. Also, the word of God. Occasionally, a symbol of Christ.

Uroboros. *See* **Ouroboros.**

Vesica. An ellipse, the vesica resembles the vulva is a symbol of creation. It represents the equilibrium between equal forces, the interpenetration between heaven and earth and spirit and matter. It also signifies the opening to the Void.

Vessels (general). Female symbols representing generation, regeneration, or alchemical transmutation.

Violet. Religious devotion, sanctity, temperance, knowledge, sorrow, grief, old age, mourning. Christian meaning: love and truth or passion and suffering. Kabbalistic meaning: foundation.

Water. The unconscious, intuition, emotion, the psychic. The medium for formulating messages from the unconscious. A feminine symbol, water also represents life-giving and generative principles.

Wheat. Bounty of the earth, fruit of the womb of the Goddess. In Christianity, the body of Christ.

Wheel. Divine power, the eternal turning. The sun, a source of spiritual illumination. Equilibrium of contrasting forces. *See* **Circle.**

White. Purity, innocence, joy, light, life. When paired with black, it represents the polarity of light and illumination.

Wolf. Valor, guardianship. Wild energy, instincts. Also, evil.

Wreath. A symbol of nature and, by extension, the Goddess.

Yellow. Glory, fruitfulness, goodness, wisdom, illumination, light. Also intellect, generosity.

Zero. Nothingness, the unmanifest. The Cosmic Egg. *See* **Egg.**

Zodiac. With its circular shape, the Zodiac represents continuity, wholeness, oneness, perfection, and other attributes of circles and wheels. Like the Ouroboros, the Zodiac represents renewal and rebirth. It also is a wheel of life, being divided into twelve units represented by constellations, each of which symbolizes stages in life or in the spiritual journey.

Sample Readings

Here are two sample divination readings to show how the Tarot can be applied to various situations. Both readings were done with the Celtic Cross spread.

Reading No. 1

I gave this reading to friend of mine, a successful man who was contemplating starting his own business but was holding himself back with doubts and fear of failure. Here is how the cards fell:

1. Five of Wands
2. Page of Wands
3. Justice
4. Knight of Cups—reversed
5. Three of Wands—reversed
6. Four of Pentacles—reversed
7. The Hanged Man
8. Two of Swords
9. Six of Cups
10. The Fool

What struck me immediately, and which I regarded as a good sign, were the cards in the seventh and tenth positions. Obviously the decision to start a business would be a dramatic change in this person's life, and although The Hanged Man indicated that he was afraid to make the break, I took it to mean he was ready to face his fears and make the jump. Similarly, The Fool card, taken in its most literal meaning, gave a strong sign that he should "go for it" and make the jump.

With that as my starting point, this is how I read the entire spread:

1. **The Cover.** The Five of Wands indicated that this person was a competitor and used to winning, especially in the face of tough odds. In his new business, he'd obviously face some tough challenges, but if he stood his ground he could be successful.

2. **The Crossing.** The Page of Wands is a card of new beginnings—again another strong sign that he would be making the right decision, because this position represented the influences that would be working in his favor in the future.

3. **The Foundation.** One of the reasons for wanting to make the break was because he felt he was pushing himself too hard in his current job and no longer getting the kinds of rewards he was truly seeking, which is exactly what the Justice card said was the basis for his question.

4. **What has passed.** The Knight of Cups, reversed, suggested that he realized that in his current job he was in the wrong place, pursuing the wrong rewards.

5. **What may come to pass.** As a card indicating what his future holds, I took the Three of Wands reversed to suggest that he'd be facing some tough challenges in the early stages of his new enterprise, and that he should be aware of the risks and not have false expectations for the short term.

6. **What you must face.** Similarly, the Four of Pentacles reversed signified a potential drop or loss of income at the outset as he built his business.

7. **What you feel.** The Hanged Man, as previously mentioned, was a sign that he was afraid of such a drastic change. However, I read it to mean that a change was indicated and based on the totality of the spread, it was the right change for him.

8. **What others think.** Because he had chosen to keep his plans confidential—and there were few people around him to whom he could disclose much—the Two of Swords card indicated that he was getting little help from others.

9. **What you want.** Despite his reasons for wanting to leave his job and start fresh in his own business, the Six of Cups card showed that he had positive feelings about the time he had spent with his current company and had learned a lot and he wanted those same positive feelings and knowledge to carry him forward into his new venture.

10. **The Resolution.** As the outcome card, he couldn't have a better predictor than The Fool. That was a definite sign that the risks were worth taking.

Reading No. 2

On another occasion, I was asked by friends to use the Tarot to help them decide whether they should try to sell their house so they could move to a larger home in a new neighborhood. They had told me that they had been pondering this decision for several months but couldn't make up their minds about what to do. They desired a change but were fearful of taking on a greater financial burden. The matter was further complicated by a slow housing market. Here is what the cards said:

1. Two of Swords
2. The World
3. Three of Cups
4. Six of Cups
5. The Moon
6. The Hanged Man
7. Strength—reversed
8. The Lovers
9. Two of Wands—reversed
10. Page of Cups—reversed

I didn't see any immediate signs from the spread, with the exception of the Strength and Page of Cups cards reversed as an indication to me of mixed emotions about this decision, plus some doubts about the real reason for making the move. This is how I read the entire spread:

1. **The Cover.** The two of Swords suggested they were indecisive people, which—no surprise—was why this decision was hard for them to make.

2. **The Crossing.** At the same time, The World card indicated that they had to make up their minds sooner or later—they just couldn't spin their wheels forever—or other events would render their plans inopportune.

3. **The Foundation.** The Three of Cups showed that these individuals had done well financially and that this would be a good time to make a move.

4. **What has passed.** The Six of Cups suggested that they had enjoyed their current home for a number of years and they were ready for something new.

5. **What may come to pass.** The Moon card was another strong indicator that they had to clear away the doubts and confusions about the real reasons for wanting to move or else they'd find that they deluded themselves into making the wrong decision.

6. **What you must face.** The Hanged Man card was a sign that the only way they could resolve a lot of the questions surrounding the possible move would be to commit themselves to a course of action.

7. **What you feel.** The Strength card reversed suggested that they were too timid to act, which I interpreted as a result of the doubts surrounding their decision.

8. **What others think.** The Lovers card was in keeping with the support they had received from their parents, with whom they had spoken about the move and who thought it would be good for both of them.

9. **What you want.** I read the Two of Wands to mean that they were looking for someone to tell them that they'd be making the right move—and they that they didn't want to make the wrong decision by relying on their own instincts.

10. **The Resolution.** As a card predicting the outcome, this card indicated that the move would be fine for material gain, but not for emotional satisfaction because of the many doubts they still had to work through.

APPENDIX C

Crystals, Stones, and Metals

Crystals and stones are popular objects to use in conjunction with meditation and divination, and simply to wear or keep for luck. For a discussion on the occult lore associated with crystals and stones, see Chapter Seven, "Tarot Rituals."

The most common uses of stones in times past were for healing various physical and mental illnesses and for protection against bewitchment, the evil eye, disasters, and bad luck. In addition, some have been associated with other properties, such as divination, wisdom, and psychic powers. Listed here are crystals and stones whose lore ascribes them attributes and qualities that lend themselves to general purpose work with the Tarot. Also included are some organic substances and metals. Try one or more, and experiment until you find ones that feel right for you. You can also change crystals depending on the nature of the Tarot work.

Amber. In myth, amber, a fossilized resin, is associated with the sun (which in turn symbolizes spiritual illumination and intellect) and with immortality.

Amethyst. Purple crystalline quartz commonly used in ancient times to prevent drunkenness no matter how much alcohol was imbibed. Placed beneath a pillow, it would induce pleasant dreams. Perhaps because of its purple color, amethyst is believed to have spiritual qualities, enhance psychic faculties, and ward off negative energies.

Apache tears. *See* **Obsidian.**

Aquamarine. *See* **Beryl**

Beryl. Once used to aid divination and incantations. Beryl is found in different colors, which are known as emerald, aquamarine, golden beryl, goshenite (colorless), and morganite (pink). During the Renaissance, most scrying "crystals" were fashioned of beryl. *See* **Emerald.**

Carnelian. *See* **Chalcedony.**

Chalcedony. The general name of a variety of a type of quartz, including carnelian, agate, jasper, onyx, bloodstone, sard, chrysopase, and others, all of which have long histories of magical uses. Carnelian, for example, is usually associated with blood, the flesh, or sexual desire; the ancient Egyptians, however, associated it with the blood, virtue, and magic of Isis.

Copper. Metal once sacred to Aphrodite, and used to fashion mirrors for divination.

Cross stone. *See* **Staurolite.**

Eilat. A blue-green copper mineral that is intergrown with malachite or turquoise, and is a form of chrysocolla. Despite its lack of ancient lore—it is too soft to be worn as jewelry—eilat nonetheless makes an excellent meditation stone. When polished, its texture is almost creamy smooth and pleasant to the touch, and its blue-green color is soothing to the eye.

Emerald. A rare form of green beryl, a true gem, with ancient sacred, mystical, and magical associations. Emeralds were holy to Goddess, especially during spring festivals; their green color symbolized the renewal of the earth. Hermes Trismegistus, the mythical author of the Hermetica, is said to have inscribed the axiom of Western occultism (part of which states

"That which is above is like that which is below") on an emerald called the Emerald Tablet. According to legend, the emerald was one of four stones given to Solomon by God. In medieval times, legend had it that the Holy Grail was carved from an emerald that had fallen from Lucifer's crown when he was cast out of heaven by God.

Fairy stone. *See* **Staurolite.**

Gold. Metal associated with the sun, solar power and light, spiritual illumination, intellect, and divine power. In occult lore, gold has always symbolized immortality.

Holed stones. Any stone that has a naturally made hole in it has long been associated with clairvoyance, magic, luck, and healing. According to legend, Coinneach Odhar, a seventeenth-century Scottish seer, obtained the power of clairvoyance with the help of a holed stone. The story goes that he was cutting peat one day for a farmer, and stopped to take a nap. He woke up with a mysterious holed stone resting upon his chest. He looked through the hole and saw a vision of the farmer's wife bringing him a poisoned meal. When the woman really did arrive with the food, Odhar fed it to a dog, which died. From then on, he had the powers of second sight every time he looked through the stone. In the Earth religions, holed stones are considered a lucky piece bestowed by Goddess.

Lapis lazuli. Cobalt-blue rock with ancient holy associations. Lapis lazuli was sacred to Goddess in Sumeria and Egypt, and later, in Christianity, to the Blessed Virgin Mary. The throne of God is said to be made of it, as was the throne of Horus, the child of Isis and Osiris. Because of its sacred associations, lapis lazuli is believed to enhance spiritual qualities and inspiration in the wearer.

Malachite. A stone of rich variegated green, reputed in ancient times to possess great magical and protective powers. Drinking from a malachite cup enables one to understand the language of animals, according to a Russian legend.

Moonstone. Milky, opaque feldspar that the Greeks associated with the lunar goddesses Aphrodite and Selene. In European lore, it foretells the future during the waning moon. Moonstone is white, silvery gray, blue-white, pale yellow or yellow-pink, and brown in color.

Obsidian. Not a crystal or stone but a glass, shiny and usually black in color, formed from volcanic effluent. In ancient Mexico, divination mirrors were fashioned from polished obsidian. In the sixteenth century, John Dee, the royal astrologer to Queen Elizabeth I, is said to have practiced scrying with an obsidian mirror brought from Mexico by Cortez. Another term for obsidian is *Apache tears*.

Opal. Iridescent gem highly valued by the ancient Romans, who believed it would bestow the powers of foresight and prophecy. In the lore of the Middle Ages, it was believed to confer invisibility. Because of this association, the opal is believed in modern occultism to promote psychic powers and astral projection. Black opals are believed to be particularly lucky and also magically powerful. The opal also has undeserved associations with the evil eye, sorrow, and bad luck, which are perhaps due to references in Walter Scott's fictional work, *Anne of Gierstein*.

Pearl. Organic product of oysters, once sacred to various aspects of Goddess; "pearls of wisdom" were given out by Aphrodite Marina through her priestesses. Even as late as the Renaissance, it was believed that pearls were formed by an interaction between the sea and the moon, and thus pearls have associations with the moon and lunar powers. Some people do not like to have real pearls, however, because of practices in the pearl industry. Many oysters are cultivated just for their pearls, and those that are farmed have a high mortality rate.

Quartz.　A rock crystal that appears in various colors, including pink, yellow, brown, purple, white, and green as well as colorless; the latter is the most widely used variety. The place of quartz in this list is dubious, because most of its popular occult lore—especially concerning the colorless variety—is of modern origin. Quartz is attributed with an amazing array of properties and abilities, such as "programmability," protection, attracting and transmitting energy, and "clearing" energy. Ancient peoples gave it no such associations. The Greeks, according to Pliny, thought clear quartz was petrified ice. It did have practical purposes, such as focusing sunlight to light fires and cooling hands on hot days, and was used in various medicinal remedies. Small crystal balls set in metal bands are found throughout Europe and the British Isles, and perhaps were worn as amulets, although no one knows for certain. According to tradition among some Native Americans and Indians of Mexico, quartz is inhabited with spirits (as are other things in nature, a characteristic of animism) and are used in divining and hunting. Quartz is also used to make rain by shamans in Australia and elsewhere in the Pacific. *See* **Beryl.**

Rhodochrosite.　A stone found in a wide range of pink shades, which gives it a mystical connection to love.

Rose quartz.　Another pink stone with mystical associations with love and the heart center.

Sapphire.　A corundum most commonly thought of as deep blue, but also occurring in white, green, orange, brown, yellow, and pink; red corundum is called ruby. The sapphire has a long history of repelling bewitchment, the evil eye, sorcery, and all manner of negative influences; in fact, Pope Innocent III (pope from 1198–1216) ordered all bishops to wear sapphire rings in order to resist "inharmonious influences."

Silver. Metal associated with Goddess, moon magic, and psychic powers. The Egyptians, who revered silver more highly than gold (most likely because silver is not found in Egypt), used it to make scarabs, rings, and other religious and magical objects. In folklore, silver protects one from evil forces.

Staurolite. A mineral also known as "fairy cross" and "cross stone," which has a long history as a lucky charm. It is formed by intergrown crystals that cross each other either as an X or as a Greek cross (equilateral arms). The name "fairy cross" comes from the legend that the stones were formed by the tears shed by fairies at the news of the crucifixion of Christ, knowing that their pagan religion was doomed. According to Brittany lore, the stones fell from the sky. As an amulet against sicknesses caused by witchcraft, the stones were once worn in little bags tied around the neck or kept in the pocket. Three U.S. presidents were known to carry staurolite as a good luck charm: Theodore Roosevelt, Woodrow Wilson, and Warren G. Harding. Staurolite can be easily faked from carved feldspar, so buyers should exercise caution.

Turquoise. A green, blue, or blue-green stone considered a holy stone by Native Americans of the Southwest. In Middle Eastern lore, turquoise is a lucky stone.

For additional no-nonsense information about crystals and stones, see Barbara G. Walker's *The Book of Scared Stones: Fact and Fallacy in the Crystal World* (1989), which presents accurate data together with historical lore, and points out the fallacies in channeled material.

For a magical perspective, see *Cunningham's Encyclopedia of Crystal, Gem & Metal Magic* (1987), which offers a wealth of magical and ritual lore and ways to use stones and metals for a variety of purposes. Scott Cunningham's book also features a "stone Tarot," in which the author corresponds the cards of the Major Arcana to various stones based upon complementary attributes. You can substitute the stones for the cards in layouts or use them in individual card meditation. You can also devise your own stone Tarot, using Cunningham's list as a guide.

A book that contains much ancient stone lore is *Amulets and Superstitions*, written by the late Egyptologist, E. A. Wallis Budge in 1930 and reissued in 1978. Most of the book's lore concerns ancient uses for healing and protection.

APPENDIX D

For More Information

U.S. Games Systems, Inc., is the largest publisher of Tarot decks. Their 48-page color catalog can be obtained for $1.00. Write to:

U.S. Games Systems, Inc.
38 East 32nd St.
New York, NY 10016

Llewellyn Publications also publishes Tarot decks. For information, write to:

Llewellyn Publications
P.O. Box 64383 Dept. 709
St. Paul, MN 55164–0383

For information and a catalog of books, monographs, and tapes by Manly P. Hall, contact:

The Philosophical Research Society
3910 Los Feliz Boulevard
Los Angeles, CA 90027

For information about the Alchemical Tarot by Bob Place, write to:

Bob Place
P.O. Box 541
Saugerties, NY 12477

Bibliography

Barrett, Francis. *The Magus*. Secaucus, N.J.: The Citadel Press, 1967.

Bonewits, Isaac. *Real Magic*, rev.ed. York Beach, Me.: Samuel Weiser, 1989.

Budge, E. A. Wallis. *Amulets and Superstitions*. New York: Dover Publications, 1978. Reprint. (First published in 1930.)

Burns, Litany. *Develop Your Psychic Abilities*. New York: Pocket Books, 1985.

Butler, Bill. *The Definitive Tarot*. London: Rider & Co., 1975.

Campbell, Joseph. *Myths to Live By*. New York: Viking, 1972.

Campbell, Joseph and Richard Roberts. *Tarot Revelations*, 2d ed. San Anselmo, Cal.: Vernal Equinox Press, 1982.

Case, Paul Foster. *The Tarot: A Key to the Wisdom of the Ages*. Richmond, Va.: Macoy Publishing Co., 1947.

Cirlot, J. E. *A Dictionary of Symbols*. New York: Philosophical Library, 1971.

Connolly, Eileen. *Tarot: A New Handbook for the Apprentice*. Van Nuys, Cal.: Newcastle Publishing, 1979.

Cooper, J. C. *An Illustrated Encyclopedia of Traditional Symbols*. London: Thames & Hudson Ltd., 1978.

Cunningham, Scott. *Cunningham's Encyclopedia of Crystal, Gem & Metal Magic*. St. Paul, Minn.: Llewellyn Publications, 1987.

Eliade, Mircea. *From Primitives to Zen: A Thematic Source Book of the History of Religions*. San Francisco: Harper & Row, 1977.

Eliade, Mircea. *Rites and Symbols of Initiation*. New York: Harper & Row, 1958.

Eliade, Mircea. *Symbolism, the Sacred, & the Arts*. Diane Apostolos-Cappadona, ed. New York: Crossroad, 1988.

Eliade, Mircea. *Patterns in Comparative Religion*. New York: New American Library, 1958.

Ferguson, George. *Signs & Symbols in Christian Art*. London: Oxford University Press, 1961.

Gawain, Shaleti. *Creative Visualization*. New York: Bantam Books, 1982.

Gray, Eden. *A Complete Guide to the Tarot*. New York: Crown, 1970.

Gray, Eden. *Mastering the Tarot: Basic Lessons in an Ancient, Mystic Art*. New York: New American Library, 1971.

Gray, Eden. *The Tarot Revealed*, rev. ed. New York: New American Library, 1988.

Greer, Mary K. and Rachel Pollack, eds. *New Thoughts On the Tarot*. N. Hollywood, Cal.: Newcastle Publishing, 1989.

Greer, Mary K. *Tarot for Yourself: A Workbook for Personal Tranformation*. N. Hollywood, Cal.: Newcastle Publishing, 1984.

Greer, Mary K. *Tarot Constellations: Patterns of Personal Destiny*. N. Hollywood, Cal.: Newscastle Publishing, 1987.

Greer, Mary K. *Tarot Mirrors: Reflections of Personal Meaning*. N. Hollywood, Cal.: Newcastle Publishing, 1988.

Guiley, Rosemary Ellen. *The Encyclopedia of Witches and Witchcraft*. New York: Facts On File, 1989.

Guiley, Rosemary Ellen. *Harper's Encyclopedia of Mystical and Paranormal Experiences*. San Francisco: Harper San Francisco, 1991.

Hall, Manly P. *Meditation Symbols in Eastern & Western Mysticism: Mysteries of the Mandala*. Los Angeles: Philosophical Research Society, 1988.

Hall, Manly P. *The Secret Teachings of All Ages*. Los Angeles: The Philosophical Research Society, Inc., 1977. Reprint. (First published in 1925.)

Hamilton, Edith. *Mythology*. New York: New American Library, 1940.

Hope, Murry. *The Psychology of Ritual*. Longmead, Dorset, Eng.: Element Books Ltd., 1988.

Jayanti, Amber. *Living the Tarot*. N. Hollywood, Cal.: Newcastle Publishing, 1988.

Jung, C. G. *Psychology and Alchemy*, 2d ed. Vol. 12 of *The Collected Works of C. G. Jung*. Princeton: Princeton University Press, 1968.

Jung, C. G. *The Archetypes and the Collective Unconscious*, 2d ed. Vol. 9, Part 1 of *The Collected Works of C. G. Jung*. Princeton: Princeton University Press, 1968.

Jung, Carl G., ed. *Man and His Symbols*. New York: Anchor Press/Doubleday, 1988. (First published in the United States 1964.)

Jung, C. G. *Memories, Dreams, Reflections*. Recorded and edited by Aniela Jaffe. New York: Random House, 1961.

Junjulas, Craig. *Psychic Tarot*. Dobbs Ferry, N.Y.: Morgan & Morgan, 1985.

Kaplan, Stuart R. *The Encyclopedia of Tarot.* New York: U.S. Games Systems, Inc., 1978.

Kinney, Jay and Timothy O'Neill. "The Imperator of AMORC: An Interview with Gary L. Stewart," *Gnosis.* Summer 1989, no. 12, pp. 33–35.

Knight, Gareth. *A Practical Guide to Qabalistic Symbolism*, vols. I and II. New York: Samuel Weiser, 1978.

Lammey, William C. *Karmic Tarot: A New System for Finding and Following Your Life's Path.* N. Hollywood, Cal.: Newcastle Publishing, 1988.

Le Shan, Lawrence. *How to Meditate.* New York: Bantam Books, 1988. First published 1974.

Masino, Marcia. *Easy Tarot Guide.* San Diego: ACS Publications, 1987.

Neumann, Erich. *The Great Mother: An Analysis of the Archetype*, 2d ed. Princeton: Princeton University Press, 1963.

Nichols, Sallie. *Jung and Tarot: An Archetypal Journey.* York Beach, Me.: Samuel Weiser, 1980.

Noble, Vicki. *Motherpeace: A Way to the Goddess through Myth, Art, and Tarot.* San Francisco: Harper & Row, 1983.

Ouspensky, P. D. *The Symbolism of the Tarot.* New York: Dover Publications, 1976. Reprint. (First published in 1913.)

Peach, Emily. *Tarot for Tomorrow: An Advanced Handbook of Tarot Prediction.* Wellingborough, Northamptonshire, Eng.: The Aquarian Press, 1988.

Peale, Norman Vincent. *The Power of Positive Thinking.* New York: Prentice-Hall, 1952.

Peale, Norman Vincent. *Positive Imaging: The Powerful Way to Change Your Life.* Pawling, N.Y.: Foundation for Christian Living, 1982.

Pollack, Rachel. *Seventy-eight Degrees of Wisdom: A Book of Tarot*. Parts I and II. Wellingborough, Northamptonshire, Eng.: The Aquarian Press, 1980, 1983.

Reed, Ellen Cannon. *The Witches Tarot*. St. Paul, Minn.: Llewellyn Publications, 1989.

Samuels, Andrew, Bani Shorter, and Fred Plaut, *A Critical Dictionary of Jungian Analysis*. London: Routledge & Kegan Paul, 1986.

Sargent, Carl. *Personality, Divination, and the Tarot*. Rochester, Vt.: Destiny Books, 1988.

Schueler, Gerald and Betty. *The Enochian Tarot*. St. Paul, Minn.: Llewellyn Publications, 1989.

Sharman-Burke, Juliet and Liz Greene. *The Mythic Tarot*. New York: Fireside Books, 1986.

Silberer, Herbert. *Hidden Symbolism of Alchemy and the Occult Arts*. New York: Dover Publications, 1971. (First published in 1917 as *Problems of Mysticism and Its Symbolism*.)

Smith, Caroline and John Astrop. *The Elemental Tarot*. New York: Dolphin/Doubleday, 1988.

Stewart, R. J. *The Merlin Tarot: Images, Insight and Wisdom from the Age of Merlin*. Wellingborough, Northamptonshire, Eng.: The Aquarian Press, 1988.

Symonds, John and Kenneth Grant, eds. *The Confessions of Aleister Crowley, an Autobiography*. London: Routledge & Kegan Paul, 1979.

Trigg, Elwood B. *Gypsy Demons & Divinities: The Magic and Religion of the Gypsies*. Secaucus, N.J.: Citadel Press, 1973.

Vaughan, Francis. *Awakening Intuition*. Garden City, N.Y.: Anchor/Doubleday, 1979.

Von Franz, Marie-Louise. *Alchemy: An Introduction to the Symbolism and the Psychology*. Toronto: Inner City Books, 1980.

Waite, Arthur Edward. *The Pictorial Key to the Tarot*, 2d ed. London: Rider & Co., 1971.

Waite, Arthur Edward. *A New Encyclopedia of Freemasonry*. New York: Weathervane Books, 1970.

Walker, Barbara G. *The Book of Sacred Stones: Fact and Fallacy in the Crystal World*. San Francisco: Harper & Row, 1989.

Wang, Robert. *The Qabalistic Tarot*. York Beach, Me.: Samuel Weiser, 1987.

Wang, Robert. *Tarot Psychology: Handbook for the Jungian Tarot*. West Germany: Urania Verlags Ag, 1988.

Wanless, James. *Voyager Tarot*. Carmel, Cal.: Merrill-West Publishing, 1984.

Whitmont, Edward C. *The Symbolic Quest: Basic Concepts of Analytical Psychology*. Princeton: Princeton University Press, 1969.

Williams, Thomas A. *Eliphas Lévi: Master of Occultism*. Birmingham: University of Alabama Press, 1975.

Woudhuysen, Jan. *Tarot Therapy: A New Approach to Self-Exploration*. Los Angeles: Jeremy P. Tarcher, 1979.

SYDNEY OMARR'S 1995 DAY-BY-DAY ASTROLOGICAL GUIDES
18 Months of Daily Horoscopes From
July 1994 to December 1995

Let America's most accurate astrologer show you what the signs of the zodiac and Pluto's welcome transit into Sagittarius will mean for you in 1995! Sydney Omarr gives you invaluable tips on your love life, your career, your health—and your all-round good fortune.